A TATTERED COAT
UPON A STICK

0624-BREN

A TATTERED COAT

UPON A STICK

William Brennan

To order additional copies of this book, contact:
Xlibris Corporation
1-888-7-XLIBRIS
www.Xlibris.com
Orders@Xlibris.com

CONTENTS

FOR BARBARA, MY LOVE AND
COLLABORATOR IN ALL THINGS.

PROLOGUE

An aged man is but a paltry thing,
A tattered coat upon a stick, unless
Soul clap its hands and sing

William Butler Yeats

If it had not been for this thing, I might have lived out my life talking at street corners to scorning men. I might have died unmarked, unknown, a failure. Now we are not a failure. This is our career and our triumph. Never in our full life could we hope to do such work for tolerance, for justice, for man's understanding of man, as now we do by accident.

   Our words-our lives-our pain: nothing! The taking of our lives-lives of a good shoemaker and a poor fish peddler - all! That last moment belongs to us—that agony is our triumph.

Attributed to
Bartolomeo Vanzetti

CHAPTER 1

'Private Emmet Magawley, Headquarters Transportation Company, Headquarters, American Expeditionary Force.' That's how I reported when we were fightin' the Germans in The Great War. It came out like I'd been recitin' it every day for the last seventy years. Of course, I can't snap to attention like I did then—I look more like a question mark than an exclamation point.

I was born in 1897 and, last month, I turned ninety-three. I'm a patient here in the long term care facility of the Brockton Veterans Hospital—that's shorthand for an inmate in a nursin' home for old soldiers.

I'm remembering out loud for a young fellow, Kevin Carney. He teaches history at the high school over in Avon. He's goin' for a master's degree at the State College in Bridgewater, and he runs around the ward with his video camera lettin' us World War I survivors talk about our lives.

This oral history is his thesis project. It's not just about World War I but how going off effected the rest of our lives. While the war set off changes in America for all time, the alterations in my life and in many others only unfolded long after we came home from France.

A reality of old age is that nobody gives a damn about what you think; everything about you is simply cute. Christ, if I called for a Bolshevik revolution or sterilizin' all the morons, everybody'd just snicker, 'Ain't he awful?' Having someone show interest is a breath of fresh air.

Kevin says that the recorder isn't like people; it doesn't get bored or pass judgment. But he can't make guarantees for those poor professors who'll have to run through the tapes. They'll have to sift a lot of gravel to find nuggets in this old creek.

Imagine, there were more than three million of us in uniform on Armistice Day, 1918, and now we're down to just a handful. Look at us; most of the lads on the ward are sufferin' delayed shell shock. Anyway, Carney's in the right place to find what's left of the Great War, but he might be a tad late.

I've been here since '84. Came in under my own power, and, with a cane to steady me, I still get around. Oh, I've slowed and need help getting into the car when one of my grandkids takes me for a beer, but, compared to most, I'm fine.

Those of 'em who are still semi-lucid do nothin' but tell war stories—that's all we have in common—and, when I pay attention, I swear they've had their memories rebuilt. Was I the only doughboy who wasn't in the thick of the fightin', shells whizzin' by his head? To give 'em a break, the stories are the product of livin' so long. They're true; it's just that what really happened can't be separated from what they're imaginin'. In any event, you're warned, don't take it all for gospel.

The boys who went off with me are dead—Tommy Mullins, Rene Dupuis, Mike Flynn—all of 'em. This ward's the last station in the processing of what remains of the American Expeditionary Force. Here, the remnants are trundled in, kneaded, sliced, and—finally—spread as fertilizer on the pitch pine copses of the Cape Cod National Cemetery. As a wag said, 'A war's not over till the last soldier's dead.' Well here's where they keep the tally.

My war wasn't like the one these boys describe. They babble about the trenches, the machine guns, the artillery, and, of course, the poison gas—we were all gassed, you know. But it wasn't like that for me. It was big; God Almighty, how many of these fellas do you think knew General Pershing, himself? Surely, I'm the last of that crowd. I was in the headquarters with the son of a bitch—the line of those who despised him extended from Berlin to Washington—where he made the life and death decisions for the doughboys.

A lot of 'em saw it up close—Mother of God, more than fifty thousand were killed. That may not compare with the French, British and the boches—our nasty name for the Germans; still, many a tear was shed on this side of the pond. But it wasn't something I couldn't put behind when I returned to Boston.

For some, though, it was so big that nothing could dislodge it from their minds. Thousands of 'em returned shell shocked, and a good number of those never made it back to reality. Some of these old lumps could've been in hospitals since 1918. You couldn't pry it out of the VA; everybody avoids that stuff.

It's not news Kev, but an overwhelmin' experience can freeze the mind. You've seen it in ordinary things. Fellows get into something important and everything after is anticlimactic. It doesn't take much—a lad becomes president of his school class—master of a lodge; there's a million of 'em, but war's in a sphere of its own—just check the stacks of any library.

I've got stories about the war and it's aftermath, and they're as interesting as those of the others—frightening, too, but in a different way.

The war unleashed changes that have yet to pass. Many improved the lot of all; others undermined inviolable traditions. But it was after the war that the great events in my life took place, and if I hadn't gone off, I'd have had no chance to understand 'em.

How many of these boys do you think were honest to God bootleggers? Oh, the guts to be a real gangster like Al Capone may have been lacking, still, I was a genuine rumrunner and dealt with real outlaws, too.

But most important, Bartolomeo Vanzetti was my friend. I was with him and Nick Sacco the night they were executed. Today, Sacco and Vanzetti is just a couplet that in some vague way stands for injustice. But they were flesh and blood, and what happened to them was an inequity that rended hearts and changed the lives of millions. From the instant I met Bart, my life was forever altered, and his sufferin' haunts and moves me to this day.

But it was the war that set off the fireworks in my life. Ridiculous as it may seem, the fuse was lit by a schoolboy crush on my classmate, Mary O'Reilly. I couldn't breath when she was near, so, just to suffer that exquisite agony, I transferred from the manual arts curriculum to the clerical program taken by Irish girls whose families harbored lace curtain aspirations.

Mary lived in Little Dublin, a neighborhood only one step up the social ladder from mine, The Bush.

Naturally, within two weeks, she had tossed me over, and I was stuck in a harem of lovelies whose collective goal was to drive me out into the factories where I obviously belonged.

Of twenty-six students in the program, I was the only boy. But I had eyes only for the lovely Miss O'Reilly. Imagine, a lad perhaps five feet—three and eighty pounds with a crooked back; arms and legs set at the most creative of angles; wearing spectacles; and armed with only a sharp tongue to offset these imperfections, yet only one girl in a quarter of a hundred was worthy of my affection. Clearly, I had a sound understanding of my place in the universe.

As you might suspect by now, my wilding was not confined to course selection. The toughs in my neighborhood, including me—naturally, were among the first to recognize the health and social benefits of tobacco. Smoking near the school was prohibited, but that didn't deter Tommy Mullins, my closest boyhood pal, or the rest of us from partaking in the deep shadows of the school steam plant.

For talking my way out of the jams created by these midday smokers, the principal, Old Man Thatcher, hung on me the appellation that stuck until I left the old neighborhood forever. In a flash of insight, the old buzzard went straight for my heart, "You've an easy way with words—blarney as you people call it, and always seek the easy way out—`Easy' Emmet Magawley.

"You had me fooled, but you're just a four flusher seekin' the point of least resistance...I should worry? The shops or docks will straighten you out."

That was unfair, my goals in school, as in life, were simply to live and let live. Suffering under no illusion that I was meant to be any kind of success, I lined up for a place in a factory or, if my grandfather, Pat, held on as city councilman, for a job in the public works department.

But the stars of Mary O'Reilly, the Kaiser, and anarchists everywhere, together with a dash of pluck, combined to cross up Thatcher, and I escaped the factories for a life of books. Still, since my great station was that of clerk in a financially precarious bookstore, the old man's accounting might not have been that far off mark.

I always loved books, and—look at the stack near the bed—I'm still at them. And typing, like printing, was a great source of information; I got to read a lot of interesting material. The method worked for Ben Franklin—perhaps a slightly brighter and more disciplined lad and many other luminaries; why not for Emmet Magawley?

Typing changed my life, and I am ever indebted to Mary for setting the course for my life that was filled with joy and sorrow.

CHAPTER 2

I was born in South Boston, Southie to the uninitiated, and carried off to Charlestown when less than a year old—a start dreamed up by leprechauns. But these were but two of our many ports of call as my Da chased work at shoe factories and textile mills all over Eastern Massachusetts—Lawrence, Lowell, here in Brockton, and elsewhere. But, because of my grandfather's political connections, it was to Boston that we gravitated. When I was seven and living in Lawrence, a job opened in the Boston Water Department. Saved, Da didn't spare the horses in gettin' there.

With lock, stock, and barrel, we arrived ready for the new century. After but a few months with Gramma and Grampa, we assumed lordship over 71 Mulberry Street, our new home in The Bush.

My father, Billy, was the fifth son of a ward heeler from Boston. The old fellow worked tirelessly to take care of his boys, but Da, being lowest on the pole, had to wait for the older ones to be placed and fend for himself till he could feed at the public trough. A good man, Billy had what it took to get along—not as slick as his own Da but steady and decent. With his wife, Nellie, and three babes, Bobby, Eileen and, last but not least, me, he had to swim till life preservers came flyin'.

Laboring in factories and mills and rubbing elbows with Guineas, Polacks, and even a few coloreds gave Da a broader view than most that, in the long run, worked to his benefit. He was forced from the homestead, with its smotherin' protection and countervailing demands. A cut above the other Magawleys in brainpower, he savored the Post each day and, like me, everything else he could get his hands on to read. More direct than his brothers and father, it was a sure thing that he'd never make a politician.

When lit up, Da dropped clues on how the neighborhood functioned and how little we'd changed since we were chased into the bogs. When sober, Billy never let on, but, when 'the creature'—beer or whiskey, it mattered not—prowled the shadows of his brain, he explained the elaborate dancin' by his Da, Pat, and John Moran, the democratic linchpin in the neighborhood. "We've never trusted government, and when we got here, we created bosses to intercede for us—to take the place of the kings.

But his greatest secret was how to keep the priests in their place. "Kiss up to 'em - they've no defense for that. Keep 'em on the Almighty and off of road repair. John and Grampa will handle the small stuff."

Billy was always quick to remind us how lucky we were to live in The Bush. "Between city hall and the church, there's no relief without a champion, and John Moran's a damn good one."

Our empire, The Bush, and Boston's sixth ward shared boundaries and values and were perfectly synonymous—a typical Irish enclave. At its heart, St. Michael's, a gothic replica—proclaimed by its pastor, Father Joseph Muldoon, to be the most beautiful church in the city, rose majestically from a slight eminence near the center of the community.

Since a parochial school had yet to be established by St. Michael's, public school students such as myself who weren't holy or prosperous enough to be drummed out to St. Ann's school in Little Dublin had to attend Mass and Sunday school in the basement chapel. For that indignity, my friends and I determined that the authorities would pay for ruining perfectly good days off.

In the autumn of my sixth and final grade of Sunday school, I stumbled on the button for sending the young curates into overdrive. Many times during Mass, we'd recite The Lord's Prayer. In a rolling cadence that moved the foundation of the chapel, the girls and mama's boys yammered, "Our Father who art in heaven. Hallowed be thy name. . ." All the while Tommy Mullins, Joe Flynn and the rest of us hooligans saved our strength until the

finale. The priest and the field thundered across the line with, "...
but deliver us from evil. . ."

At that instant, we fired, "For thine is the kingdom, and the
power, and the glory for ever," the version we were required to
recite in public school each day.

The hunt was on. Scarlet faced, the poor priest charged the
length of the lower church, skirt flying. "Who said that?"

Naturally, we weren't about to confess, and even the goody
goodies, under the weight of the age-old Irish hatred of informers,
sat like stones. "That is heresy. By embellishing on the 'Our Father' you condemn your souls to eternal damnation. The 'Our
Father' was given to us by our Lord, Himself. That pernicious
ending was added in the Middle Ages by a monk who thought it
strengthened it.

"The words of Our Lord need no boost from heretics racing
down the road to hell. Never repeat that—in church...or in school.
Never!"

Each week the angry cleric augmented his force to flush us.
After a month, the four curates and half dozen of the holiest parents hovered like guards in a prison mess, but they couldn't keep
us all under surveillance, and often the blasphemy escaped.

Late one Sunday afternoon as I returned from play, Da was
sitting on the stoop—unusual as there was a chill in the air. Closing, I shot him a wave that was not returned, and he was without
the smile that invariably graced his countenance. He rose, and
long autumnal shadows sharpened the already bird like features
that is our mark.

"We'll take a turn."

Shaken, I asked, "What's the matter?"

"Father Muldoon came by and said that you'd been given up
by your friends for leading an uprisin'. Are you guilty?"

I stammered through half a dozen openings while Da, never
interjecting himself, walked on grimly.

After two blocks of fits and starts, he asked sharply, "Is it that
complicated? Are you the one?"

It was another fifty yards before I delivered, "We meant no harm."

"You meant not to give the priests apoplexy. Meant not to be shitty. Why I'll tell the old buffoon to bugger off."

Squirming to avoid the worst I said, as contritely as humanly possible, "I'm sorry."

"Sorry for what? That you're caught?" The words dripped.

"No—the whole thing." By this time, I was, truly.

"Of course you are." The tone was now one of deep solicitation. "Sorry your mates did you in? Or because you're a cruel little snot?"

"I never thought it through."

They were no longer bombs but piercing little darts that pricked my innards. "Never thought that mocking the deepest beliefs in a man's breast would hurt? Never thought that makin' fools of the priests would bring shame on us all? Never thought that words unleashed can never be recalled? I'm merely touchin' the surface. Which aspects of it did you not think through?"

My bed. I wanted to sleep and awaken with this long behind, but there was no respite. "I'm sorry, Da."

"Did I never tell you not to conspire?" There was no pause for a response. "You're lucky. Many have spent years in Charlestown Prison unraveling this mystery. Did ya not know that the first utterance of companions in crime is the name of their ringleader—especially if he's absent from the inquisition.

"Are you too thick to get it?"

"I understand," I said, by now bearing the cumber stoically.

"Grand. Have you given thought to your punishment? I've never been one to whip you."

My prayers were answered. 'Thank you, Jesus. I'll never do anything like this again.' Had he chosen corporal punishment, there would have to be welts and blood. I could live with anything else, and I felt the life returning to my body.

"Here we are," he said mildly.

We stood at the walkway to the rectory of St. Michael's. He

turned and approached the huge house. In the living room, the priests were reading under primitive electric lamps.

"They're doin' their breviaries...You know what to do."

Instantly, I understood. "God, Da, no! Hit me—anything else. I can't."

"You shall."

"Da, please."

Mounting the steps, I felt ill used. Turning to my tormentor, serenely observing his youngest climb the gallows, I screwed up my courage and knocked on the door of the worst week of my young life.

Returning home after my public confession, he placed his arm around my narrow, crooked shoulders and said, "It'll be a while, but, for one so slight, I believe that you'll make a large man." Despite the resentment, his absolution was sweet balm.

Ever after, with but modest success, I kept my felonies as private as possible and paid far greater attention to the lessons on survival that Da placed before me.

It's not just the Irish who challenge the notion that just because history is chaos incarnate the future cannot be managed; we've merely raised it to an art form. Blessed with a naivete which permits us to believe that, despite all evidence to the contrary, if we conform to tribal teachings, the future will be assured.

So, in June of '13, I reported to my grandfather's house to receive the secular sacrament of confirmation. I had quit school, and it was time for the great event—a bar mitzvah for Celts entering the work force.

Old Pat, a prototypical ward heeler, knew every person in each of the precincts. He deferred to all, regardless of station, and for those few biddies remotely appearing old enough to have borne him, nothing was left undone by the party or city departments to make their winters as comfortable as possible.

His loyalties to God, country, party, tribe and family—in ascending priority—were beyond question. In these, he took direction from Big John Moran, funeral director and—as I said, Kevin—

democratic boss in an area covering two city wards. The answers to all questions of politics, law, and morality—in descending import—were proclaimed by Moran, and, while Pat bowed and scraped before the priests and the mayor, they might as well be bayin' at the moon when it came to changing the direction of anything not approved by Moran. Similarly, fading brown likenesses of the Pope and Woodrow Wilson commanded places of honor on his sideboard, but they would have to leap to the floor and beg on bended knee before their views would be worth a fig.

Even before the famine and continuing into this century, lemming like, the Irish scurried to the States and to nowhere more densely than Boston. By the time I reached the age of reason, all who could personally remember the famine were gone, but the images were as fresh as if it were yesterday, and the animosity toward the English and their surrogates in Boston festered still.

Gaelic ghettoes were established wherever the housing was drafty, the rent cheap, and the scent of work even remotely in the air. Except for the topography, an Irishman would have felt at home in The Bush or any of the scores of such places in the State's industrialized cities. When the sacrament of work was offered, a thousand down on their luck men from these neighborhoods lined up at the factory door—their women and children champing to join them.

The houses in The Bush, including 71 Mulberry Street, were three-story, three family, detached, clapboard clad aircraft carriers—'triple deckers'. Typically, the utilitarian flat tops were owned by the residents—title holders on the first floor and sons or daughters and their spouses and children occupying the second and third floor cold water flats.

Family values and tribal loyalty were the building blocks of The Bush, but even a cursory review revealed a network of cracks in the foundation. In addition to families, the neighborhood was home to many single parents—widows and the wives of alcoholic or defeated men who had 'gone to the store' and lost their way, forever.

Young Celts were on the make and also on the move, and many of the Irish lads trickling from college and law, medical and dental schools were forever lost to The Bush.

Invariably, houses owned by families with mother and father present were well kept, while those occupied by renters suffered from advanced atrophy. A stroll by enabled even casual observers to glean the social and economic status of the occupants of any structure.

Pat's home exemplified the qualities that the old fellow wore on his sleeve—a man of the people, not one whit more worthy than any unemployed laborer living in a drafty room on the frontiers of the neighborhood. On the other hand, a lifetime of service to underdogs in the community had brought a few small comforts acknowledging the esteem in which he was universally held.

The elder Magawleys' first floor apartment was pleasantly decorated but never approached lace curtain; it had the welcoming feel of the lovely people they were. But it was the lamps that impressed me most—art nouveau with beads hanging from the best ones and with fur bearing wires leading to the raised brown outlets.

After hugs, kisses and solicitations for my Ma and siblings, Gramma seated me at the simple maple kitchen table to await the great man. At sixteen, I didn't rate an audience in the parlor—even if I was a direct descendant. Still, Mary fluttered as if John Moran, himself, was the honored guest.

After a brief wait, shorter than warranted by my status, Pat popped out of his bedroom. "Emmet, you're lookin' well. Thanks for comin' to see a tired old man." The tiny heron approached as if gliding to an awkward landing in a marsh. Not five-three—and, like all of us with rounded back and arms and legs whose angles were never quite correct, he bore the sharp features of that same bird with which he stamped the males of the clan. But beneath the zigzags was a heart straight and true. No doubt, I had inherited his bones, but I hoped that some of his internal power had devolved upon me as well. But I harbored doubts—as did others.

Mary, as round, soft and straight as the old man was hard and crooked, placed doilies before us and served tea for himself and milk for me—and, like a hockey referee, dropped three little cookies in between for us to scrap over. On the wall above the table, Jesus, pointing to his sacred heart and giving the Boy Scout salute, served as arbiter.

Gramps, wearing a suit shinier than the image intended, was serious. "You've quit school?"

The quavering affirmation confirmed that I was present to be preached at.

To, "You'll need work?" there was no reply.

"They say you're a smart one. Many of them are goin' on now. Billy's not so flat that you couldn't stay in school. Educated lads we need more than factory workers.

"Did you really take the girls' course?"

"Typin's not just for girls—it's not." It came out half an octave higher than I had reached for. "And...I'm not suited for school. I never liked it, and Thatcher and the teachers return the feelin's."

"God, a sharp Irishman without skills or discipline... Useless. Times are changin', Em. There're opportunities, and the Yankees can't fill 'em all. And they ain't as afraid of us as they are of the Dagos and Polacks. We're the nearest thing to white they've got, and they're happy to let us ward off the immigrants.

"To hell with them. You could be a lawyer—that's what I'd do in your place."

I tried to reason with him. "I try but always founder. Besides, who am I to be a lawyer? None of us have ever put on anything, and I won't be the first." The words cut, but they just melded with older and deeper furrows.

The old man never missed a beat. "It's sad, but you're among the majority."

Lowering his voice to protect the hard-earned gems from prying ears, he intoned, "Loyalty got us here. It'll always be the coin of the realm. Brains are way down the line. And typin'—Jesus, Mary and Joseph, what were you thinkin' of?

"The kids would have been like us, but we wanted more for

'em. We gave our backs to make them lawyers and doctors. But, quick as they made it, off they ran to Milton and Dedham and put The Bush behind.

"They'd change their names to Adams, but the Yankees can spot 'em a mile away."

Though I'd heard the pastoral from many, I listened again, as he set up and destroyed the aged straw men.

"Any who hung with us is taken care of. Look what bein' thick has done for us. Your dad's set at the water works. Pat's a lieutenant, and Johnny'll be fire chief one day. And look at Tommy and Jocko—big jobs down't'the hospital. Stay close; you'll be fine, too." He looked around for confirmation, but no one was listening, except me—and maybe Our Lord.

"I'll call. Remember, loyalty...Then we'll see about usin' your brains—if you have any...Mother of God, typin'." Feigning anger, he shook his head.

He rose and clapped me on the back. Failing at whatever was intended, through habit, he went on as if welcoming home the prodigal or converting a colored heathen. Mary rushed in and joined in sending me off.

CHAPTER 3

Not two weeks after my indoctrination into tribal manhood, I found myself ensconced in the back office of John Moran's funeral parlor. Had it not been for the typing, there was no way that John and Grampa would have placed me anywhere but on the city payroll—if there had been a job open—never a sure thing. Mary Moran, John's most trusted advisor—as well as secretary and bookkeeper—was my boss, but, as there was not that much office work, I was soon helping with everything from grounds keeping to the back breakin' drudgery of hoistin' coffins up the two flights of the triple deckers for waking the contents in their own parlors.

The Morans noted in me a talent for mourning far beyond my years and quickly exploited it. Clad in a coal black suit from John's closet, I was a natural at looking heart broken during graveside services. It was a challenging way to spend an hour, and I'd do anything to avoid real work—which I couldn't define but recognized whenever impressed into it.

Each Saturday, Mary, with a wink and a nod, "Ya done good, Em - better than yer Grampa led us to believe ya would," - slipped me six crisp dollar bills - mind this, with most evenings, Saturday afternoon and all day Sunday for myself—and I joined Moran's minion, including Grampa and most Magawleys, atop the money chain with lettuce straight from the garden. By the time the cherry tree vandal wended his way from Clancy's to Dorchester Heights and Bunker Hill and back to Fallon's grocery store clutched by wizened crones, the father of our country looked like he'd really been through a revolution.

But since I couldn't bear to enter the embalming room while the magic was being performed, there wasn't a chance this arrangement would become permanent. It would be but an interesting interlude until my true calling made itself known, whatever that might be.

Big John gently guided his friends and neighbors through their most difficult hours, accomplishing far more than simply disposing of what remained of their loved ones. A giant, nearly six feet tall, crowned with an unruly crop of graying auburn hair, he easily topped two hundred pounds. Heavy jowls and a high and friendly forehead gave him the appearance of an orangutan. Carrying his frame and generous front porch with surprising grace, he swept up mourners, his long arms easily girding even the most buxom of widows. In those times, using a funeral parlor for a wake was the exception, and there was horrified whispering for them that did. When The Bush was in flower, a body was prepared at Moran's and transported to the deceased's own parlor for viewing by neighbors, friends, and Democratic politicians.

In the course of the evening, the pastor or a curate, depending on the rank of the survivors, swept in and led a rosary for those trapped by the surprise attack.

When not participating in funerals, I smoked whenever I felt the need and suffered none of the back breaking and mind numbing drudgery of factory work. The smoking caused pain for my family and the Morans. You may think the world never changed before the Great War, but let me tell you there were tensions everywhere, including in The Bush. High on the list of abominations for the lace curtain crowd was smoking, the primary symbol of degeneracy among the young. Of course, we loved shockin' 'em.

Buzzing round The Bush with smoke pouring from seemingly every orifice, I was a walking advertisement that the Magawleys couldn't control their own, let alone manage the neighborhood. While John and Mary despised the filthy weed as, in their view, it stunted the growth and shortened the breath of partakers, they tolerated self-inflicted vices as simple human frailties. For this, they suffered the wrath of the most pious elements of St. Michael's and St. Ann's, especially the clergy, who felt badly used under

Moran's easy hand and who sought the moral heights to counter his secular power.

Mary, a wren in size and energy, loved the opportunities my assistance provided. She showered her grandchildren with presents and played the grande dame. "They're God's greatest creations, Em." And why shouldn't it have been so? Wasn't she the wife of the most successful man in The Bush?

Life was good for the Morans; they'd made it thus with hard work. They resided in a comfortable apartment upstairs over the funeral parlor. Mary's taste in decoration was impeccable—beauty without excess. Today, people recoil at living above a mortuary, but, in The Bush, the grandeur of their house—God, it was Tara to me, columns and all—outweighed the niceties that might seem compromised by sharing their home with their late friends. For all their business and political acumen, they were simple people dedicated to family and the residents of their domain.

The two Moran girls, Helen and Gert, married well and produced three boys and two girls for Mary and John to dote on. John and Mary's only son, Jack, would soon be off to Boston College where the Jesuits broke the finest of the wild Irish colts, and, later, he would stun the empire by gaining acceptance to Harvard Law School—a pearl beyond price. The Yankees were beginning to comprehend that co-opting the Irish was more effective than bludgeoning the beasts, and Jack was everything that an upwardly mobile Gael could be—handsome, graceful, kind...ah, on it went.

Jack was courting Peggy Mulligan, the prettiest girl in the neighborhood—God Almighty, just lookin' at her would take your breath away—and one day they would join the two most successful families in The Bush. That none of the Moran offspring wanted to take over the funeral business struck a nerve, but, in his heart, John understood and moved on.

During school breaks, Jack and I became friends. He was several years older but treated me as an equal—and me not even a high school graduate. Often, we took the Mack truck down to the rail yard to pick up a load of coffins or such. A powerful man, he outworked everyone, so there could be no ill will for having to carry the boss's son.

John, an easy taskmaster, provided an ample living for all the hangers on in the domain. Even more than today, it was a mark of gentility to be driven about, and my lack of interest in the core businesses—unlike the politicos on the payroll who were a constant threat to her sway—prompted Mary to have him make me his chauffeur. Soon, I was carting the great man to appointments in the elegant 1910 Franklin and guiding the brand new 1913 Model T Ford flivver on errands for herself—trailed always by a heavy cloud of tobacco smoke.

The stable also included a 1912 Model 10 Buick, a direct competitor of the Ford in those years and, of course, the Mack truck for transporting our late friends and other heavy loads. The day of the horse in Boston was far from past, but the end could be seen in the distant shadows. The draft animals were the last to go, which was contrary to how I thought it would happen. The light Hackneys were the first to trot into the glue factory, their owners having switched early on to the self propelled wagons, but the cobbled streets in the neighborhood and downtown were the province of the working breeds until long after the war.

Many magnificent horses plied our streets. Mike Mulligan had four gorgeous Percherons whose dappling was a joy to behold. Those good grays were the foundation for his moving and storage business that survived into the late sixties. But my favorite was Bob, a huge golden Belgian with a beautiful blond mane, who trotted Arthur Baxter's milk route each morning.

Baxter, a wiry little Yankee treated the Irish equitably and was rewarded with their business for as long as he lived. He flew up the stairs on quick little pistons, delivering milk to each family, as Bob trotted on to the next house and waited for his master. What a pair!

I was the envy of my peers. We had all quit school at about the same time, but, to a man—really they were boys—they had been swallowed by the factories, docks or fishing boats. They could only hope that Big John would find them something with the state or the city.

The liquor laws, lightly enforced in the ghettoes, did not preclude factory hands from drinking. Numbed minds and insufficient funds were considered essential for meeting production goals, and, while drunken carelessness occasionally yielded eyes, fingers and hands to the predatory machines, anything was better than labor problems. Besides, it was a Celtic predilection to chase the demon, so the system worked to everyone's advantage. The owners had opiated workers, and the Gaels satisfied their deepest guilt. Tommy Mullins and I spent evenings and Saturdays in Clancy's on Melrose Avenue, the principal tavern in The Bush, pondering this and other arcane management theories.

We were welcomed at Clancy's when we approached our mature height—obviously, I was older than most. Mere apprentices, a couple of lagers sufficed. 'The Creature' would prowl amongst us later, but in the beginning it was strictly for laughs. Heavy curtains, grimy windows, low lights, and a blue gray cloud supporting the rafters irritated our eyes and easily transformed noon to night. At each session, a new tacky layer was blown onto the oily veneer of the already heavily tarred walls.

The decor, art deco—authentic and cheap—was the product of Jimmy Clancy's over-exuberance at coming into the business and substantial cash when his Da paid his final visit to Moran's. Jimmy, in reaction to the old man's frugality, redecorated from top to bottom in the latest style; so far as I know, it was the only Irish tavern in town so decked out. But in the decade following, the quality of the furnishings showed through. The gray linoleum no longer held even a temporary shine, and the soft wood under flooring, blackened by countless spilled flagons, exposed two distinct paths, the first beginning at the barmaids' station where the lager was loaded; the other focused on the men's room door. Clancy's pioneered recycling.

Early in the century, Clancy the Elder, an entrepreneurial genius, opened the second floor of his establishment for the improvement of the toughs of the neighborhood. 'The academy', its nom de guerre, was the classroom in which the skills required of young Celts—swearing, smoking, cards, and pool—were lovingly honed. Entrance could be made directly from the tavern, but, until a lad qualified for drinking at the bar, he was required to make the long climb up the open exterior staircase.

Apprenticeship in life's most prestigious arts began at the door. Lads tall enough to stand over a table and in possession of two pennies for rack rental were welcomed with open arms. In the binary world of The Bush, the admissions committee screened the mama's boys and nonconformists, accepting only those capable of withstanding the great matriarchs. I know it takes a stretch to see me as a rebel, but, even in prize fightin', surely you know there have been great featherweights.

On the first day, a language arts examination was held. Naturally, our betters were concerned not at all with our swearing—providing it was done out of earshot of the weaker sex—fully cognizant of our genetic propensity for vile rhetoric. Oaths, scatology, and blasphemy were introductory subjects. Mixing categories, extended strings, invective, and rounds were usages in which we apprenticed ourselves to the older lads. I was thought a prodigy and called upon to demonstrate my power for the men. Master of all facets of the skill, on my first day, I used the 'F' word repeatedly—noun, verb, and adjective in proper tense and perfect agreement. Some thought I might be the stuff of legends, a tiny clarion soloist within a great choir.

Regrettably, shortcomings were soon discovered. Almost as quickly as my vocal talents were recognized, it became obvious that I was but an ordinary smoker. After letting out a string of oaths asserting readiness, a weed was produced for my first communion. After but a single drag, the consumption that had plagued us for generations made itself known. Four whiffs and the old problem with my inner ears appeared. This was initially suppressed by sitting and holding on, but when my chronic dyspepsia materialized, the dash for the throne was lost. The cruel barbs of the adjudicators were terribly unfair. "That's a lovely shade of green you are, Em."

Eventually, I became adept at drawing deeply on those little nails but had no talent for blowing smoke rings, exhaling through my nose, or for talking with a weed hanging from my lips - all academy requirements. I'd blubber as the butt danced, but, invariably, the damn rattlesnake coiled and struck me right in the eye. I found these prized skills to be difficult and disagreeable all of my life, but the affinity for tobacco was snuffed out only when I was in my late sixties and ordered, unnecessarily in my view, to desist. Naturally, as the academy was a private preparatory institution, economics played a significant role, and cigarettes were the dearest commodity. Those talented at pool used winnings to secure them. Without ability at the tables, I had to work for my keep. Cleaning toilets, washing Clancy's Buick, and running errands were bartered for weeds.

The popular press described Irishmen as beasts, and, while lace curtain types found this reprehensible, academy members reveled in the consignment. Many true toughs matriculated, but with a glance from those myopic eyes into Ma's mirror at the bumpless biceps and scrawny neck, my membership in the company of hooligans collapsed like a punctured balloon.

Despite its reputation and in contrast to much of what I've said, The Bush was a place of extremely high morality. A streak of puritanism runs deep in the Irish mind, and I found it strange that the Celts couldn't get along with the old Yankees. My guess was that they simply couldn't get past the animosity from their trials in the Old Sod and the wage crimes here.

But righteousness was never eradicated from the enclave, and there was an abiding resentment of exploiters of the down and out, the foundation stones on which The Bush had been built. Every night, rage against the injustices committed against the poor—our own—broke out, and, as the Irish courage flowed, Big John inflamed the oxygen starved minds of the regulars. The big fellow drew tears from the hardest hearts with his descriptions of

the methods of the Black and Tans, the Penal Laws still persecuting the poor devils in the old country, and the cruelty of the Protestants during the famine. Clancy's could have served as a recruiting station for the IRA when Moran was holding court, but, thank
God, I was blessed not to have been cut from that bolt.

So it went, night after night and year upon year. Even after
putting four dollars on the table for Ma, there was plenty for rai-
sin' hell. By 1917, I was up to eight bucks a week, and a real thirst
could be satisfied with the four in my wallet.

Along the way I smiled at one Millie Moynihan and damned
if she didn't return it. It was a minor league Romeo and Juliet as
our families were rivals. But I was enthralled by her embrace. All
that I fantasized with Mary O'Reilly became a reality with this
gorgeous creature from Little Dublin.

After the initial addiction eased, I assessed my situation. Truly,
Millie was an uncommonly well put together colleen with an open
round face and a smallish turned up Gaelic nose in its center.
Balancing that plucky little thing were beautiful blue eyes and the
most tempting lips I'd ever seen. Of course, not enough can be
said about the attractiveness of a woman with perfect posture, such
as Millie's, to one whose back resembled an old country road.

Fighting my way to sanity, I discovered she was a living, breathing human being with desires that did not always coincide with
my own. The adjustment from flying into her arms from across
the floor at St. Ann's weekly dance to acceding to the dreaded
demand that I enter the lion's den when the beast was in the lair
was sufficient to clear my synapses, and I began to understand
some of the more practical elements of our relationship.

The pretty little led me through the gauntlet of her brothers
and mother right into the grasp of the Capulet butcher where I
learned again all of the pithy wisdom of the Irish in America. The
only difference from the lessons laid upon me by my Grampa and
this load was the charge that there were false prophets among the
Celts in Boston. They remained nameless, but the clever might
infer their identity—I guessed 'Magawley'.

Emerging with but a shred of dignity, I conjured an equally unpleasant fate for my sweetheart. Torn by affection and anger, I postponed her punishment until a later date.

Even as empires crumbled and millions died in Europe, we could observe few changes in our lives, but Millie was no longer a secret. Courtship among Celts went on forever, even the most intense of them. The Irish are very repressed and most can stifle their urges indefinitely. Enough beer, crying, and laughing make five years but a blink of an eye for a couple headed for marriage. But we are a fecund people who marry late, have a minimum of sex and produce a huge number of offspring. As you know, Kev, times have changed; there aren't nearly so many babies these days.

Millie's family was on par with mine in the pecking order of democratic politics—the Magawleys ran The Bush, and the Moynihans were in charge of Little Dublin. The two neighborhoods made up the kingdom. So, as you might expect, John Moran's younger brother, Joey, served as the state representative for the district and did the king's bidding on Beacon Hill.

On the surface, relations between the clans were cordial, but there was little love lost as they were competitors for John's affection and largess. Alright, boyo, I'll out with it; the Moynihans were too goddamn cute for the more straight forward Magawleys—that's Irish 'cute'—goddamn devious. I don't mean to knock people I was headed for joining as family, but three of the four men were just plain shitty.

Sean, Millie's father, was the Councilman from Ward Eight, Little Dublin. Brothers, Mike and John, were police officers. Mike was already a sergeant, and the youngest, Billy, who was my age, had just become a guard at the Charlestown State Prison.

John was, at best, taciturn, Mike was downright surly, but Billy was another story, accepting and right away in my corner.

It came to be understood all around that Millie and I would someday marry. That someday could be very far in the future, but we never discussed the contract while keeping to the road inevitably leading to the altar. It would be the joining of the houses of two princes, and there were hopes in Moran's headquarters that the match would heal old wounds, or at least buff some of the angrier scars.

After the initial rush, Monday, Wednesday and Friday nights—if I wasn't needed at Moran's, which was seldom—were spent with Millie, mostly at her place. We had sing alongs around the piano—The Mrs. played the spinet quite well—or played cards. If Sean was home—thank God for public duties that kept him out often—and 'six sheets to the wind', we would be subjected to a repeat performance of the talk. Millie's eyes would roll, but I got perverse pleasure from it, finding it hard to believe that Sean and Pat could say the same words with virtually the same inflection. It was the Irish, Democrat gospel according to Saint John Moran.

At the end of the evening, Millie would apologize, and I'd insist that it was nothing. We'd kiss and kiss again and again. The gentle press of her firm little breasts on me was my reward for putting up with the harangues. Some times, if I'd had a couple of beers, my hands roamed, demonstrating that I was alive. There'd be some hell to pay for that—after a good check of the topography. That was the way it was—with exceptions, of course. We placed our women on higher pedestals than any tribe in the world until it came time to work them to death.

No matter where we spent our time, the great diversion was cards, whist. We played it aggressively and well—women, men, girls and boys went at it—at Clancy's, at home, and at parish hall whist parties. We even partook while waiting for tables at the academy. This parent of bridge was a passion shared by all—all with any brains, that is. While it could not compare with the academic majors—it was, after all, played by women and old men, skill in the art was admired. For sharp play, my ledgers, bankrupted by lack of facility in smoking and billiards, were added to, at least a smidgen.

I believed that nothing would have changed had it not been for the war—three evenings and all day Sunday with Millie and three at Clancy's and, before you know it, it was 1917. There was little talk of the conflict, except in economic terms. We bore no hard feelings for the Germans. But it was a Hobson's choice, as the King was waiting at the door and being championed by the democrats. There could be no rational look at the Kaiser's case, as he was charged with—and was guilty of—drowning kin from both countries on the high sea. Regardless, after the fistfight, most nights we came down on the side of prosperity.

America was doing very well with work for all. Every shoe that could be stitched and every yard of cloth that could be woven was on the way to England or France before the last thread could be cut. From about '14, unemployment was nonexistent, and, while prices shot up, wages more than kept pace. Why should we have to choose between 'em? There was no interest in Clancy's for anything but letting them exhaust themselves while America made out very well—and us with it.

Well wouldn't you know the Brits could screw up anything, and it was common gossip that we'd soon be sidin' with the King. Wilson was putting out grand explanations on why we might have to fight the Germans, but by the time they got to Clancy's, they were thinner than old Pat Magawley's shoe leather.

I paid little attention until war was declared in April of '17 and the following month when we had to register for the draft. My God, what a start - not only did my number come up early, but, regardless of my value to Big John, I was classified 'nonuseful' by the board. Jesus, Mary and Joseph, how could anyone with half a brain not see that causing Mary Moran to return to work full time would be anything but a calamity. 'Nonuseful'—Mother o' God, Wilson was right; Western Civilization was threatened.

Off they'd go to war. The Post, the Globe, the Transcript and the others printed pictures of the smiling civilians on the way to some God forsaken place in New Jersey—inhabited by devils, I'm told—to be transformed into soldiers of sufficient ferocity to scare the hell out of Kaiser Bill. They got to me in June and, by then, the pictures were routine and hardly noticed, except by those who loved them. Still, Tommy Mullins and I were the first from The

Bush to be selected, and the denizens were determined that we'd be sent off like the heroes we would surely become. Now that we were in it, there was no sympathy for the Krauts.

My health was far worse than those with similar symptoms, but it mattered not; the army hacks weren't interested in the terrible problems I'd been having with my dyspepsia, myopia, and near consumption. I would never have pointed these out to avoid service; I was simply under the impression that they were seeking perfect specimens and didn't want standards lowered on my account. In exasperation, I asked the examiner, "Don't you know that Wilson said, 'There is such a thing as a man bein' too proud to fight.'...I am that very lad."

The quack laughed and offered, "You'll do just fine. Let's see... five—six, a hundred and nine with the chest of a bully. A match for ten Huns."

Sonofabitch!

I was to report for induction on a Wednesday, and, that Monday, Millie said there would be a dance down at the A.O.H. Hall—that's the Ancient Order of Hibernians, saints every one. Longing to be alone with her, I didn't want to attend. That I was in love with her was forming in my consciousness as well as in my heart, and I desired nothing more than to hold her close. Anyway, off we went. I saw a big crowd through the windows—including my Ma and Da, but damned if I wasn't shocked when they screamed, "Surprise!" God, what an innocent! They caught Tommy off guard, as well.

The place was decked in red, white, and blue bunting. The wooden folding chairs were set on the perimeter leaving the center floor clear for dancing. Three locals played the latest dance tunes and all the old sad songs from Ireland.

What was a fellow to do? Pound the lager and dance with all the girls that's what. After I was well lubricated, the speeches started. Grampa began with, "I've got strong words for the Kaiser, himself, I have. 'If ya don't call it quits by Christmas, our two lads from Little Dublin 'll tie a knot in yer monkey tail.'" Oh, the cheers and clappin' for that one. Moran told them there was none finer in the Bush and how he'd miss me.

I was crying from the accolades and the beer when Sean got up in front of the neighbors and the entire Magawley clan and said he was going to welcome me into his family as soon as we won the war. That drew huzzahs from every democratic throat. Millie grabbed onto me and smiled like an angel. It was now both public and official. I danced with my cousins and aunts and all of the Moynihan women. By the time the crowd thinned, I could barely walk.

Fall down drinking was never my style. Oh, I got lit up lots of times in the army but never again as stupefyingly as on that evening, and, after the war, even on the gloomiest of nights, I was never again as subject to 'the creature'. Not that I was too good, I just couldn't stand the pain or the familiarity with Thomas Crapper's new invention.

Millie hauled me to her house, and we were overcome by the desperation of the war. Fortunately, the lager maintained her standing as an honest woman.

I remember nothing of Tuesday except the pounding head and nausea from the grippe that had been going around. That evening, alone with Millie, our love came out in sad little asides. I promised that I would live and return. Of course it wasn't for her alone that I made the pledge to take no unnecessary chances. It had become clear to me that rear echelon support was of equal import to facing down the Germans, against whom I had nothing anyway, and it was from this vantage that I vowed to serve. My war began.

CHAPTER 4

Some twenty bedraggled ethnics—Tom and me as well as five lads we knew from Little Dublin, a half a dozen Guineas from East Boston and the North End, and a few assorted Polacks and Krauts—reported for induction. All of them looked bigger and stronger than little Emmet, but the monumental pile of granite that is South Station dwarfed the crowd. Except for the Custom House, Boston was a low rise city, so the mammoth rail center appeared far more massive than it does today. Standing tall and holding Millie's hand, I dared not look at her. Magawleys surrounding us, we waited for the army and the railroad to get organized. Tommy's flock milled hard by us; if there was strength in numbers, we wanted it. A whistle called attention, and the inductees assembled for picture taking and speeches. Because of a mix up by the army, most of the newspapers didn't get the word, and only the Post had a photographer on hand.

In two rows, with the taller lads standing in back, we knelt as straight as possible in an effort to look as tough as possible, so that the Kaiser could gauge what he was up against and quit in time for a Christmas homecoming. I didn't know it, but they'd been going to be home for the holidays every year since 1914. Poof went the flash; we were immortalized.

A few years ago, when I last looked at that picture, I nearly fell over laughing; the St. Michael's Boys Choir had been drafted to whip the Kaiser's hordes. Not one of the Celts looked more than fourteen—with Tommy and me looking even younger. Lads didn't grow very large then, and the under-class Irish were smaller still, but, with one exception, I recall thinking that the group looked pretty formidable.

Mayor James Michael Curley blasted us with more of the blarney Pat had used at the Hibernian Hall; His Honor could charm the birds from the trees with his powerful and melodious voice. A brass band of Spanish American War vets played rousers from their days in Havana and from the Civil War. Everyone came alive for 'Give My Regards to Broadway', and when they got to 'The Stars and Stripes Forever', the fellows without girl friends damn near screamed for the train to roll. But there's nothing like survivors of past wars—especially with legs missing here and there—to inspire confidence. Yes, sir, Emmet Magawley took heart at the sight of crutches and wooden pegs among the band.

When the music petered out, we staggered through the station and the hissing beasts to the car reserved for us. Milling about, we waited for the order to board. God, the tears flowed. Millie, holding me close between sobs, demanded, "I love you, Emmet—come back to me. We've got too much in this for you not to come home." Her anger was palpable, but sensing that an explanation of the conscription law wouldn't help, I absorbed the hit.

"I will. It's just trainin'. I love you, too, Mil." There, after all the years, it was out. Tenderly, I kissed her sensitive lips and held on for dear life.

The army doesn't tear you out of the arms of your loved ones; a tooting, hissing, bell ringing, thousand horsepower steam locomotive does the dirty work, and there was nothing to do but let go. My arms stretched; no matter, Millie's sad eyes receded into the distance—forever branded into my mind.

Lumbering down the aisle, I flopped into a seat and lived in my head until the conductor yelled, "All aboard," in New Haven. Looking around to make sense of my situation, I saw that our detachment had been augmented along the way. Boys had boarded in Providence, New Haven and God knows where else; the car was filled with miserable looking lads off to war.

The child next to me, a square little fellow, dark and at least as forlorn in appearance as myself, Rene Dupuis from Fall River, had boarded at Providence along with eight other Canucks. By the time we arrived in Trenton, four of them, including Rene, were named 'Frenchy'. Uniformed soldiers were peppered throughout the other cars, but they were travelling independently and looked to be of a totally different species than us.

Frenchy and I spent the rest of the trip alternately falling into self-absorption and talking about what might happen to us in New Jersey. The conclusion was that the training would be tough, but, if the others could make it, so could we. Of only one thing was there certainty—the advice we had received from those who'd gone before us—'never volunteer for anything'.

In Trenton, we boarded buses bound for Camp Dix. When events spin out of control, the time required for making deep friendships is compressed infinitely, and the serendipitous discovery of a common interest in motor vehicles, afforded Rene and me brief periods of respite from the gnawing angst over what might be about to happen.

Entering the cantonment, the magnitude of the wartime build was amazing. Rows of two story wooden barracks were being sawed, pounded, and raised into existence by hundreds of sweat shined workmen. Confused centipedes, platoons of recruits marched in continually changing directions. The buses slowed, and a dozen soldiers lounging in front of a newly minted quadrangle of barracks came alive, predators sensing fresh meat. As we pulled up, the pride divided; a leader and three assistants moved to greet each vehicle.

The buzzing was intense. Rene and I whispered fearfully about the stark environment and the ferocious welcoming committee.

"You sons o' bitches, when I come in, there'll be absolute silence. What's your name soldier?" the man screamed at an unfortunate behind us. Mother of God, a wild beast was loose in our midst.

"Mullins," was the quiet response.

"Mullins, when we get off the bus, move to the side and give me fifty pushups. If I ever have to speak to you again for anything you're dog meat. Got that?"

"Yes." The silence was deafening. The man stared into Tom's being. . . "Yes, sir." Haltingly, Tommy tried again.

"You ignorant bastard, I ain't no goddamn officer. I am Sergeant Michaels. When you talk to me, it's: yes, sergeant; no sergeant; or no excuse, sergeant. Never call me `sir'. You got that, Mullins?"

"Yes, sir...I mean, yes, sergeant," Tommy stammered.

"Are you so fucking stupid you can't follow a simple order?"

"No, sergeant."

Horse thieves mounted bareback beneath a thick oak limb, we were perfectly focussed.

"When you people get off this bus, move like greased lightning and form two ranks. Any questions?"

There were no requests for clarification, and we raced to our places as Tommy counted off. He was strong and began with purpose. . ."Thirty-three...Thirty-four. . ." He had slowed appreciably. Eyes glued to the horizon, the drama played out in the periphery of our frozen stares.

At forty-two, it was obvious that Tom could not make another repetition. "Help that yellow bastard," Michaels snarled. Two henchmen flew at Tom and, without hesitating, picked him up and dropped him for the remaining counts. He was barely able to protect his face.

A blinding fog of horror enveloped us.

"Mullins is a trouble maker, so I'm goin' to drive him into the swamp. Then we'll hunt him down and throw him in the guardhouse. The bastards there know how to deal with yellow bellies. Anybody want to join him?"

Michaels' face flushed, and he shook in his rage. He paused—no response. "Did you hear me? Anybody want to join Mullins?"

A glimmer of understanding shined through, and the haltingly murmur, "No, sergeant," limped from the ranks.

"I can't hear you," Michaels bellowed into the faces barely inches from his own.

"No, sergeant," sprang crisply from the multitude.

"Still can't hear you," he screamed.

A cannon roared, "No, sergeant."

Michaels' disgust was palpable. "You're the sorriest bastards ever. I'm supposed to make soldiers outta this?" He threw up his hands in despair.

The surreal hours passed in epochs. Entering our barracks, we were assigned bunks. Then we were off to the quartermaster's for issuance of incorrectly sized clothing. Milling cattle in a slaughterhouse, that evening, we were herded—the drovers cruelly taunting us—to the mess hall for the driest, foulest cardboard masquerading as meat loaf it had ever been my pleasure to gag on.

Worse, the fallibility of The Bush—the academy, Clancy's, the lot—was exposed. Entering Camp Dix ready for induction into the pantheon of cursing, it took but minutes to recognize that the army was leagues ahead of my native land; oaths of a lifetime were ground viciously under the heels of our leaders. Ignorant, I believed every curse ever uttered by man was on the tip of my tongue ready for firing, but Sergeant Michaels loosed at least a dozen new ones before the sun had set—some so vile and foul that it took me until nearly sundown to master them.

Camp Dix, a gloomy swamp, collaborated with the army in breaking us. In summer, when it was my misfortune to cavort among its endless potholes and hummocks, the heat, humidity and insects tested every pore. Brain or body, only one could survive, and that, of course, was the plan. Our bodies were bent until our wills snapped.

One steamy day, as our battalion readied for war games, the companies were divided into allies and enemy to practice the tactics in which we'd been drilled. Sergeant Michaels ground us even more hatefully, swearing that weak performers would be driven, without rest, on a twenty-mile forced march.

Over the previous weeks, we had gotten to know, at least casually, troopers from other companies in the battalion. Mingling in the combined mess halls and at the post exchange in the few moments permitted away from hell, we were on waving terms with many of our fellow inmates, some of whom had been inducted with us. Be that as it may, we would defeat them or pay with sweat and tears. We were the allies and would hold defensive positions on the battalion perimeter. Our squad was set at a forward outpost to await infiltration efforts by enemy troops.

Clouds snuffed the stars, and, by eight-thirty, it was pitch black. Rene, Tommy and I shared a crater that we had stumbled upon—anything to avoid the backbreaking work of digging one man foxholes. Had Michaels found us, there would be hell to pay, but, exhausted, we risked discovery. The rest of the squad was spread out at about five yard intervals on our flanks.

Hours passed; suddenly, screaming and cursing filled the air. We jumped to assist our comrades. Two soldiers from 'B' company had been caught trying to penetrate of our lines. As required, when confronted, they surrendered. The rest of their force slinked away into the night.

We would interrogate the prisoners and deliver them to Sergeant Michaels who, undoubtedly, would issue medals of valor for all. The captor, Mike Flynn, a tough from Little Dublin whom I'd known forever but kept at arm's length because of his mercurial personality, assumed command. Though our rifles were empty, we pointed them menacingly at the captives—both of whom I recognized when Tommy pointed a flashlight at them.

Flynn, a formidable hundred and fifty pounds of muscle, was in a frenzy. "What's your goddamn names?"

They responded without hesitation.

When one refused to answer any more of Flynn's hysterical questions, and the other pleaded ignorance, Mike lost it and, without warning, punched the smaller of the two flush in the eye. Paralyzed, the rest of us said nothing.

"I mean it, talk or I'll bust you open."

I assessed the situation. Two soldiers from Company B were in our charge. One had a toadstool for an eye, and Flynn was readying to commit real atrocities. The prisoners were in shock, and no one but Mike moved. In the flash-lit moment, his eyes sparkled, and he drew back his Springfield to smash the butt into the gut of the smaller prisoner. It was surreal, everything happened in slow motion. The others were catatonic, and, much as I wanted it to be somebody else, there was nothing to do but jump between them.

I grabbed the weapon and yelled, "Cut it. It'll be our asses."

Mike prepared to reason and, without blinking, blasted me square in the nose with a straight right hand. My glasses headed for Philadelphia, and I stumbled back four steps before landing on my backside. I tasted blood from the heron beak but rose and went at him with my best stuff. "For Christ's sake, we'll all be in the guard house."

Frenchy and Tommy came to my side and diffused the situation, and the prisoners agreed that it had all been a misunderstanding. It took ten minutes to find my specs, miraculously undamaged, and we headed for Sergeant Michaels' tent. Squeezing my bloody nose with a green army handkerchief, I trailed them in. Michaels was elated, and from the animated smiles and body language, it was obvious that he knew there had been a scuffle. Rene and I exchanged glances. God pity any Germans that Flynn might capture.

Later, Tom said, "Christ, Em, if you hadn't stepped in, he'd a killed the poor bastard. Way to go."

Between snorts, I whined, "Yeah, stick your nose in and see what it gets ya...Dublin—assholes. . .This'll bleed all the way to Paris."

When we'd completed barely half the basic training, a sinking feeling descended over me; I wasn't going to make it, and a few days later, as we stood in front of the barracks, it became decision time. Corporal Brown, Michaels' chief executioner, asked the fateful question, "The clerk's been transferred; can anybody type?"

The wisdom of generations about volunteering was balanced by aching bones and the holes already blown in the lessons of home; I hesitated about a tenth of a second. "I can."

"Smart ass, himself. OK, Magawley, but if you're bull shittin', you'll be diggin' foxholes for the rest of your life—after the doc pries my foot outta yer ass."

You've heard it a thousand times, so there's little need for more details on the brutalization. Preparing morning reports, I was relieved of the heaviest training, and, on occasion, drove the company commander to the field and suppressed chuckles as we observed virtuoso performances by Sergeant Michaels on my friends—for which, of course, I paid dearly later in the barracks. Tommy Mullins made it through basic training without going to the guardhouse, as did Rene and I, and, when it was over, we were more frightened of Sergeant Michaels than of German machine guns. We had been transformed from ordinary young boys into a wolf pack under the total domination of its leader.

At our last formation, we wore our dress uniforms for the first time. Unbelievably, most had gained weight under the terrible regimen. The few who began the program overweight—very few—found the opposite to be true. Looking around, I believed that this crowd—that but weeks earlier couldn't cross a street without angry direction—would acquit itself well against the Germans. I was filled with pride.

As we stood at attention—straight as arrows, high collars not even close to our chins, baggy breeches, handsome canvas puttees wrapping our legs, and the beautiful stiff brimmed Canadian Mountie expedition hats, tilted ever so slightly—we feared little. The company commander charged us to do our duty in France, reminding us that we had received all the requisite training for success. He departed, and it remained for Sergeant Michaels to dismiss us. Snickering, he hinted broadly that he had been merely joking over these last months when stating he would tear our eyeballs from our heads and roll them in the sand. Everyone laughed; it was over.

Most of the troops were assigned to advanced infantry training at Camp Dix, and the rest were off to other cantonments for specialized training. Cooks, medics, artillerymen and a host of other occupations would be molded from this malleable mass of men at arms. Tom Mullins, Rene Dupuis and I were headed for Alabama for driver training. Who says it doesn't pay to know how to type?

Our records were replete with evidence of advanced automotive skills.

In early autumn, we were given rail tickets for Fort McClellan and, as the sun began its descent in the New Jersey sky, thanks were offered that we were headed for the sunny South. For the first time in our lives, we would not endure the cold blasts of New England's icy winter. It would be mint juleps in the gentle Alabama evenings.

Apparently, much of the Deep South enjoys an excellent late season climate. At Fort McClellan, however, that fall was worse than any January we had ever experienced. We lived in tents—actually half barracks, wooden frames enclosed in canvas—eight to a unit. The latrines were about fifty yards away, and we ran all the way to shower and for bodily functions. Cold? Envision Nome, Alaska at Christmas and you might begin to comprehend the pain of those icy stumbles in the night.

The training, however, was a vast improvement over what we'd known. While the cadre made it clear that we were of no value to the army, they didn't have it in them to grind us like Sergeant Michaels and, occasionally, even treated us like human beings. Soon we were driving through the back woods of Alabama—God, what fun. The Yankees were amazed by the red clay and did their best to spray it over all the troops we passed.

The army could spare only one heavy Mack truck for this training, so we got little time behind the wheel of that old giant. But speed was all that was prized, and we fought for turns on the little 1915 Dodge Touring models. More than a hundred of these little bugs zipped along on the Punitive Expedition in Mexico, and General Pershing was reported to love them. These were the clay-splashing champions.

The weeks flew; in a blink, it was graduation day, and we received our orders—most were headed for France. Because Rene could speak French and I had superior typing skills, we were assigned to the transportation company supporting General Pershing's own headquarters, and Tom was assigned to the Port of Le Havre where he would shuttle supplies back and forth among the allies.

The few boys ordered to posts in the States were objects of pity, for, while not anxious to mix it up with the Germans, to a man, we hungered for the adventure of crossing the pond.

Before reporting to New York for passage to France, we were given thirty days home leave, and I could hardly wait to show off my uniform for Millie. Never have trains rolled so slowly as on the long trek to Boston.

At the last hiss, Millie leaped at me and smothered me with kisses. The folks waited patiently, and she tore herself away so they could have their shots. Ma cried—as able a crier as there was in The Bush, with techniques for all occasions. Surely, it was from her that the broken man at funerals emanated. Da beamed, "Ya look grand, boy. It must be the chow." He laughed, waiting for his chance to hug me.

Mil's eyes popped at the uniform. Taller by the measure of the expedition hat, I had also bulked up to a muscular hundred and twenty, and the fright from facing Sergeant Michaels each day seemed to have straightened my back at least a tad. The way they looked at me, I began to believe we'd be home from the war in no time. The Germans could never resist us.

That evening at the Moynihan's, the Mrs. clasped me to her, and Sean shook my hand. Billy said I looked grand, and, as the evening progressed, the rest of the clan dropped in on the conquering hero. John and his wife, Margaret, were very nice, if quiet, but Mike—the bastard—came right out and spat in the soup. "You look good, Em—like them boy-scout pictures. What the hell d'ya call those wrappings on them bird legs? Better not let a fat Kraut get his paws on that scrawny neck o' yours, or it'll be into his Sunday pot with ya." He guffawed at the great joke, and, while Millie covered for him, for hours her eyes flashed daggers whenever he spoke.

If the train from Birmingham was slow, the home leave was a blur. By the time my furlough ended, many more boys from The Bush had been drafted. When visiting John and Mary Moran, I learned that Jack had taken leave from law school and reported to

Georgia for officer training. They were filled with pride, and I told them I was sure that he'd do fine.

There was a sour note, however, Clancy's was in mourning, as word was received that some kind of prohibition was to be put in place. Bible thumpin' drys had forced a law parchin' us out to support the war effort. Good Jesus, what did they think we were fightin' for? Since it wouldn't happen until 1919, I decided not to desert.

On the last day of leave, I walked past the high school and discovered a fancy honor roll listing the names of former students serving in the military. Dozens were posted, and the war was hardly under way. There was no requirement for having graduated to make the list, and Magawley was spelled correctly. I thought it a fine thing.

Millie and I had little time to pledge our love and grapple with true determination when it came time for the great adventure to begin, and damned if she wasn't fiercely angry with me again. "God, I'm sick. What'll I do if you fall?"

"Mil, I ain't pickin' my head up for nobody."

She swooned, but, in a flash, she was a hornet again, "I hate you, Emmet, you'll have girl friends in France. You will."

"Come on. You're my girl, and I'm comin' home. I promise."

She got over it, but love and anger shared her heart in nearly equal measures during those final hours.

The next day as we waited for the train, I watched a group of conscripts mill about with their girl friends and families. Straight and tall—mountie hat and puttees—I prepared for dignified good-byes while those recruits in all manner of civilian dress readied to meet their own Sergeant Michaels. They couldn't even leave Boston without help. The ride to New York was a revelation. I smoked Camel after Camel in total relaxation, and, when I looked into the car carrying the draftees, all I could observe was fear and anxiety. I was a soldier.

CHAPTER 5

In November 1917, the complex choreography of loading the Mauretania, the ship that would take us to France, commenced in march time. As the units completed their ascents of the gangplanks, ants scurrying onto a mastodon carcass, the tightly timed schedule placed additional busloads of soldiers from Brooklyn and New Jersey at the pier in Manhattan.

The coughing and sputtering vehicles emptied at a curb running parallel to the dock, as the great ship, like a prehistoric monster, loomed over all. Overstuffed kit bags caroming through the maze of metal seats, we struggled from the buses, and, by the time we formed up at the four gangplanks to the behemoth, we were sweating profusely. Repeatedly, we sounded off as our travel agents diligently checked and rechecked the rosters assuring that no one was left behind as the European holiday began.

Everywhere, sergeants barked at milling men who appeared to pay no heed. Cranes swung supplies for the crossing into the cavernous hold, while an army band played Sousa marches—amidst a cacophony of whistles and clanging and crashing metal—for the benefit of the troops and hundreds of well wishers straining for final glimpses of loved ones.

Since we were among the last to board, in no time the forearm thick anacondas slipped from the huge cleats and slithered aboard, as tugs straining against the dark hull eased us into the Hudson's channel. Heavy black smoke belching from the tall stacks enveloped us, and soot, clinkers and broken hearts drew tears everywhere.

Naturally, a Brooklyn wiseacre pointed out highlights for the rubes, but it was difficult not to be impressed by the Woolworth,

Met Life and other buildings that dwarfed everything in Boston, including the Customhouse. Soon, the great screws propelled us past the Statue of Liberty and on to the Verrazano Narrows. More quickly than I thought possible, the skyline slid beneath the waves.

South past Rockaway, we headed for a rendezvous with other vessels that would become a small component of a huge convoy forming off of Hampton Roads. As the ships gathered, the Mauretania shuddered when the engines were asked for more torque. I was filled with both trepidation and high hope at the prospect of adventure.

Steaming south for two days, we came on a flotilla of freighters, colliers, troop ships, and a host of others I could not identify. On the perimeter, porpoise like destroyers herded and protected us from the German undersea boats waiting to torpedo us. After several hours, the great school set off to the northeast. We were on our way over there.

The first afternoon, my anxieties surfaced when the enlisted men were issued Springfield rifles and ordered to remove the heavy preservative from them. Mother of God, could I set the sights on a German boy and squeeze? More important, might there be in Hamburg a heartless Hun wiping his piece and looking forward to plugging a crooked little Celt?

When finished, I sought out my sergeant and dedicated myself to preparing morning reports without so much as a single error for the duration. Typing would be my avocation in France; it had served me well, and I was full of hope that it would continue as my rabbit's foot.

The Mauretania, an aging British vessel, transformed into a troop ship and painted with irregular gray, green and blue patches to camouflage it from the U-boats, steamed into the North Atlantic surrounded by her smaller sisters and Lilliputian escorts.

The voyage quickly became a living hell. On the second day, swells rose ominously, and we found ourselves in the middle of a major nor'easter. Our great whale rose and crashed into the foam. The razor sharp bow sliced the gray green walls rising before her, and she shuddered as they crashed down upon the slicker clad seamen fighting for purchase on the slippery decks. The great ship yawed wildly, and seasickness was epidemic. However well intentioned, the troops were confined below, helpless to assist the exhausted mariners hold off the angry beast.

The maelstrom raged for three days, but, as quickly as its temper rose, it was sated, and we were bathed in sunshine in the midst of white caps and fresh winds. My longing to expire receded with the swells, and I stumbled out to the railing for fresh air. Only when I saw the smaller troop ships bob as if still in the heart of the storm did I realize the good fortune of those of us on the gargantuan Mauretania.

Tom, Rene and I were among a tiny minority of specialists on board, the overwhelming majority was infantry, the real Doughboys, and, as the days passed, they became somber. Only a few aging sergeants had ever faced live bullets in Cuba or Mexico, but the perils of trench warfare was on all minds. All their training would be for naught if they were ordered over the top into the teeth of machine gun fire. Even more frightening was the artillery; each side's blasts killed, maimed, and buried friend and foe alike.

The convoy's speed was limited to that of the slowest ship, so the crossing took twenty-one days, and, regardless of the consequences, by the time it was completed, even the most apprehensive and least dyspeptic among us welcomed landfall.

On the final day, we awakened surrounded by a pea soup fog and found that we had slowed noticeably from the already lethargic cruising speed. After hours of creeping like the haze itself, from nowhere Saint-Nazaire loomed about us. Eased to their berths, cranes began to disembowel freighters, while the Mauretania and the others spewed streams of human lava onto the Continent. Trucks and teams strained amidst a cacophony of curses, roaring engines, screaming horses, grinding winches, and slapping halyards. I was filled with mixed emotions as the doughboys, recovered from their reflections, strode purposefully onto French soil, kit bags slung on their shoulders.

Representatives of a hundred commands barked at the twisting and writhing mass. A sergeant found our names and directed us to his assistants. The time came for Rene and me to part with Tom Mullins. We'd survived Sergeant Michaels and Fort McClellan together and knew that we were to split up here. Regardless, it was difficult to believe that the moment was upon us. Tom was steady as we took leave.

"Take care o' yerself till we get back to The Bush."

He mumbled his affirmation and hopped lightly onto the back of a truck bound for Le Havre, disappearing into the soup. The wrenching in my gut was terrible.

Rene and I were driven by car into the nearby city of Nantes and given rail passes for Paris from which we would be transported to the headquarters of the American Expeditionary Force, the whereabouts of which was a closely guarded secret. We were headed for 'Somewhere in France'. Apparently, only the Germans knew the exact location.

General Pershing had moved from Paris to Chaumont, about one hundred and fifty miles southeast of the Capital on the River Marne. It was near there in Western Lorraine that American troops would engage the Germans directly. Pershing and Wilson resisted allied demands that U.S. troops be committed piecemeal to augment the tattered French and British armies and determined that the Americans would fight as a single unified force. That caused great ill will among the allies, and Rene and I heard about it many times in the months ahead.

We were fully engaged during the five-hour trip to Paris by our fellow travelers and the now bright countryside. What a life, from The Bush to Paris with a private interpreter and natives ecstatic at the opportunity to embrace Yanks racing to their aid.

A trio of lovelies from the tiny village of La Fleche—I'm not kidding—smiled on us, enthralled by tales of the Wild West—Worcester. The runty Bay Staters, late of New Jersey, had been transformed into muscular and lanky Yanks for these petite mademoiselles who giggled uproariously at Rene's accent. Our hearts broke when they disembarked.

During the trip, it became obvious that France was war weary and, without the shot in the arm provided by America's entry, the civilians would have been totally disheartened. By the time we arrived in Paris, Frenchy and I—clearly made of the stuff of heroes—had achieved very good buzzes, courtesy of our new friends. While I maintained at least a semblance of my expected role in the war, Rene was beginning to believe these drunken Frenchmen who proclaimed that he and I—alone—would drive the Kaiser back into Prussia.

We passed quickly through the capital, ignoring the great landmarks. Given the depths of our ignorance, it's doubtful that with even a week's leave we would have taken advantage of anything but the decadent sports held in such high esteem by the goons back in the swamps of Camp Dix.

At the station, sergeants pushed, dragged and carried us to a truck bound for Chaumont. Sadly, this leg of the trip, which should have been of even greater interest than the one across Northern France, went unobserved, as we slept off our surfeit.

We awakened to find ourselves in a motor pool created from an old moving and storage company on the outskirts of the provincial capital. The barns had been converted to garages and the warehouse doubled as our barracks.

This was no ordinary transportation company. The mission was to drive staff officers to and from various sub-units and pick up visiting dignitaries and carry them to call on General Pershing. Except for heavy trucks, we had the standard vehicles in the AEF inventory, but, unique to Chaumont, there was a collection of not less than fifty staff cars. The most numerous were the little Dodges, loved dearly by the great one, that had chased Pancho Villa through the Mexican countryside. In addition, Model Ts and ten Royal Mail Chevrolets, open four seaters used to transport larger parties, were kept at the ready.

Pershing demanded that everyone in headquarters advance the notion that the Americans were here to turn the tide. Looking like we could do it was the first order of business, and the drivers were expected to maintain excellent appearance and military bearing and move more smartly than our counterparts in the other transportation units.

Notwithstanding their greasy occupation, mechanics were given only slightly more leeway. This was not a difficult charge; smartness just became part of our routine. For officers, failure to measure up meant a lonely crossing back to Hoboken, while sloppy enlisted men were sent forward to combat units. On learning this, my childhood propensity for shined shoes and bright brass came to the fore, as did my resolution to continue working on my posture, if only for the sake of my prideful love.

A glance confirmed that a soldier was a member of the Chaumont contingent. Officers, especially Generals of all shapes and sizes, swept through the compound, cigarette holders casually displayed in one hand and riding crops smartly in the other. Whenever I saw these supermen approach, cape flying, I made every effort to avert my eyes and avoid saluting. Many, such as Douglas MacArthur and George Patton, became more famous in the second war. I steered clear of such dandies, recognizing instinctively that they were too courageous for my taste; the sacrifice of a platoon of Celts for the greater glory of the war effort ever loomed as a possibility.

If the Kaiser could have visited us, the war would have been shortened dramatically. Any number of staff officers in AEF headquarters wanted to encourage similar smartness in front line troops, but there were a few, including George Marshall, guarding against such directives that bubbled up from time to time. I typed a few of the more whimsical myself.

For my money, only one human being wore stars in Chaumont, Denny Nolan. We were convinced that Black Jack kept him around to assure the enlisted men that he gave a crap about them. Kev, I know you're thinking that I liked Nolan only because he was Irish, but that's not it at all. He was a damned straight shooter.

Life in headquarters resembled that in any unit - kitchen police, guard duty, and an endless array of other mundane chores.

Too dainty, I made myself invaluable by typing reports. Company clerks have always been too precious to dip their fingers in greasy water. Dishpan hands ever have been a no no for army typists.

While I was discouraged from even walking through Pershing's front office—not nearly straight enough for the martinet—my skills on the keyboard were utilized to produce all manner of reports in support of the forty-man contingent of clerks brought over with Jack on the Baltic. Today, with millions of youngsters flitting lightly across computer keyboards, it's difficult to comprehend how rare male typists were in that age.

Movie buffs know that armies always set up headquarters in castles. Black Jack Pershing determined that his domain would be second to none and made sure that his was fit for a king with an ego the size of Picardy—matching its wartime occupant's needs perfectly.

The mansion, an asymmetrical French country house, its front gable and entrance to the left of center, exuded the genteel informality of a rural home for the highest nobility. Limestone quoins on all corners of the gables and the main house framed the three story walls, adding greatly to the impact of power.

The main entrance, surrounded by beautiful foundation plantings, was but strides to the four steps leading to the doorway framed by Greek columns supporting an elegant pediment.

The foyer floor was of pure white marble, and, on either side, a staircase rose gracefully to a mezzanine enclosing the great room. Vermilion runners raced up the treads, and an Austrian cut glass chandelier dominated the center of the ceiling.

Overflowing with brilliant flowers, Ming vases sat on lacquered oriental tables at the side walls on the main level. The cuttings were changed every morning from stock in greenhouses on the grounds. The little French gardener had mess privileges and invariably sought out Rene and me to pass the hour.

Above the tables, Impressionist cityscapes casually connected the orient and Europe, and, on the facing wall, a huge painting of sheep being driven to pasture with the Cathedral at Chartres looming like a ghostly mountain in the distance impressed even the most jaded diplomat.

The library, bordered by leather bound books, served as the waiting room where visitors cooled their heels waiting for Pershing. The aides serving in it were selected for appearance—six foot, one hundred and sixty pounds were absolute minimums. They must have been denied permission to sit, as no one ever observed a wrinkled uniform exit the room. This antechamber was the source of most of the memos on the need to spruce up the appearance of the front line troops.

The salon, off the library, served as Black Jack's office. Exquisite furniture from the periods of one or another of the Louis, whom I could never keep straight, was set in a manner assuring that neither comfort or ease could be attained. I thought that this room fulfilled Pershing's napoleonic fantasy perfectly.

While in the mansion, I labored in a third floor bedroom converted into a bullpen for eight typists. Since none but the adjutant to Pershing's own adjutant ever visited, we were free to slouch and smoke as we pecked away.

The situation was perfect; my primary job was that of driver, and if not on assignment from the motor pool, I assisted the company clerk—unless, of course, my services were needed in the big house. Those with any military service can decipher the circumstance—no one knew where I was supposed to be—but assumed I was slaving away somewhere.

Rene's job was more structured. In no time, his command of both Parisian and the local dialect was perfect, and he was regularly on call to pick up French officers and diplomats at the train station. Taking his cue from the master, he, too, learned to be expected in several places at the same time.

In Chaumont, cigarettes and red wine were available at no cost to us, and each day we strolled the grounds of the beautiful villa in the midst of verdant fields and woods alive with the songs of birds. Ah, yes, this was the heart of the war zone. When we returned to Boston, we would almost certainly have to be pensioned off with combat ruined livers and lungs.

Life was not without true hardship, however, and among the worst was the poorest possible communications with loved ones. Mail service was abominable, and the army cared not at all about the impact on morale. Weeks passed when, out of the blue, huge trucks lumbered into Chaumont and dumped tons of it before us. Stained letters written months previously referring to others obviously lost were devoured with far less satisfaction than they should have provided, and queries in the incoming confirmed that many accounts of life in France had never made their way to Boston.

I corresponded almost daily with Millie and Ma, even if many of their letters failed to arrive, and I received occasional notes from others. Spirits were high at home, and I was heartened by news of the war gardens. Big John Moran had located several squashes among his weeds, and Da was apparently the first agronomist ever to plant peas and harvest carrots.

One morning, a letter from Da announced that Gramma had been found dead in her bed, and his loss was obvious, despite her considerable span. She and Grampa were pioneers in The Bush, and she had been a force in civilizing the beasts that prowled its streets—more than a few of whom she herself had produced.

Even with half of the mail lost, I found it easier to deduce changes in the old place from this alien posting than from a stool in Clancy's.

On the war front, divination was prized, and those arranging transport for foreign officers had better be able to separate wheat from chaff. When lowly French or British generals—between generals there are more gradations than among all other ranks combined—needed transport to headquarters, two of us were sent. What the second fellow was for, I never really figured out—copilot, I suppose. Often, Rene and I drew the duty, and, until we had them on board, it was a ball. We mashed the gas pedals, and tried our best to ruin the old Chevy torpedoes. A cloud of dust and smoke was the evidence of our zeal. But we never drank on duty; several alcohol related accidents had resulted in quick reassignments up the Marne where the shells were exploding.

Once, Rene and I picked up a pair of generals, a Brit and a Frenchman. I drove, and Rene popped out to greet them. Before he could utter a word, the Brit spoke for both, and they hopped in. Convinced of our ignorance, they palavered in Francais during the trip to the house.

After they left, I asked, "What the hell was that about?"

"The Yanks ain't worth shit, and they'll have to bail us out when the goin' gets tough. And they dumped a load o' shit on Pershing."

"Fuck them."

On the return, the two stars, at it again, were suddenly silenced when Rene asked in his most cultivated French if they needed anything. Christ, what a deafening hush descended on us. On a more mundane level, when I got close to the transportation company clerk, I began to lobby a transfer for Tommy from Le Havre to Chaumont. Naturally, the man blew me off, but I kept coming on—any clerk can be broken with a relentless campaign. Two months of grinding and Tom's transfer was under the captain's nose, and, four weeks later, we had the damnedest reunion imaginable.

Tommy fit right in, but, without the skills in demand in the big house, he had to pull all the details from which Frenchy, half of the others, and I were excused. Mullins learned that war is truly hell; the bastard resented the kitchen police and let us know about it, too—ingrate.

In March of '18, the Germans began an offensive against the British and French, a last ditch effort to win the war before the Americans could shift the balance with fresh manpower. The number of visitors to Chaumont doubled and redoubled in a frantic effort to speed the American buildup, but there was nothing that could be done to get the arms and men across the sea any faster, and Pershing held fast in his determination to fight with his own unified force. The panic among the Europeans was palpable, and we listened to far more sarcasm on the way back to the station. God, the allies adored the Kaiser compared to Black Jack.

At about that time, the Russians collapsed, and the Germans were free to wheel great numbers of men and masses of material to the West for a knockout punch against the exhausted British and French.

Finally, in late spring, after panicked appeals to Wilson in Washington, even Pershing saw the desperation of the situation and ordered the AEF forces to shore up French positions on the southern flank. I don't know how much good the decision actually made in the battles raging at places like Noyon and Castel-Cantigny to our north, but our visitors were far friendlier to the drivers. Still, none of them could bring themselves to say a kind word for Pershing—but, of course, neither could we.

Within days, the war commenced in earnest for the Americans, and casualty lists lengthened. Foreign correspondents crawled about headquarters, and we picked up bits and pieces of what was happening. The upstairs typists became engulfed by citations for bravery, and, since many were for boys who would never read them, the work was abhorred.

The American force grew daily, and by April there were more than a million of us in France. West of Chaumont, French officers and sergeants trained the doughboys for the combat they would find at the front.

At the company, the call for transportation to and from the front became heavier. This duty was hazardous—more so for our passengers than for us, however. We picked up officers at the house and headed to the northeast where the battles raged. Dropping them to the rear of the line, they were escorted on foot or carried in motorcycle sidecars to the front where they'd have a look for Pershing.

Since, until near the end of the war, penetration by the combat forces of both sides usually covered only hundreds of yards with each assault instead of the miles typical of the next war, and because air support was primitive and under allied ascendancy, unless we got right up to the front, there wasn't much danger of coming under fire. After turning our charges over to the fighting troops, we'd retreat to find cover for our vehicles and wait for their return.

But once, in the summer of 1918, I came upon the real war and was filled with terror and disgust. The heaviest combat involving Americans was raging along a line running roughly from Belleau Wood and Chateau Thierry northeasterly toward Reims. Our second and third divisions were taking the brunt of the last great drive by the Germans, and the give and take was unbelievable. On this day, however, the Yanks were clearly in command.

My passenger was a major, and I expected nothing more than the usual drive in the park. Nearing the combat zone, the pounding of the heavy guns could be heard and felt over the banging and coughing of the engine of the little Dodge, and, on this lovely clear day, a great storm appeared in the distance. Dark thunderheads of fire, soot and smoke from artillery bursts, the lightning bolts of the horizon to horizon conflagration, awakened the realization that there was a war on. Still miles from the battle, we turned easterly on a road leading to the front and fell in with a column of trucks, guns, and other vehicles of every size and description, mechanized and horse drawn. The going was slow, as only one lane was open heading into the thick of things. On the side of the way to our right, fresh doughboys, concerned but steady, strode faster than us toward the Germans.

The broken line on our left told a different tale. Ambulance drivers leaned on horns and screamed epithets to speed their passage to medical stations. Beside the rolling litters, exhausted troops being relieved by the fresh fodder struggled toward rest and safety, showing none of the bounce of their comrades only twenty yards away. Filthy with tattered uniforms, some had lost their weapons and helmets; bandages stemmed—partially—the flow from the wounds of those for whom there was no room in the ambulances; Walking wounded were hardly curiosities, but there was no panic.

At first glance, dried mud worn by the troops in both lines seemed a common garment, but nothing could have been further from the truth. Those marching toward their great adventure bore the marks of splashes cavalierly deposited by chauffeurs of careless generals rushing to order charge before the traffic had bogged down, while the muck worn by their weary comrades had been garnered in the loving embrace of mother earth. As the bombs burst and the machine guns cut, they had pressed themselves to become one with it to avoid the screaming metal; some were never released.

Closer to the battlefield, we were surrounded by dead horses and shattered equipment, the flotsam of desperate conflict, pushed aside to decompose into the scarred soil. While the human corpses had been collected, no such niceties could be provided for the horses until later. Already, their bellies were distended and the sickening sweet scent of burnt flesh mixed with the smells of fire and powder. Nausea rose within me.

At a road junction still miles from the fighting, a lieutenant collected my major, and I pulled off and parked far from any dead animals, settling in for the long wait for my passenger.

During such spells—in my unbiased view, a handsome figure, straight as nature permitted, cigarette at a tilt, steel pot at a rakish angle—I looked toward the front and observed the grunts as they passed. This time, however, I had no stomach for posing; the poor devils being relieved had looked hell in the eye. While those fresh from the training sites trod doggedly to the front; they saw the chewed up remains of their comrades staggering away from the horror that waited for them. Smoking, I hunched over and averted my eyes from the poor bastards dragging themselves to the rear, hoping the day would pass quickly.

Bobbing buzzards—engineers, artillerymen and quartermasters—scavenged broken guns, limbers and caissons for parts and unexpended shells. Occasional rifle reports rang out as dying horses were destroyed. This taste of war was too much, and I was nowhere near the raging battle. Suddenly, I felt sorrier for those advancing than those whose mission had been completed.

"Emmet!...Emmet!" A voice rang out from a particularly ragamuffin gang passing to the rear.

To no avail, I searched the faces but heard it again emanating from a boy assisting his buddy. Helmet gone, weapon slung over his left shoulder, he was one of the most bedraggled on the road. They stopped, and I approached. The poor lad attempted a smile, and, with that, I knew it was Mike Flynn. "Mike, good God, boy, you look like shit." With an instant to think, I'd have never said such a stupid thing, but it was out.

Tears streamed through the sooty mask, tiny rivulets of pain. "Jesus, Emmet, they killed Joe Riley and half the others from Little Dublin. He was just a step ahead of me, and we were runnin' at 'em, and then he had no head. He just sat down—without his fuckin' head.

"I don't remember anything else till I found myself standin' with poor Pat holdin' on to me."

Mother of God, I hadn't recognized Pat Ryan. I was only casually acquainted with him, as he was two years ahead of me in school and in another platoon at Camp Dix, but we'd knelt side by side for the picture in front of the South Station. "Pat, it's me, Emmet. Pat?" Nothing...Thinking he might be deafened by a shell concussion, I touched his shoulder, but he offered no reaction. Slack jawed, he just stared.

The retreating soldiers stumbled by, and I led the boys to the side of the road. "Sit down. I've got water."

Flynn pulled Ryan down beside him while I ran for the canteen. Mike drank deeply and tried to pass it to his partner. Struggling mightily, he forced some into Pat, but there were no signs that Ryan comprehended anything.

"Rest a minute. There's an aid station just down the road. They can take Pat."

"His fuckin' head was gone. He sat down like nothin' happened, but his head wasn't there."

"Forget him. He never felt a thing. Worry about yourself—and Pat...Nobody can help Joe."

Ryan sat and scanned the horizon while Mike stretched out on the soft grass and closed his eyes. This wasn't the Mike Flynn who'd bloodied my nose—the wild man from Little Dublin. While still outweighing me by twenty pounds, he was gaunt and drawn, and I saw no trace of boy in him. A passing sergeant shouted, and we stumbled into the disorganized column.

Slinging Mike's rifle over my shoulder, I took Pat's hand. In the first half hour, we'd covered only about a mile, when, without notice, Mike lurched to the side and dropped near a shattered caisson with four fallen horses still in the traces. The smell gagged me, but the Dubliners seemed to notice it not at all. They were exhausted beyond human endurance, and I vowed to get a hold on my nerves. Placing the rifle in the grass, I eased Pat down.

Ryan stared and Mike continued his mumbling to the world at large, "His fuckin' head was gone—like he sat down for a butt...One swing of the machine gun and all of 'em were cut down like fresh green grass."

Unable to stand it, I began prodding them to move on when I saw that one of the horses was alive—the leader on the off side lying furthest from us. In a trance, I approached the poor devil—a huge Belgian—it could have been old Bob from home—whose blood oozed from numerous punctures. Covered with earth, his blond mane was matted with mud and caked blood, and his broken right foreleg was thrown at a right angle. Flies were at the festering wounds and the mucous draining from his flared nostrils. Breathing shallowly, he observed me with alert but pain filled eyes. For an instant, I thought he might attempt to rise, but the poor beast was long past that.

"Mike!" I screamed, "Mike! Here!" Tearing my eyes from the doomed animal, I saw Flynn babbling, giving no sign of having heard. Sprinting to him, I yelled, "One those horses is alive. You've got to shoot him."

Instantly alert, he puffed up with indignation and contempt and, looking me in the eye, spat, "Half the boys from Dublin are dead, and you're worried about a fuckin' horse?" He turned to Ryan. "The assholes from The Bush never change...Not an ounce of sense, eh, Pat?"

With no time for niceties, I snatched the rifle and ran to the horse. Placing the barrel in the center of the white diamond on his forehead, I squeezed. With the flash and explosion, the lights dimmed in the beautiful eyes. Staring for a moment, I turned away and puked.

When I returned to my companions, Mike's head was shaking with an overwhelming sadness, and he cackled sardonically, "The asshole can't even put a horse out of his fuckin' misery, Pat. The Bush...What the fuck do ya expect?"

The rest of the hike to the aid station passed in a blur. Pat was identified for the medics, and I patted Flynn's shoulder and was off without a word. I fell into the faster paced line of troops headed toward the front.

Before I could begin to sort out what had happened to my neighbors, I was in the Chevy watching for my major. As the sun settled, he returned wearing a broad smile. We exchanged salutes, and he said, "The war's over."

On the long road to Chaumont, he chattered incessantly. "We're showin' those frogs. They were praying for the old man to fall on his face...Bastards." He completely overlooked my lack of interest in the prattle, however positive.

It was now a race between the war and medical science. Which would give first, the Germans or our livers. If the war lasted into 1919, the enlisted men in Chaumont would be in mortal danger from the elephants and lions crawling from the woodwork in their barracks, but the word was out, the boches were done.

Suddenly, a new crisis confronted the AEF, the worldwide influenza pandemic hit. Since the bug had made well-publicized stops across the globe, killing millions in the process, there was no surprise when it arrived, but we were nearly helpless to oppose it. Initially, it struck the Germans. Perfect targets, they were poorly nourished and had fought without proper rest or sanitation for years. Soon every fifth Kraut in the divisions facing our troops was down, and the mortality was horrendous.

In less than a week, the flu broke out among our prisoners of war, and soon the guards were collapsing as fast as the poor Huns. Within days, it struck our front line troops and turned on us in Chaumont. Naturally, the British and French suffered almost as badly as the Germans, but, their problems were their own, it was AEF headquarters that worried me.

One morning, we found Tommy vomiting over everything. A quarter of the platoon was unable to stagger to formation, and the sergeants were helpless to respond. Fortunately, the headquarters facilities were excellent, and eight or ten of the those most ill from our barracks were evacuated to the field hospital. While there was no cure, the resources in Chaumont permitted rehydration of those most ill, keeping fatalities down considerably. Regardless, the dying commenced.

It was very sad; the disease struck the youngest soldiers hardest. The older men, sergeants and officers, were almost immune while the privates fell like flies. Panic was everywhere, Mother of God, I'm still ashamed when I think of how I held my breath and shunned friends, but I was no worse than the others.

After three days, Tommy rallied and was soon able to take on soup. Rene or I'd get a canteen of broth and bring it to him, and soon he was gulping it down.

A few days later, I returned from the villa and found Rene confused and suffering with a high fever. Tom said that he'd been hurling over everything, and the fellows had been working like dogs to keep ahead of him with mops. They'd called for a medic, and, minutes later, a doctor came for him and the others who were down. We were ordered to sponge him down and get water into him.

By morning, Frenchy was delirious and burning up. While one of the boys went for a car, we soaked him again. Tom and I lifted him into the Chevy and raced to the hospital, but, since a quarantine had been instituted, we were not allowed to go in with him.

That night, Rene Dupuis died. Chaumont was the safest place in France in 1918, and, while hundreds of thousands allied and enemy soldiers were slain, not a single soldier from my company had been killed or wounded. Broken bones caused by crazy driving were the extent of our casualties, but, now, my friend, my buddy, was dead—without as much as a smile or wave goodbye. My heart had been wrenched from my body, and a glance confirmed that the impact on Tom was equally heavy.

Poor little Frenchy—from the train ride to Trenton until his death, we were rarely apart. We'd suffered together in New Jersey and sprayed mud in Alabama. We'd laughed through a war that was almost over, and he'd bayed at the moon as we drove back to our barracks after wild nights on the town. He was dead, and, to this day, I occasionally fly awake from a nightmare in which his disappearance is but a cruel hoax perpetrated by a miserable sergeant.

It was a hell of a siege, and the influenza won. More than sixty thousand American boys died—ten thousand more than had been killed by the Germans in a year of savage fighting. It hit hard back home, too, but it's terribly sad for a boy to die without a loved one to hold a hand or pat a brow as he's consumed by the heartless foe.

The war raged on, but the news brightened each day, and Chaumont overflowed with confidence. Oral attacks by allied officers on Pershing ceased—though more than a few clerks still wanted a chance to catch him bent over. He'd never done anything to me, but the sight of the cold sonofabitch striding through the compound, put in command by God, Himself, was enough to place me among them.

As the front moved quickly away from the big house, Pershing transferred his command post into a private railroad car to better enable him to maintain contact with the rapidly receding war, and Chaumont became a backwater for paper pushing.

More time was spent typing than on the road, but we suffered little pressure in the pool, as those in charge had little interest in determining what our output should be. Establishing a reasonable rhythm, I typed deliberately, with hourly smoke breaks. Not thinking about the posthumous citations enabled us to get through the difficult days.

Flicking a butt into the cool air of a late September afternoon, I climbed the stairs to finish the day. Grabbing a handful of awards, mindlessly, I pounded away. Within minutes of knocking off, I decided to complete one more. Glancing at the hand written cover, I stopped. 'Second Lieutenant John Moran, Second Platoon, C Company, First Battalion, 189th Infantry Regiment, Third Infantry Division . . .Lt. Moran was killed while rallying his platoon to repel an overwhelming enemy attack. For gallantry in action, Platoon Leader Moran is posthumously recommended for the Silver Star. He entered the service in Boston, Mass., and his next of kin has been notified.'

After struggling through the body of the citation, itself, I placed it gently on the desk. This would have to wait. Toward sunset, having skipped the evening meal, I staggered along the bank of the lovely River Marne. My thoughts were on the trips to the rail yard to pick up caskets. At this moment, someone somewhere was delivering a coffin for poor Jack Moran. Mother of God, the crown prince was dead—no world was safe. Dropping at a particularly lovely spot, I thought of Mary and John. There was nothing to inhibit me, and I sobbed uncontrollably. Back in command and, as always, thinking of myself, I dreaded my next encounter with the Morans.

The war, that lovely adventure, was now the bleakness about me. My pledge to return safely to Millie would be fulfilled. Aside from that terrible day I'd driven near the front, I never saw a gun fired in anger, but, now, I was revolted by everything in France. I couldn't wait to escape the ghosts of Jack Moran and Frenchy and return to The Bush where the greatest pain was in failing to sink the nine ball. I dreamed of holding Millie and crying about Jack and Frenchy, and for Mary and Big John, and poor Peggy Mulligan, and Mike Flynn, and Pat Ryan, and Joe Riley—still sitting somewhere without his head, and for the Dupuis of Fall River, whom I'd never even met. As the sun set over the shimmering water of the meandering river, I pounded my fists helplessly into the dew-softened turf. My quest for the exotic was fully satisfied. In a trance, I shuffled to my quarters.

By mid-October, rumors that the war would soon end were flying about. It was said that German feelers for an armistice were overwhelming the British and French. But a major impediment surfaced—John J. Pershing, himself. The officers said the old man didn't want to let the Krauts off the hook without demonstrating to their civilians back home how horrible war had become. If we didn't, Jack said the Huns would be back at us in twenty years. God, how I wanted to kick some sense into the crazy martinet.

Pershing was overruled—naturally—given the exhaustion of all the armies, except our own, and the armistice was signed. I thought him a maniac, out only for personal glory. Still, there was no choice for the governments but to end it. But I still believe that half of those idiots sweeping through Chaumont, caped comic book crusaders, didn't give a damn if peace ever came so long as they could order charge. More than once I heard the old canard that the only thing sadder than defeat was victory. But the Great War ended on all fronts, and we were going home. Pershing had long departed Chaumont, and most of the automobiles and drivers had moved out to support him in supervising the Armistice. Those of us remaining at the old moving company were of little use to anyone and soon received orders to return to Saint-Nazaire for transport home. None too soon, as the dissipation evident without the presence of the top staff was patent. I, for one, no longer feared being caught without shined shoes or a wrinkled shirt, and the threat of being sent to the front no longer obtained, not that I ever feared the Krauts or Pershing anyway. By mid January 1919, the army could find no excuse for detaining us, and we joined the parade home.

Logistics for the return to America were almost as complicated as the trip to France. By mandate of General Pershing, the strictest military bearing and readiness was to be maintained. Enforcement of that baloney gave the sergeants something to do while waiting for their own orders. Disappearing experts, Tom and I found little to dread in such foolishness.

Prior to boarding, we were given health examinations. As you can imagine, these physicals were as thorough as the one I'd been given in Boston and looked past the impairments acquired in making the world safe for democracy. After the command to cough, the doc commented on its depth, and I advised him of the many cases of consumption in Chaumont. The bastard found that humorous.

Tom and I would ride home in style. By coincidence, we were assigned to return on the Baltic, the vessel that carried General Pershing and his AEF staff to France. While boarding was as complex as that of the trip on the Mauretania, efforts to assure that we made the trip were not nearly as rigorous. The authorities were somehow more certain of our desire to go home. In nothing flat, we were ready and under way. There was none of the looking for company as in the time of misery; the captain simply pointed her at New York and revved the engines to cruising speed. We were alone—no flotilla, no escorts, and no effort was made to avoid detection. The weather was fair, and, after only a week, we spotted Montauk.

Steaming near Rockaway at cruising speed, I feared we might follow the bow wave onto Staten Island, but the narrows opened, and the Statue of Liberty waved us home. Jesus, Mary and Joseph, in spite being the color of seasickness, itself, she looked mighty good to us. We waved and yelled as the docking progressed, and, cinders in both eyes, I was razzed for being a Mama's boy. The closer we approached, the more we pounded on each other, and even the surly among us seemed pleased.

As a foretaste of post war life, we found a dock strike under way, and the Governor had mobilized the State Guard to unload us. As we stepped ashore, not one damn soul—not a band, not a mayor, not a single speechmaker, nobody cheered; the deflation was palpable. The bus driver was friendly but, obviously, just doing his job, and, as we passed through the East Side and Brooklyn, few waved. The Great War was already passing into history.

The hours on the train were passed determining what to do with the rest of our lives and, more importantly, the munificent fifty-dollar federal bonuses for unstinting, even heroic, service.

Tom began, "I'm gonna sleep for a friggin' month. No, first, Ma'll make a pot roast—she's the best. Then I'll sleep for a month. Then I'll see Big John about bein' a fireman. They're good jakes— no orders, takin' or givin'. What about you, Em?"

"Tommy, boy, I'm returnin' to the bosom of my love, literally. I want to die in her arms. If I ever wake up, then I'll think about it."

The nonsense passed the miles and hours. We were veterans— with mustering out pay and fifty more, and we could do damn well as we pleased. We would need work—but neither desperately nor soon. Tom hit it on the head. "For damn sure, we ain't goin' to be put in our place no more. There ain't no place no more. Right, Em?"

I assured him there was no longer a place. We were returning to The Bush, but it was a new world in which no bull would be tolerated. We were Irish and as good as anyone—not one whit better but just as good.

At Providence, I said, "Poor Frenchy. If only he could be here."

We remembered in silence, but the train rolled on through ever more familiar stations—Foxboro, Walpole, Norwood, and Dedham—and our thoughts turned to The Bush. Outside it was cold, and the people leaned into the biting wind, but there was no sign of misery. How could there be? They were home.

As we neared the city, we felt the crush of Boston—the people, commerce and housing. The dynamism swelled in the starts and stops of the cars and trucks and from the horns that pierced the single pane window of our car. Far more than when we left, not two years before, the horses looked out of place among the herky-jerky motor vehicles.

The train slowed as we switched across tracks and entered the rail yard separating Dorchester and Southie. Carson Beach told me that we were closing in on Millie. Still more slowly, we rolled toward the Fort Point Channel. The massive South Station rose before us. "Tommy, we made it. I'm never leavin' home again."

Tom smiled more broadly than I'd ever seen, and his eyes sparkled. "Write it down, Emmet. Make book on it."

We struggled for position at the door and strained to see those waiting. In seconds, a crowd waved but then disappeared into the breath of the huge beasts. Then in a break, I saw her. "Mother of God, Tom. Have you ever? Jesus, she's waitin' for me."

The tortured eyes that were seared into my soul fifteen months before were filled with joy, but, again, she disappeared into the vapor. I willed my eyes to penetrate the cloud, but she was lost. Then I saw Ma and Da and Grampa, too, lifting his tired old wing. She reappeared, and I saw the lovely smile. Unable to bear it, I leaped to the platform and raced into her arms. No, I didn't die, but had I, they could have lowered me into the ground without a dirge.

The Great War was over, and it would be smooth sailing from now on for Easy Emmet Magawley.

CHAPTER 6

For two days, Mil and I were imprisoned in each other's arms. Her embrace alone sustained me, and I couldn't bear a moment's freedom. Her kisses were more precious than life itself, and the prophecy that I had returned to die in her arms ripened. No matter, for more than a year, I had fantasized this incarceration, and it was all that I had dreamed.

"Every night, I fell asleep fearing you'd fallen. But, thank God, you're home."

"Mil, the Krauts and I had an understandin'. I didn't attack the fatherland, and they didn't shoot me. There was no way I wasn't comin' back."

Naturally, such passion could not be maintained and reality slipped through the bars. The word that set off the warning siren was 'marriage'. The alarm emanating from the lips of the lovely Millie Moynihan bounced off my ears, and I rose for air. It dawned on me that I was headed for the altar.

When, temporarily, I had shaken her spell, it was time to face the Morans. If the visit were postponed too long, questions concerning loyalties would arise, so I screwed up my courage and forced my reluctant feet to their doorstep. Mary flung open the door and threw herself in my arms, her eyes welling with tears. "John! It's Emmet. John! Mother o' God, thanks be for delivering him."

The shadow of the rough old beast filled the doorway, and he brachiated down the banister, flying over the stairs, "Thank God, ya made it, boy." He enveloped me in his great arms. "It's a great day for The Bush. More important, it's time for a brew."

Mary fluttered like my old Gramma, and both of them fawned

over me as if I were the Prince of Wales. Most of all, they tried every ploy to sniff out my intentions toward Millie, and, when I admitted to a settled contract, I thought they'd burst. This would solve many of the problems that had nagged the district from time immemorial, and they extolled the value of both families to the city, the party, and, most important, to the local organization.

We talked of Boston, and John went over the changes, but, most of all, he talked about the social and political volatility in the country. "The country's goin' to hell. Damn reds everywhere. Sixty Thousand strikin' in Seattle. The Goldman woman—agh! —And that damn Bolshevik, John Reed, stirrin' up the workers—there's no end." The most ebullient man in The Bush was in a deep depression. "For generations, we've given our all to convince the Yankees that all we wanted was a place at the table. Now the scum are mockin' us. 'To hell with the Yankees. And their toady Irish.' It's sickenin'."

But deep within the lament, I sensed a determination to fight for what he had been shaping.

"The saddest thing's that many of ours are with 'em. Even our police are radicalized. They may even strike. That rascal Curley's stirrin' the pot. Idiot, he'd bring us all down to get elected again."

He carried on through three long beers and seemed saddened when I was slow to leap to his banner—finding even a smidgen of merit on the other side.

The end of politics came into view; it was time to address what we'd been avoiding. Mary entered the living room and sat, and we turned to the pictures on the baby grand. Jack's was in front, straight as an arrow in his officer's uniform, made seemingly invulnerable by his Sam Brown belt.

"I learned about it only days after it happened. My heart broke for yuz. You got my letter?"

John blubbered, "It was a great comfort...He was a hero, Em. Let me get the citation." He hurried into the bedroom and returned with the beautifully framed document.

I recognized my work but, saying nothing, took a long time to read it as if for the first time. "He was a wonderful man, and it was a great loss not only for yourselves and Peggy but for the country, as well."

We all cried.

The first to recover, Mary came alive. "They've established a prize in his name at Harvard. It will be awarded each year to the outstanding young man in the second year of the law school. For-ever, Emmet—for all time. His classmates endowed it. For Jack Moran, an Irish Catholic—Harvard. Isn't that wonderful?"

"It is. It's a fine thing."

We pulled ourselves together, and I took leave as gracefully as possible. It had been even more difficult than my visit to the rec-tory concerning the 'Our Father', but I'd made it through. As soon as I hit the street, I drew deeply on an overheated cigarette.

In dire need, I headed for Clancy's. Three days home and not a minute with the lads, what the hell was going on? Even from a distance, I saw that big changes were brewing at the bar. Piles of lumber lay about and saw horses pointed in all directions. I charged in and saw that the rear of the tavern had been closed off for reno-vations; there was nearly as much carpentry underway as when I arrived in Camp Dix.

A wall dividing the front and rear of the old place into equal parts was nearly finished. The support timbers were heavy enough for a bank, and the planking and paneling had been carefully carved around the bar. The room would have two entries, one behind the bar and the other in the center of the floor, and the thick doors standing against the wall gave evidence that there was to be an impregnable vault in the back.

Jimmy Clancy was supervising everything. "Jim, boy, was there a revolution while I was in France? What are you afraid of, the Germans? We won, you know."

Grabbing my hand and pounding my back, Jimmy yelled for me to be set up. Turning back, he explained, "It'll be the finest family restaurant for miles—pizza, too."

"Pizza? For Christ's sake, Jimmy, what the fuck are we, friggin' Guineas?"

Clancy touched my sleeve, whispering conspiratorially, "Times are changin', Em. Already, there're a couple of Italian families livin' here—lovely people, and, really, the pizza's very good. The Micks love it."

He went on, almost as quietly, "There's this other thing, too. I know it's crazy, but we won't be allowed to sell booze after July—part o' the war effort. It's friggin' nuts, and the prohibition's certain to be made permanent."

"This is what we fought for?"

"Don't jump out the window yet, boy. The room in back might make it possible for close friends to sip old stock, if we could locate any," he said with a wink.

Slow as I was, I got the drift. It was my first encounter with a speakeasy. Jimmy shouted again that mine was on the house all day and got back to his supervising.

"Emmet!"

Two men sat in the deep shadows of the front booth, and as I closed on the greeting, I recognized Mike Flynn sitting opposite another man. Extending my hand, I half shouted, "Mike, what the hell are you doin' in Clancy's? Dubliners need a passport." Laughing, I turned to his companion. Mother o' God, it was Pat Ryan. "Pat! How ya doin', boyo? The last time I saw you, you were under the weather, but you're lookin' fine now."

Flynn spoke, "Shit, Emmet, if you think it's bad in The Bush, the Guineas have taken over Nolan's. We're movin' out. Right, Batty?"

Haltingly, in a child like voice, Ryan said, "...Movin' out."

"What did you call him?" I asked incredulously.

"We call him Batty Patty now. He likes it. Don't ya, Batty?" he asked, without shame.

"...call him Batty Patty now."

I blanched and said, "If ya don't mind, I'll stick with Pat for a while."

Mike smoothed it all over. "Batty's come a long way since that day in France. He don't need a hospital or nothin'. He may not get any better, but he's good enough right now."

I couldn't say what was on my mind and slid in next to Pat and the waitress brought my beer.

"When did ya get home?"

"On one of the first boats after the Armistice. Made it for Christmas. Batty was already at the VA hospital in Rutland, and they turned him loose a couple o' weeks ago. Right, Batty?"

"...turned him loose. Right?"

"Have you really quit Nolan's? It's older than this joint."

"Goddamn right. Perch at the bar and a droopy mustached Dago parks his anarchy preachin' ass next to ya. Right, Batty?"

"Right. . .parks his ass," Pat echoed his master.

I had a couple, made my good-byes, and made a beeline for Millie's.

That night, after drinking too much with Sean and Billy Moynihan, I got home at two in the morning. At about eight, I found that simply turning my head set it to pounding. It couldn't compare with the night at the A.O.H., but it was bad. I closed my eyes, intent on not moving a muscle till it passed, even if it took all day.

But in the distance, I heard the footfall of a trotting horse, heavy clopping—a big draft animal. Ignoring the drumbeat of my temples, I leaped up, pulled on my trousers, and sprinted barefoot through the kitchen, all the while tucking in my underwear and burst out into the cold air. Right at me, came old Bob, trotting easy and blowing clouds o' steam into the bright morning. He stopped right at the door, and I ran to him. "Bobby, boy," I draped myself on his powerful sweaty neck and drew heavily of his rich scent.

The fog rose from the great back and heaving flanks, and, calm as he was, the big Belgium was shocked by the show and shook his head to rid himself of the tiny pest. At that instant, Arthur tripped out of Sullivan's, and, when he saw me, he put even more zip into his trot. "Emmet, I heard you were home. You look swell, but what the hell are you doin'?"

"Nice to see you, Arthur...Nothin'. I thought a lot about Bob in France and couldn't wait to see him. I'm happy the both of ya are still at it."

Confused, Arthur filled his rack and moved hesitantly toward my house. Bob, still perturbed, kept nodding, and, when I stepped aside, trotted on to get away. Hands and feet pained and reddened from the cold, I danced inside—my headache gone.

Ma was waiting. "What in the name of God was that?

"Nothin'...Bob's been on my mind."

She rolled her eyes. "John Moran wants you at Clancy's tomorra mornin' at ten. Tommy, too. Be on your toes; it's about work. There's nothin' round, so don't be particular."

With little to do until the next day, I gravitated to the Moynihans' and found that my whirling dervish had already involved all her friends in the wedding production. I don't recall agreeing to a date, but there was no doubt that it would happen on Saturday, June 22, 1919. She informed me that she'd chatted with the pastor of St. Ann's on the day after the Armistice—the Moynihans were far above dealing with curates, and he'd reserved the church for us.

The Nuptial Mass would be of the most solemn and highest type—my very favorite. The news must have been in one of the many letters that never found its way to Chaumont. The Mrs., with all of her ins, had already claimed the A.O.H. Hall for the reception. Millie would have six attendants. A conservative colleen, at that she was slighting half of her friends, and it was up to me to lasso a best man and five ushers. A virtual recluse, except among the few I knew well, I gave thanks for Tommy Mullins, my brother, Bobby, and cousins, Johnny and Mike, and two to be named later. If it hadn't been for Tom and the gift of a large family, I'd have had to depend on one or two of those shitty Moynihans—not countin' Billy—to stand with me.

"Love, would it be better if we waited till I get a job?"

"Don't start! John Moran will take care of that. Seekin' a re-lease are ya?" She was in my face, nails at the ready, prepared to discuss it.

I was home for but three days, and the corner I'd painted myself into was already shrinking rapidly. "Oh, Mil, I was thinkin' only of appearances. June's fine. Somethin'll turn up before then." So it was set, just as I had wished since my days in Chaumont.

As Ma said, work was not easy to come by when the war ended. The procurement that went with it, including that by France and Britain came to a screeching halt. The result was an explosion of layoffs, and everywhere labor unrest was evident. The shoe and textile orders were halted with half stitched shoes and remnants of bolts of cloth still in the machines. The worst fears of the Yankees and many of the Irish, now inching their way up the social ladder, were coming true. Our own were angry, and an immigrant tide was rising. Any swarthy face could be the mask of an anarchist—every Slav a potential Bolshevik.

The Bush was torn as never before. Always, the old place fa-vored the working man, but now its more intelligent sons could see light at the end of the tunnel. Soon the trickle of boys heading for Boston College would be a healthy stream. Solidarity in the old place was threatened. Many workers left behind had little trouble seeing themselves as socialists—Christ, they couldn't do any worse, but the brighter lights saw that the worst was over and there was promise, if only they could hold on. As the most daring lit out for Milton or Dedham, the old neighborhood gave the impression of being worse off than ever.

Only the elders remaining in the ghettoes could provide sen-sible leadership, but, as there was a changing of the generational guard, their credibility was slipping. The beheading of the leader-ship of those most impacted by the economics left the ignorant and disaffected more vulnerable than ever to socialist malarkey. Foggy as my perception was, I felt that by sucking the best of the lads into the middle class, the Yankees and the kings were creating even greater problems for themselves in what had been left behind. But, of course, there was no alternative as our aim all along had been full assimilation.

The next morning, I walked into Clancy's on the hour and found Tommy slumped in a booth sipping on a glass of water. "Kind o' early for the hard stuff?" I slapped his shoulder.

"This is the first time I've been sober since I got off the train. And restin' my liver ain't a bad idea anyways. Besides, d'ya think Moran would appreciate me crawlin' across the floor to ask for work?" His fingers shook as he raised the glass, and his red rimmed eyes demanded hydration.

At ten past, Big John blasted through the door, his two councilors, Gramps and Sean Moynihan, in tow. Poor Pat had a hard time keeping up with his partners, but he was game. They parked at a table in the center and motioned us over.

John got right to it. "I know ya need work, boys, but I'll lay it on the line. There's damn little out there. Pat and Sean have gone to the mayor—nothin'. I sent Joey to the State House, and it's the same thing.

"But here it is. I found a couple of temporary jobs at the prison, and I was hopin' you'd consider them.

"Emmet, it's ninety days—half in the office and half as a guard for you.

"Tom, you'd drive a truck half time and the rest would be in the lock up. What d'ya say?"

Tom was quicker than I was. "I appreciate what you're sayin', Mr. Moran, but it never even crossed my mind to be a guard. I don't know if I could do it."

"Damn it, Tom, you're a veteran. Call me John. You've been to France, for Christ's sake.

"It's temporary. There's nothin' else. Tell 'em, boys," he ordered turning to Gramps and Sean.

They mumbled their agreement under their breath, aging altar boys bowin', scrapin' and yappin' in what might as well have been Latin as John presided at a High Mass.

"What d'ya say?"

I screwed up my courage. "When would we have to start?"

"You're just home, and they'll hold 'em a couple o' weeks. I'll see to it.

"Before the three months are up, somethin' else 'll turn up. Everybody wants to do the right thing by the boys."

CHAPTER 7

On the Ides of March 1919, Billy Moynihan dragged Tommy and me across the Prison Point Bridge to the monstrous Charlestown State Prison. Designed by the great American architect, Charles Bulfinch, to instill terror in the hearts of malefactors, the great pile of stone succeeded with me. It was its great bulk that was most frightening. The primordial beast rose to devour us—an enormous granite octagon with brick arms readying to ensnare and rend any foolish enough to enter. Even on this bright and windy day, my thoughts were of forbidding Transylvanian castles and their daimonic residents. Regardless of the reality, once inside, I wondered if I could make good my escape.

"I can't do it, Billy."

"For Christ's sake, Emmet, everybody feels like that the first time, but, it's nothin' like what you're thinkin'. It ain't a life sentence. Three months—and half of that in the office. Come on. You'll have stories for a lifetime."

"Yeah—right. But not the kind I was lookin' for."

We were swallowed by the great maw that gaped its welcome like the whale for Jonah and passed through its many iron sphincters, swinging before and slamming after us. One last door and we found ourselves in an office standing before the warden.

The benign looking middle aged man in a dark gray suit, spoke without interest. "You come highly recommended—everyone does. First stop will be the infirmary for a physical—we can't be charged with infecting our wards. Then you'll draw uniforms and equipment. When you return, Captain Healy will describe your duties. Any questions?"

Neither Tom nor I responded, and we were hustled off for processing. In the poorly lit and vile smelling infirmary, the doctor touched the frozen stethoscope to our chests and pronounced us fit for duty. His speed and dexterity were both amazing and alarming, and, for a moment, I thought he might shout, 'You're it,' in some ghoulish game of tag. The trip to the equipment room was nearly as confusing as drawing supplies at Camp Dix, and, in a daze, I responded to demands from prisoner clerks for shoe, shirt and trouser sizes. Next, we were delivered to a damp and deteriorating locker room where we changed and then were led back to the office.

I was outfitted as a guard in the penal system of the Commonwealth of Massachusetts. My impression of the costume was that it was long and gray—long gray pants, long gray shirt, and an especially long gray coat. On top of it all was a half size gray cowboy hat that matched my head size perfectly.

"Christ, Em you're ready for your audition as a Confederate cavalry trooper for D. W. Griffith."

"Ya, and you ain't such a vision yerself, asshole."

I had never felt as phony as I did at that moment—'Emmet Magawley, fraud, reportin' for duty, I thought, almost aloud.

Captain Healy read a list of do's and don'ts. 'Don't make friends with the inmates. Don't be overly familiar. Don't turn your back. Don't, don't, don't. Be clear in your demands. Do, do, do.'

Healy, an angel of mercy, then said, "For the first day, Magawley, you'll work here in the office, and, Mullins, you'll go to the garage for indoctrination."

Never, certainly, were two recruits ever so happy in their first day's chores as Tom and I. The time passed as if in a dream much like that first day we spent in the swamps of New Jersey so long ago. Yes, sir, nothin's too good for the boys who served their country in its time of greatest need.

That night, Billy collected us and led us back into the world. My new uniform smelled as if worn for a month without cleaning. Ten hours of simple office tasks, and I was exhausted. My partner in correction, the great truck driver, Tom Mullins, once again looked as if he'd spent the day doing pushups for Sergeant Michaels.

My first assignment inside the prison proper, equal in unreality to my initiation to the institution, demonstrated for all to see that Healy had wasted his breath; the do's and don'ts were violated at every turn. Guards made small talk with prisoners, and, everywhere, familiarity abounded. Later, I got a look at the cells and concluded that old Charlie Bulfinch must have been a pretty nasty customer. Only tiny slots in the bricks admitted outside light to the cells and that for but a few hours on the brightest days. The barred cubicles could not have been darker, and the few inmates who enjoyed reading truly suffered cruel and unusual punishment.

Only later did it come up that the architect whose buildings I'd always admired was something of a crime freak. Charlie was a selectman in Boston with an inordinate interest in criminal justice. In addition to this resort, he had designed numerous jails around New England. The great man was none too dainty in his choice of entertainment and apparently enjoyed occasional hangings and maimings. Slicing off ears seems to have been a standard method of rehabilitation, and, of course, flogging served to restore law and order and improve the circulation—to say nothing about raising the spirits of public officials. Ah, morning in America when its artists had great souls.

My rookie assignment was that of supervisor in the tailor shop. I performed under the watchful eye of an old Yankee whose name is long forgotten, patrolling the cluttered shop, gabbing with the sewing machine operators and cutters as they created uniforms for both prisoners and guards. Looking casual, I dared not expose the probationer I was. The inmates knew exactly what was going on but were not at all intent on driving me out of the business during that first shift.

That evening, I maintained a stiff upper lip for Ma and Da, but, later, when alone with Millie, I almost broke down. But I trekked across the river the next morning and the next and still one more. In just a few weeks, I saw that the sentence could be served, but, when payday arrived, I counted the ten fivers for the fifteen days of incarceration. Prison management would never do for a man marrying into the Moynihan clan. Well, at least it didn't cover room and board in the big house. Depressed, I didn't raise the financial questions with Millie but trusted in the future and in Grampa and good King John.

Days off were rotated, and I vividly recall one free Tuesday in April when, after crawling out of bed, dressing and coming out of my room for breakfast, a great commotion broke out at the back entry. Ma rushed to answer the insistent knock and opened it to a breathless Ripper Dooley, Millie's next door neighbor.

"Johnny Moynihan's done. Shot dead. Millie sent me for Emmet."

Instantly, Ma broke down and sobbed, "Mother of God, it can't be true."

I jumped to her side. "What happened?"

"I can't say for sure, but, late in the night, a Guinea gunned him down."

"Oh, God...Thanks, Rip. I'm on my way."

Poor Ma swooned, and Eileen, who had not gone off that morning, helped me console her, and, supported by both, she took to her bed. I left Sis holding the bag, literally, and took off for Dublin.

I trotted the half-mile and entered without knocking. Huddled together, their weeping was terrible. Seeing me, Millie broke away and dove into my arms. "I'm sorry, so sorry."

Billy spoke for the disconsolate girl, "He was makin' his rounds in the alleys in back of Scollay Square—near Joe and Nemo's. He tried a door. It gave, and he shocked this Dago who just up and shot him," he said, desperately trying to hold himself together.

"He had enough left to drop the bastard cold. Somebody heard the shots and called the cops. He was sinkin', but he got it out. He never made it to the hospital."

The blow, swift and heavy, left the Moynihans reeling. Sean held the Mrs., and Billy shored up Sean, and all of 'em consoled poor Margaret, the shocked widow. Ripper and his wife made the rounds with water and hugs where they seemed most needed.

Within minutes, Father Harrigan, the pastor of St. Ann's, flew in and led us in Hail Marys and Our Fathers. All the while, I held my poor love. The pitiable sobbing which emanated from deep within bore witness to the pain, and she heaved against me spasmodically. I tried to ease her into a chair, but all she wanted was to be in my arms.

Half an hour later, John Moran entered. The balance of support shifted radically as he gathered the wounded flock under his protection.

The kitchen door flew open and Mike, in uniform, burst in, lookin' grim. Sean broke free. "Anything new?"

"An anarchist from Lynn. The bastard just opened up. There's nests of 'em up there. I swear, I'm goin' to wipe 'em out."

A horrified look crossed Dolores's face, and she broke from the scrum to restrain him. But she passed into babbling and dropped into his arms.

John Moran stepped into his face. "You'll do nothin' of the kind. No foolishness now. You're needed here."

Mike railed, but I saw that he was in command of himself, and he carried Dolly to his mother's side. There was no consoling the woman, and, each time the door opened, it sent her into new paroxysms of grief. But somehow, the day ended, and the family settled down, and the rest of us took our leave. It was time for the worst to begin—the wake would be held the next night. When I arrived home from work, the family was ready, Da in a dark brown suit, and Ma wearin' a tasteful deep blue dress that hung to near the ground with a great royal blue hat with a great crown that went up and over her head creating the aspect of an angel about her. I never knew they had such clothes but learned they'd stocked up when Gramma died. Bobby and Eileen, preparing for duty, sat in the parlor waiting to move out. It was obvious that Ma was pleased that we were going to have a show of force for our new allies and buzzed about how happy she was that the past was dead.

"Mary Moynihan will be pleased. You're makin' me proud, you are."

It would be a somber night, but I was impressed that Ma was in command of her emotions.

Da had acquired a flivver, but, after a long discussion about who could ride and who would have to walk, it was determined that we would all proceed on foot.

As we plodded along, only Ma had need to unburden herself. "I can't believe that a man could gun down another without so much as a 'how-do-you-do?'. When we were young, Da, you could walk anywhere in Boston as if it was your own back yard. These immigrants have no morals," she said with such sad intensity that the rest of us just dropped our heads another notch.

With heavy hearts, we arrived at Moynihan's. Ma was amazed at the crowd and the dozens of officers needed to direct the extremely heavy traffic. All Boston was paying its respects to the Moynihans and to John's widow, Margaret.

Ma was bursting from adrenaline. "Look at them in their uniforms. Ain't it grand how much they liked John? This'll be the finest funeral in twenty years. Eh, Da?"

Da said nothing, but I couldn't contain myself. "Ma, he's dead—shot full o' holes. It ain't a vaudeville act. He hasn't got a clue."

"But look how they loved him; they must be very proud."

Eileen pinched my arm, and I said no more as we made our way. After crossing the piazza, we would enter through the front entrance, something done only on the most solemn occasions—such as your wake. The body lay at the bay window of the parlor. After paying our respects to the relatives, we'd view the body and disperse by age and sex into the other rooms for a period of mourning. Approaching the walk, we came on an honor guard of police officers in a line from the street up the front steps and into the parlor where the family took over.

Ma addressed the only person capable of responding, "Em, have you ever seen anythin half so grand in your life?"

"No, Ma, I haven't," I answered honestly. "Now let's just get done with it."

The line stalled as we reached the steps; there were more mourners than I'd ever seen. The crowd was orderly, and, through the windows, I saw Sean and the Mrs., Margaret, Millie, Mike, and John's children. As we moved into the parlor, Da expressed our condolences and outrage at the act that brought us. The rest of us just mumbled, and the Moynihan's thanked us for coming. I held Millie for just a moment. They were all running on empty, so I helped Da move Ma and Eileen along as quickly as possible. Da needed little proddin', and John Moran, hoverin' behind the Mrs., gave thanks with his eyes, as the whole affair was far tougher to manage than most.

With the gauntlet past, we came face to face with the uniformed corpse, and a plaintive cry arose in front of me. A banshee screamed into the night for its own. Now, I'd been at the prison for several weeks and had heard some baleful sounds emanate from those black holes, and my time in Moran's employ had taught my ears a few sounds that could not have been produced by the human breast. But this was tragedy, and I thought for a moment that it might be Johnny Moynihan come back for revenge. No such luck; it was Ma—Ma who had talked rationally only moments before. Da moved to increase his hold—and I reached to clamp the horn—and Bobby jumped to assist us both. But there was no sustaining the racked and ruined woman. Dead weight, she was now in full wail, "Virgin Mary, Mother of God, intercede with your son, our Lord, Jesus Christ. Restore this poor man to his lovin' family."

Bobby, Da, and I were paralyzed, and only Eileen had the presence to push us past the body where John Moran, having scooted around, opened his arms like a harbor to save us and direct us into the living room where the ladies had circled the room. I thought then that there might be a chance to calm her, but I was naive. As soon as we got her through the doorway, the other biddies sitting like mice broke into communal support of their shattered sister. In a fog, we dumped her on a chair and left Eileen to control the maddened crowd. Moran fled back to the parlor, and the three of us staggered into the kitchen where the men were holding forth.

The Magawleys, outlanders—but not strangers—in Little Dublin, nodded around and kept to our chairs and ourselves. Bobby and I smoked to cover our discomfort—Da, of another generation, had never taken up the weeds, and we whispered amongst ourselves, ignoring the wailing that bounced into the kitchen, where we were hiding.

The scene quickly sorted itself out. Chairs were set around the large kitchen, and bands of men were caught up in cliques of three or four. Three principal topics of conversation with only slight variations were on every tongue.

A man opened with, "Ain't it awful. The poor lad never had a chance."

The reply, "Cold blooded Guinea bastard. Too bad John killed him. I'd love ta nurse the sonofabitch back to health and fry his ass in Charlestown."

The second began, "Everything's goin' to hell. Immigrants—anarchist bastards..."

The response, "All of 'em should be sent back to wherever they came from."

The next group listened to ribald tales of John's youth. When the round was done—musical chairs, the stories—not the men—moved to the next group.

During the first two topics, the sadness tempered by anger was palpable, while the group listening to the tall and dirty stories laughed uncontrollably, the humor heightened the emotions rampant during the morose occasion.

The Magawleys were polite and reserved—even though well known to most all in Dublin. All the while we listened to the wailing in the living room—led by a terrible sad voice that had a most familiar ring. When we'd stayed the appropriate time and had been caught by St. Ann's pastor for a rosary, we reversed the process, gathering Ma and Eileen, both fully spent, and made our good-byes. By this time, Millie was composed and able to see us off without incident. I whispered, "I'll come back as soon as everyone's put away."

Walking back to The Bush, silence and contemplation reigned until Ma began blubbering, "Have you ever seen more flowers in your whole life? John Moynihan never looked better. Didn't the family do good? Mary Moynihan was stronger than I'd have been. My God, what's the world coming to?" This went on until we got her into her bed.

After everything settled down, I returned to Millie. The crowd gone, she waited at the back door. All that the poor girl wanted was to be held close. After a long while, I said, "I'm sorry about my mother. She's never done anything like that before."

"Don't worry. My Ma thought it was the nicest thing that anyone's ever done—the wailin' was just what was needed to show proper respect."

Convulsed by a terrible laughter, it took all the muffling we could muster.

The next morning, the Magawleys arrived early at St. Ann's where a huge crowd had gathered. Moving into a pew in the middle of the church, we sat lost in our thoughts. The rear half of the church was cordoned off for uniformed officers who also waited for the Mass to begin.

As they prepared for the procession to the altar, I turned to observe. For me, the most impressive moment in each funeral is the placing of the shroud over the coffin. Great or mean—pine box or bronze casket—comin' down the aisle for the last time, covered with plain linen, they're presented to God and congregation as equals.

The pastor had the unhappy task of directing John to his reward. When the Solemn High Requiem Mass was done, more than a thousand police officers, eight abreast, escorted the body, to Calvary cemetery. Police departments from as far away as Hartford and Portland, Maine, sent representatives to pay homage to a fallen brother, and more than two hundred uniformed fire fighters joined in the mile long parade. Pipes and drums, packed between the companies, sounded the dirges.

After the long graveside service, Ma could barely contain her pride in the City and John Moran for orchestrating the magnificent send off. She chattered all the way home about how wonderful they all looked in their uniforms.

The Moynihans got through the ordeal, but there were important changes in our lives. A big wedding was out of the question. Millie and I proceeded with the date, but it was a quiet private affair conducted in a side chapel of St. Ann's. Even more traumatic, as was customary, Margaret, the grieving widow, and her brood moved back with her own family, the Nolans. They would bear the greatest share of the burden of supporting her and the children, standard at such terrible turns.

An unexpected blessing emanated from the tragedy, Millie Magawley inherited the vacant third floor apartment in the homestead. There was, however, a down side to this benefit, Millie was about to marry a certain Emmet Magawley who was not exactly thrilled to be moving into that nest. There was no choice but to put on a brave and friendly face.

As the wedding approached, cannibalization of Magawley and Moynihan households for furniture and furnishings for our love nest began in earnest. Margaret donated her double bed; I thought that above and beyond the call of duty, and it made me uncomfortable. Grampa sent his maple table and chairs that had been in storage since he moved in with Pat Jr.'s family. Even with the downplaying of the bridal shower, we would be able to set up at least a primitive level of housekeeping.

The day came, and we were married. It was a sad occasion that brought home the great loss. Poor Mil, wearing a gorgeous tan shift, looked lovely, but the murderer had denied her dream of marrying in a wondrous flowing gown, attended by friends and witnessed by half of Little Dublin. Only the immediate families were present, and I felt terrible for my poor little girl.

Through no one's fault but the killer's, even our two day honeymoon to New Hampshire was filled with grief. Da lent his flivver, and we were off in a shower of rice. But it was a far cry from the romantic interlude that the poor lass had fantasized, and our walks along the banks of the lovely lakes were interrupted by torrents of tears.

But we were married and ensconced in our little bower. John Moran had arranged an additional ninety day appointment at Charlestown, and our new lives began, even if not very auspiciously.

CHAPTER 8

Each day I became more comfortable at Charlestown. The reality of working in the prison was not nearly so dreadful as I'd feared. In the years since, newspaper and television exposes describe a prison world alien from that we knew. The social compact between the inmates and the guards has fallen on hard times. Sure, Charlestown had its sociopaths, bad actors and total lunatics, but they hadn't succeeded in dividing the world between guards and inmates or among themselves by gang, race, or religion—God, we'd have fallen over if we ever met a Muslim.

Most of the prisoners had been caught in crimes of necessity and were ignorant unfortunates—far less clever than they thought—unable to feed, clothe or shelter themselves and their families in an ever more complex world.

The prisoners and guards knew the bad apples in both populations. Troublesome inmates were dealt with easily; we locked them up, especially the crazy ones. It was a simple solution, but you have to remember that they had few of the protections in the Bill of Rights available today. The constitutional guaranties that we take for granted were pie in the sky when the Great War ended.

Dealing with the sadists among the keepers was a more difficult problem, but the management did its best by using them on the guard towers and other jobs requiring minimal interaction with the prisoners. Of course, that meant they were always armed and ready to shoot, but, silver lining, knowledge of this kept prisoners with a yen for wall climbing closer to home.

Familiarity between staff and inmates was forbidden, but little effort was expended in enforcing it. Guards and prisoners laughed and scratched their way through the days in the shops, and, when at the close of day the inmates returned to their cells, checkers, cribbage and other two man games between prisoners and keepers were played on every block.

In the world outside, newspapers catering to well-to-do described how economy was improving rapidly, but those of us dependent on the Post felt little of the good times in Little Dublin or The Bush, except for the rampant inflation in prices. The government was still buying ships and that helped the New England shipyards. But the factories and mills of the working stiffs from ethnic neighborhoods were clamped shut like the rat- traps they were.

The paltry incomes of cops and prison guards that hadn't been raised since 1913 bought less each day, but, surprisingly—to me, at least—little support for raising their pay could be found among the pols in City Hall and the State House. A hundred dollars a month might have been acceptable, perhaps even munificent, when it was established but didn't place nearly enough bread in the mouths of families of five or more in 1919. As nice as she was, even Millie complained how little could be bought with the load I placed on the table on the first of the month—and us about to be joined by another mouth in the spring of '20—ah, the Irish in our little warrens.

On the job and at home, the restlessness in the police force that John Moran had alerted me to became evident. The issues were simple. The police demanded higher pay and recognition for their union. To the establishment, the former was unwelcome and the latter an abomination. Mayor Peters wasn't up to the crisis, and the responsibility fell to his police commissioner. With none of the sensitivity of modern labor disputes on either side, we stumbled drunkenly toward a strike that everyone wanted to avoid but no one seemed capable of sidestepping.

All summer, the parties tossed bigger and bigger bombs at each other. Law and order types promised to fire any officer who blinked and have the State Guard crush any support for the cops. All the while, the unions, led by the big boys in the AF of L headquarters in New York, grew more strident in support of the patrolmen. The terror of a general strike filled every conservative breast, and the papers stoked the fires of fear.

Governor Coolidge helped not at all. If he'd come out against the boys right at the beginning, the strike might have been avoided, but he fed us baloney that could be read both ways. The Post, the Cardinal's megaphone into Irish homes, and the other papers with democrat leanings couldn't find a way out. They were for the working man and supported raises for the officers, but, out of the other side of their mouths, they defended the respectability that the Gaels had only recently won.

One September morning as I made my rounds in the tailor shop, I got a start. While shootin' the breeze with a Polack sewing collars to inmates' shirts, he suddenly changed the subject. "Will the cops walk?"

An Irish question was my parry. "It looks that way, don't it?"

"It ain't the pay. It's the split," the Polack snickered. "If the coppers get a livin' wage, half the speakeasies will fold overnight."

"I don't follow."

"The speakeasies are paying off the pols and captains, but the boys on the beat ain't gettin' a fair shake," he said with a superior air. "The sergeants are fat as pigeons, but the patrolmen have to sweep up the crumbs."

"What are you sayin'?" I asked, shocked to my shoes.

The Polack laughed in my face. "God, what an innocent. You've got no future in this game." He couldn't control his glee, and others in earshot joined in.

A Mick named O'Brien, knowing that I was related to cops, said, "Ask about that at Sunday dinner, and you'll find yerself on the couch."

A grand time was had, and I had to get shitty to get them back to the machines. But, poking about with the older guards, I found broad hints of a widespread system of payoffs for cops and politicians in connection with the booze.

As my eyes opened, the situation became clear. The big property holders and homeowners were pushing to keep taxes down, and the politicians were happy to oblige. The winners were those who controlled the flow of liquor, and the police were left to hold their hands out where they could. Without a living wage, they saw little choice but to turn down the road to corruption.

After serious reflection, the conclusion was that, if I'd been in the shoes of the men in blue, I'd have done the same thing. To me, drinking was but a self inflicted vice, yet pious fools from the Bible Belt had taken it upon themselves to butt into the lives of people about whom they knew nothing. Fortunately, bein' but a temporary prison guard meant that my ruminations on the matter were of importance to no one but myself. But Jesus, couldn't I use another fifty a month for lookin' away from activities that I didn't believe were wrong?

At home, the Magawleys and the Moynihans feared the worst as the affair careered towards a brick wall, but neither family was in the front lines. Johnny Moynihan, the only patrolman in the lot, had been taken from us, and his brother, Mike, and my uncle, Pat, were too highly ranked to be involved. With our clout on both sides, all of the relatives, except Billy and me, were higher up functionaries ready to ride out the storm and curse everybody from the governor to the man on the beat.

Most of the guards, including Tommy, Billy and me, supported the lads, but the two of us from the House of Moynihan had to watch our tongues. Inside the walls, Tom and I were in the enviable position of being rookies, so our views were ciphers and never solicited. But there was nothing but brotherhood in the dank prison air; the louder and brasher—and less senior fellows—talked about going out in support of the cops. While the older men wept as their pensions prepared to fly away between the bars.

By early September, the front pages covered nothing else, and the threats and counters were spelled out in the most minute detail. Bakers, printers, fire fighters, and dozens of others supported the men in blue, and the AF of L promised solidarity. Wobblies and anarchists stood on street corners screaming for a New World order. On the other side, the establishment and the lace curtain Irish—including, God Almighty, all Magawleys, Moynihans and King John—called for draconian measures in crushing any strike. The scene scared the dickens out of me, since all I wanted was few more bucks a month.

After the weeks and months of talking about how tough they were, the preliminaries ceased and the fateful day arrived. Tommy and I changed into civvies after work and stopped at Clancy's to watch the show play out in the neighborhood.

Flynn and Batty were in the second booth. "Afraid of lookin' like cops when the fight starts?" Mike laughed.

"...lookin' like cops..." echoed the little boy voice.

We ordered brews and ignored the taunts. "Think they'll go out?" I asked.

"They ain't got the balls," snapped Mike with his usual antipathy for anything connected with authority.

"...ain't got the balls."

"They'll walk, and we'll have the damnedest fight ever," Tommy pitched in.

"The yellow bastards'll march to the line and do an about face...A buck says they don't." Flynn grew angrier and louder with every statement and fresh glass. "Let's run over to Roxbury Crossin'. They're loud farts, and I want to watch the sons-of-bitches back down."

It sounded innocent enough to Tom and me, so we settled up and jumped in the back of Mike's old Model T. A huge crowd milled in front of the station house, and Mike had to park blocks away. We sauntered down, breathing in the electricity.

Out of control, hotheads yelled and screamed into the night. Fist fights and shoving matches broke out everywhere, but, of course, inside, the cops were too busy singin' labor songs to break them up. It had rained and puddles were everywhere. Hooligans sloshed and kicked mud on each other. Finally, the dam burst, and out they came in single file. To a man they hit the street without their shields and nightsticks. They'd done it; the strike was on.

The mob reacted to each new morsel. A lad would come out and face it. The huge and angry moray eel writhing and swaying in convulsive contortions opened its vicious jaws, and the forlorn copper, bereft of badge, would be swallowed and drawn deep into the innards of the beast. Demonstrators pelted the poor bastards with mud balls as they ran covering their faces while vile names bounced off their ears.

Mike enjoyed himself immensely firing sloppy missiles at them. Batty played in the mud and tossed gobs into the crowd setting off screams of rage everywhere within his limited range. Tom and I stood dumbstruck observing the anarchy. I asked, "Are they all fuckin' nuts, or should we be pickin' a side?"

Over the taunting, Tom yelled, "Grab Babe Ruth. Let's get the fuck out o' here."

Tommy drew Pat gently by the hand, and I approached Flynn who was pitchin' fast balls at the heads of every blue coat in sight. "This is out o' control. Let's head back to Clancy's."

"Just a couple more. I'm waitin' for one in particular." He said through a menacing smile.

"Dig in, the bastards have it comin'." Mike, happy as a newborn, moved closer with each offering.

The mayhem continued while, surrealistically, the three of us stood and watched as the frenzied mob slobbered madly. Suddenly, Mike turned to us, and bellowed, "Here's my boy."

A striker strode toward us, looking neither right nor left, ignoring the taunts and the mud missiles. Suddenly, Mike flashed into his path and pounded a straight right fist into the middle of his face, flattening him like he was shot.

"That's for the ticket, you sonofabitch," Flynn screamed as he set to put a boot in the downed man's ear. The vicious kick missed by but a fraction of an inch. "Up, you yellow bastard. I'm payin' the fine in trade." It was like old times, I jumped on Mike to save the poor devil, now bleeding profusely from his nose and mouth, but, this time, I protected myself and didn't win my own bloody reward.

We struggled to get the enraged Flynn back to the car. Silent, Tom drove back to Clancy's. Barely controlling my anger, when we jumped out, I faced him. "You're the biggest asshole in Boston. No, I am, for gettin' caught by you again. If I never see you again, it'll be too friggin' soon." I raised my hands to fight and die.

"The little shit wants a fight, eh? Well here's my chin," he taunted me like a prancin' Mussolini. "Make it good, or I'll plant your skinny ass like a fuckin' spud."

"...like a fuckin' spud."

Returning to sanity before me, Flynn slowed down. "Easy. I've had my fun. Besides, I ain't lookin' for target practice," he said sarcastically through a huge grin.

"...ain't lookin' for target practice." The tiny voice wafted softly into my consciousness.

After an eternity, I wheeled and stomped off homeward, Flynn's laughter fading in the background. Full of fire, Millie waited. "Where've ya been. I held supper for an hour. Just what do think you're doin' not even sendin' word."

A short summary from between clenched teeth, steam hissin' from both ears, I stormed past her and dove into the bed in hopes of finding sleep to cool my white hot rage and sooth my awful shame. A sensitive lass, she let it pass.

Around the city the tragedy began to unfold, looting parties bounced all over Beacon Hill, and toughs took over the Common. Coolidge had no choice but to call in the State Guard. The papers told of smart alecks playing craps right in front of the State House, and, when done, the toughest scooped up the dough and taunted the rest to take it back. It was anarchy, and the Yankees and the Irish responded to the mayor's cries for help in acting as volunteer police. The zealous posers directed traffic to the limits of their ability, and state police and officers from nearby towns made stands where they could, but there were too many wild ones for them to have much success. All the unions were takin' votes on whether to go out in support of the cops. It was a day to remember.

The next morning, we crossed the bridge not knowing how

the day would play out. The guards were meeting and threats were flying, but the consensus was that they'd walk only after another union made the first move. Apparently, the butchers, bakers, and candlestick makers were of a similar mind, and the tough guys from union central in New York were having second thoughts. A pattern emerged, all who'd been tellin' the cops they were behind 'em were so goddamn far back you couldn't see 'em, and I began to comprehend that the poor devils were flappin' like sheets in a raw wind.

After the shift, we trudged across the river, skirted Scollay Square, climbed the hill in back of the State House and moved around to the Common. The scene was one of total anarchy. Squads of the State Guard, obviously not even partially trained for civil insurrection, engaged gangs that ran through the park like wild beasts seeking to commit mayhem. Each knot of protozoa split into new cells that slid around the flanks of the troops. I felt sorry for the poor lads, tryin' their best to look like seasoned doughboys ready to do battle, but they were no match for hooligans from South Boston and the North End. We ambled among the cells that divided amoeba like as quickly as they were routed. While fearsome, we enjoyed ourselves, sucking up the energy. We were in uniform, and the sea of rioters, thinking we were cops, parted before us.

We crossed into West Street where a company of guard prepared to move in support of their weary buddies. Three platoons were being inspected by their lieutenants, and we snickered at the display of power. This was not the Yankee Division that I'd known in France. It was a hundred and twenty Emmet Magawleys not yet battered into shape by Sergeant Michaels. A quarter of the little boys had failed to press their knickers, a few wore glasses thicker than mine, a dozen puttees wouldn't stay up, and none of 'em looked up to dealing with the rabble on the green.

From the roofs above the formation, foul mouthed and laughing toughs, looking for all the world like Townies to me, guffawed at the frightened boys. We were on the side of the soldiers but enjoyed their discomfort. Most respectable people in the city were confined to their homes, so it was just ruffians streaming past us toward the State House, waving and hooting to those on the low flat roofs. I thought that most on the loose were simply on a lark, neither looters nor anarchists. They didn't look too menacing to me, and I felt little need for protection.

The troopers sharply snapped the Springfields for inspection. The officers flipped the pieces and looked with hawk eyes for specs of dust or rust before jamming the rifles back into the hands of the soldiers. An arduous process, neither those on the roofs nor we could maintain concentration on the entire routine in view of the colorful parade. Just as I turned back to the examination, a trooper grabbed his freshly reviewed weapon, slammed home the bolt, and, to complete the process, pulled the trigger.

The people of Boston, or at least that portion of them on West Street, heard a repeat of the shot heard round the world. The flash and report were followed by the crash of the sign shot off the corner store. The toughs recoiled from the roof's edge, and the crowd panicked. I looked at the poor lad whose rifle had discharged and saw only fear and disbelief. The officer, back to, stared for a long moment and, without a word, moved on to the next recruit.

It was time to head for home, and we watched the roofs clear. Apparently, the lads on the parapets thought it suppertime, too. As we descended to Washington Street, we sensed that the crowd was now with us and that those heading for the Common were clearly in the minority.

I won't say that shot broke the strike—far from it, but it was typical of what happened across the City. Frightened guardsmen shot into a number of taunting crowds that night, killing two and wounding four or five others. It took a committed anarchist to face a panicked eighteen year old with a loaded weapon he didn't know how to operate, and the demonstrations lost a lot of their fizz.

The cops had walked, and it was time for their backers to put up. The final position of the AF of L was that a strike against public safety wasn't what they had in mind. They were still for the patrolmen, mind you, but they couldn't bring themselves to hit the bricks; it wouldn't be right. The butchers, bakers, and candle stick makers who'd goaded the lads into the streets concluded the public would not be well served by not having beef, pies or lighting, so they deferred their strike until a later time. The guards, who'd been swearing brotherhood and solidarity the day before, had second thoughts at the tough words emanating from Silent Cal Coolidge. Besides, they never did say they'd absolutely walk when the cops did. They said they'd vote on it when the strike went into effect.

Many Irish leaders, like Moran, had worked, silently, in league with the Yankees. Their constituency was divided, but they knew where they'd come from and where they were going. The quiet alliance across party lines was old but known to only a few of their closest supporters. Coolidge's minion had placed a number of Moran's boys in state jobs, including Billy, Tom and me. While James Michael Curley was making much mischief in proclaiming support of the strikers, Moran and a good many of the Celts understood where the stunning alliance was headed. The Governor, recipient of many Irish votes, knew that he could count on more during his lucky jaunt to 1600 Pennsylvania Avenue. But the cops had to be sacrificed, and they were. Of course, I couldn't see it that day.

The cops were fired. That was it. They were gone. The dance played out over days, weeks, months, and even years, but they were history. The Police Commissioner, the Governor, and pols like John Moran had cut them off at the knees. The public didn't realize the result for some time, but, the instant they struck, they walked into new lives—many none too pleasant. About a week after our trek across the Common, word was received that Moran wanted to see Tommy and me. The next evening, with ample notice for Millie—not that I feared her—we arrived at Clancy's. The construction had been completed, the great doors locked and barred. We knocked, and Jimmy, himself, manning the latest technology in peepholes, opened up with great ceremony. "I'd appreciate it if youz'd change from them uniforms in the future, boys."

Gramps accompanied John. A couple of empties sat among the wet rings in front of Moran, but old Pat was having trouble finishing his first. Drinking was no longer permitted in the front of the restaurant, but, since the deepest clamps of prohibition had yet to be felt, if your name was Moran or Magawley, Jimmy might make an exception.

Moran, direct, as always, began, "I know you're buddies, so I wanted to take this up with ya together. This'll sound cold-blooded, but they'll be replacing all the cops. Veterans'll have first call. Tommy you're a shoo-in, but, Emmet, those glasses and your size will make it impossible. What say ya, Tom?"

I was stunned—not by my lack of qualifications, but by the realization that the cops were history—but Tom was as ready as he could be. "I was wrong about Charlestown. If the truth be told, I'd rather be a guard. I'd welcome the chance to be made permanent,..." He got stuck trying not to say Mr. Moran, but finally stammered, "...John."

I said, "I'm with Tommy, the prison ain't as bad as it's cracked up to be. If you could make us regulars, it would be swell."

"You boys're easy." Moran flashed two fingers at the waitress.

Gramps, long silent, opened up, "I'm glad you like it. Good work is a fine thing.

"Emmet, you're the first in the family to know, I ain't goin' to stand again. I'm tired, and the party would do well with new blood."

I didn't know how to react to the end of an era. "Are you ok?"

"Sure. I just can't go out nights and all. It's time, really."

Moran jumped in, "Pat's the finest the city's ever had. I tried to talk him out of it, but he wouldn't have it. Too bad you're in Dublin, Em. We'd ask ya ta run if you were still in the homestead. Magawley's magic in The Bush."

It was just buttering up, but it was nice, just the same. "Who's goin' to run?" I stammered, havin' trouble gettin' the `John' out myself.

"There are many fine fellas, we won't have trouble fieldin' a good candidate. No one could take your Grampa's place, mind you, but a good one, nonetheless.

CHAPTER 9

As in Chicago, New York, Philadelphia and other cities laden with spicy ethnic flavoring, there was little support for the notion of prohibition in Boston. Even the greatest Brahmin opinion maker of them all, Henry Cabot Lodge, denounced the effort as pure folly.

But there was applause for the drys from the cops and lower level pols; these staunch defenders of public morality knew right from wrong. Besides, couldn't they use the protection revenue? It was clear from the outset that the great experiment in godliness would improve the character of the nation and its people.

Not an ounce of respect for the law could be found in Charlestown, Southie, Little Dublin, or The Bush, and, surely, it was the same in Guinea and Polack neighborhoods around the Commonwealth. There was little criticism of those who worked against the beast, except from them too chicken to play and who burned with envy for those who did. So it was that Tommy and I, along with my brother-in-law, Billy, got to serve the people again— this time in the combined land and naval forces.

Kev, boy, there's no topping the St. Valentine's Massacre or the wars in Cicero, but I can spin a yarn on how the great experiment worked down in The Bush and Little Dublin. Long before, I'd learned the terrible truths Da taught concerning conspiracies, but I wasn't the leader in this and knew next to nothing about its inner workings. By the time I got involved, the risks were clear; I'd be takin' no real chance, except gettin' canned from the rock pile where I had almost no pension vested anyway. The State, in its munificence, gave us a hundred dollar a year raise in the aftermath of the police strike—such generosity.

So it was that on a pleasant evening in March of 1920, I came home to find Da and Grampa in the kitchen. I thought they'd be uneasy in the Moynihan lair, but darlin' Mil was charming them. The three of 'em were carrying on so that you'd think that she was the Magawley; at that instant, I was struck by how deeply I loved the girl, now heavy with her first child. They were staying for supper—wondrous for me as they were packing four quarts of ale, three of which were in the ice box in the back hall while the first finished its death throes.

Millie had boiled a smoked shoulder on Sunday, so she laid out the remains as a feast fit for kings, from whom we were all descended. It was a grand time, and, expansively, I played the host, like I'd done all the work. The talk was the usual, 'The country's goin' to hell with all the immigrants,' and 'Can you believe it, it'll never be legal for us to buy booze again.' The palavering went on till nine o'clock when the purpose of the visit was slipped in under the door.

Gramps was the messenger. "Emmet, will ya bring Tommy and Billy over to the warehouse tomorra? Mulligan's got a few odd jobs, and yuz might be able to pick up a bit o' loose change."

Ever the innocent, I agreed without a second thought, and when they left, I swept Millie up in my arms and kissed her softly. "You're a wonder, Love." She was bursting for pleasing me, as well as from other causes.

The next evening, the three of us crammed ourselves into Mike Mulligan's office. A single weak bulb hung over his sagging desk that was heavy with untidy piles of papers; it wasn't the office of a wealthy man—at least not as I had envisioned one.

Mike opened with a friendly, "Beer, boys?"

None of us had ever turned anything down, and the lubrication commenced in earnest. He had won the council seat vacated by Grampa and was now Moran's main man in The Bush. A mighty man was Mulligan, but, like his Percherons, he was gentle as a lamb. A huge florid Santa Claus face surrounded by white curls, he was an easy laugh. His broad shoulders and thick trunk had been the basis for starting him in the moving game, but it was his agile brain that made it a going concern. "Ain't that sweet?"

"It's good, but what's this all about?" I asked.

"We need a few part time drivers, and thought, on occasion, you might see your way clear to help."

Tommy responded, "There was no need for the buildup, Mike. Don't be cute, we can handle it."

Rarely was Mullins that straightforward, but it was obvious that we were being recruited to run booze, so there was little need for dancin'.

At that Mulligan dropped it. "So be it. We need yuz to run from here to Vermont and back. And we need help bringin' stuff in from beyond the three-mile limit. There'll be little risk. If they catch ya, the worst that can happen is you'll be canned, and, of course, we'd take care o' ya. It's simple and'll be worth your while. If you don't want to know more, it's time to leave." We could never claim we didn't know what we were doing.

Mike let it lay a few seconds before asking, "Well?"

No one blinked, and, after another pregnant moment, Mulligan went on. "It's so simple morons could do it, so you boys'll have no trouble," he was barely able to get it out, as he choked with laughter. We didn't think it was that funny and had to winch up weak smiles.

"Emmet, get your Grampa the schedule of when you'll be in the office and what days all of you'll be off altogether. A fella'll call and say his name's Revere. He'll say it's a one and name the time. Then be at the back of the warehouse. You'll drive from here to Burlington and back in one day.

"If it's to be a boat ride, he'll say it's a two. In that case, just drive to South Station at the appointed hour and, one by one, walk across the bridge. Where Sleeper Street cuts back to the channel, a boat'll be waitin'. Lend your backs. That's it."

Mike went on, "Em, confirm the orders by askin' our man to repeat the number. He'll say one if by land and two if by sea. Get it?"

It was simple but there was too much elementary school cleverness about it for me.

Weeks went by, and the conspiracy crawled into the recesses of my mind. I was a committed bootlegger but felt no different than before, especially, since I had yet to be frightened out of my wits.

Each night, I hurried home. The baby was due any day, and I wanted to help as much as possible. Mil's mother was on the first floor, so she was in good hands, and Mike asked the local patrol to check in on their rounds. We couldn't have asked for more support in our circumstances. Doc Murphy had delivered hundreds of babies and said she was doing just fine.

On April 6, 1920, I was drawn up the stairs by the wail of a newborn. The baby had been born only minutes before, and there were happy looks all around the still frantic kitchen. The Mrs., scurrying madly, said in passing, "It's a boy. Everything's fine with the both of 'em. I've sent for your Ma. . .Now keep outta my way."

I had trouble stickin' to the chair, as the Mrs. sprinted back and forth between the kitchen and the bedroom assisting Doc who was speaking soothingly over the howling. I was revved up but held back for almost an hour. Never so happy, I thought I'd die if leashed any longer, but, finally, the door opened and the Mrs. beckoned.

I shook hands with the doc and flew to the bed. Under her eyes, poor Millie had circles so dark and deep, you'd have thought she'd gone ten rounds with Mike Flynn. I put on a brave face and told her she looked lovely, but, truly, it was a frightening picture. I kissed her gently, and she smiled weakly. Turning to the baby, I was horrified; the little fellow looked like a big purple rat.

"Ain't he beautiful?"

I pulled myself together. "He is—the spittin' image of your Da."

Hearin' that, the Mrs. smiled on me as if she cared and shooed me out.

After a bit, Ma clumped up the stairs and rushed in with a big hug for her own baby. "I'm so happy for ya."

Millie and the baby were sleeping, so Ma was parked with me for what seemed an eternity, her motor racing, as the Mrs. had all the fun. I felt old enmities bubbling as Ma stewed.

The baby, Bobby, announced supper, and we ran for a look. Ma and Millie hugged, and Ma grabbed Bobby in her arms. "He's beautiful, Emmet. He looks just like you."

I puffed up and peered at him again. Unfortunately, in my view he still had the aspect of a rodent, so, once again, I laid him at Sean Moynihan's doorstep—temporarily, of course.

Da came and made of the pair and congratulated me for siring my own likeness. By then, I was able to absorb the shot without cringing. It was late when they all left, and the greater family Magawley slept and dreamt in their first night together, but at the stroke of midnight, Robert Emmet Magawley made his first major political outburst.

In the office at Charlestown one afternoon, I was pecking away on the Underwood when the phone startled me. The voice announced that it was Paul Revere; I almost collapsed. It was one lantern in the belfry of the Old North Church, and we were to be at the warehouse at six the next morning. On the way home, silence reigned. It was to be my first true felony and probably Tom's and Billy's, too. In my mind, I played out my part under the lights in the station house; it wasn't a pretty scene.

As agreed, the three of us, together for support, sauntered over to Grampa's before splitting up and making the final dash to the rear of the warehouse. Last in, I discovered a surprise party of Magawleys waiting on me. Mike and Jocko, looking not at all like hospital managers, sported the guilty smiles of boys caught rummaging through their sister's undies drawer.

Mulligan introduced the dark stranger with a droopin' mustache who would be our leader, and I watched the confidence drain from the home boys as the reality sank in that a federal felony would be committed under the direction of a Guinea. Mother o' God, what had we gotten ourselves into?

Six sedans were lined up and ready, and the Guinea, a native

Bostonian by accent, gave us a run down of the route to Burlington. If the schedule held, we'd convoy to a farm near Lake Champlain south of the city where we'd load up and then head back shortly after noon. If there were breakdowns, we were to flash our lights and stop. The Guinea would assess the situation and make whatever decisions were necessary.

He finished with, "I know that this is everyone's first time, but, remember, we ain't carryin' nothin'. The trip up is just practice. This is small time stuff anyway, and we'll never ask you to run the border. Mulligan says you're sound, and I guarantee that you'll do fine. Now, let's roll."

I cranked up a new Reo, and, by the time we made it into New Hampshire, my nerves had settled considerably. I loved the car. There was power to spare and the transmission was smooth as silk. The double clutching was a pleasure, and the stick moved like it knew where to go. Wherever the road permitted, we pushed hard and got up to at least forty before the convoy spread out too far for the Guinea's comfort, but the Reo had a lot more left. It was my first trip through the mountains of New England, and I was diverted often by the passing bucolic scenes—but never tempted to move into the godforsaken countryside. The Irish had had more than enough of fields and rocks and now were committed to life in the cities of America. The hours flew, and, soon, we neared Burlington.

Standing fourth in the convoy, I observed the Guinea in his Packard leading the way. Approaching Burlington, we slowed and left State Route 2 and headed for Shelburne. After about a mile, we turned into a dirt road and dropped down toward the lake. In second gear, we proceeded at perhaps five miles an hour. A farm came into view on the left, and, as we approached, the barn doors swung wide. The two lead cars drove in, and the rest halted behind them, outside. I saw Lake Champlain in the distance and would have liked to have walked down to it, but that was out of the question, given our mission.

After a couple of minutes, the Guinea waved us inside. Two

men worked furiously pulling cases of liquor from huge stocks stacked against the walls and placed them beside the first Packard that had been driven onto blocks. Another man struggled with the undercarriage of the vehicle, and, finally, a low gate on the side of the frame opened, displaying a false bottom. The first two fellows emptied the cases and began packing the bottles into the chamber. It went swiftly, and I was shocked by how much the car would hold. When they finished with the bottom, the cloth covers of the passenger and rear seats were removed, and metal seat forms were lifted out exposing additional space. The expert loaders placed dozens of bottles into the hiding places using straw for packing. When finished, the car was driven off the blocks and out the rear doors.

In less than an hour, the cars were fully laden and had been gassed at the farmer's pump. We were felons; what the hell, it was the Volstead Act. Heading back toward the highway, I felt the Reo struggle. Each car carried perhaps twelve cases of the finest liquor, weighing eight hundred pounds or more. Entirely without incident, we retraced our route to Boston and pulled into the warehouse shortly before seven o'clock. Unloading was left for another crew.

Crawling into bed, I felt as used up as on the first day inside the prison. I wasn't cut out for a life of crime, but the business was so vast that recruiting had to extend even to the chicken coop. It was sobering, however, to find that the party who delivered to Millie the envelope containing the four five dollar bills was Da, but, obviously, it had to fall to the Magawleys and Moynihans to supply both labor and protection. If we were to drink and prosper, we had to play a role.

During those times, on Sundays, the Moynihans, like most self-respecting Irish families, held communal dinners. They were rotated up and down stairs, apartment by apartment. The hostess did the cooking, and the two other women set the table—expanded and moved into place in the center of the kitchen by the men.

Donning our best suits, we repaired to the parlor and smoked as the women worked. The jackets were singled breasted—we'd seen pictures of the swells in their double-breasted blazers—just one obvious sign that we hadn't made it to the leisure class. Sean would break out a quart, and we'd sip away from unmatched tumblers and puff up a storm—cigarettes for the young men and a pipe for himself. On summer days, we'd be in shirtsleeves sitting in the shade of the huge sugar maple in the back yard safe from the prying eyes of busybody neighbors. In those days, sports were nowhere near the pastime they became after the second war and only occasionally did we talk about the Red Sox. It was them damn anarchists and the price of illegal booze that occupied us.

When dinner was ready, the hostess called. Sean led the way and would kick off on how wonderful the spread looked; I never remember one of those feasts that didn't appear welcoming. The women would be all atwitter as we buttered them up about the table and how nice they looked in their Sunday best. The Mrs. and Dolores, Mike's wife, were wondrous cooks, and Millie was learning fast. They could get all there was out of a smoked shoulder or corned beef and had dozens of recipes for the slowest pullet from the backyard.

While waiting, I observed the Moynihans. I was at home with Billy who was now almost as near and dear as my brother and Tommy Mullins. Sean was more complex than I'd imagined, abrupt rather than mean; he kept the Mrs. jumping with his inconsistency. I couldn't understand how the man could have ever been a successful politician until the first time a neighbor wandered into the yard. Jesus, you'd 'a thought Sean's younger brother had returned from the wars the way he fawned on him.

But it was Mike Moynihan who was the rock of the family. He could be counted upon to be a perfect son of a bitch on every occasion. If the bastard worked in Charlestown, he'd be the first sent to a tower. As we waited in the yard or parlor, he kept his hating focused on the Guineas and Polacks, but when we assembled and were trying to be nice for the women, he'd train his sights on Billy or me. "Looks like young Bobby's takin' after ya, Emmet.

Won't be long before he'll be down at the pond stabbin' frogs with that beak."

That would set Millie off. "You think you're funny. Bobby's beautiful, and Emmet's got a very nice look about him."

The usual retort was, "Just kiddin', Mil. No offense, but you gotta admit, the Magawleys walk like they're wadin' in knee deep water."

Of course, he wasn't out for me alone and let Billy know in no uncertain terms that he was too soft for prison work and should be harder on the inmates—much harder. Billy always began by feigning indifference, but, invariably rose to the bait.

"Are the anarchists gettin' their readin' material, Billy?"

"I don't have anything t'do with that."

"Are they gettin' enough exercise to keep up with their bomb throwin'?"

"Come on, Mike. Let's eat."

Dear old Emmet hunkered down as Billy got his. It could have been worse, a Magawley could have been on the griddle.

Millie had a weekly offering, "For the love of God, Mike. We're supposed to be respectable. Do you think the Protestants are babbling on about unpleasant subjects at their dinners?"

"Well we ain't Protestants. Besides, at least they built the prison to teach those thugs a thing or two, but, now that Charlestown's in the hands of softies like Billy and Emmet, it's hardly worth pinchin' anyone the way they're mollycoddled."

Billy pleaded, "For God's sake, it's still prison. They're locked up in that hellhole. We come out, but they can't." The plaintiff tone was raw meat for his tormentor.

"Put me in charge, and they'd be locked down permanently. We'd slide 'em the gruel and throw away the keys. You treat murders and anarchists like they're naughty boys. Show some guts. Treat 'em like the animals they are."

"Ya can't run a prison like that; there'd be a revolution."

Mike pounced. "There. He admitted it...You kiss up to 'em. You're afraid."

When the Mrs. could bear it no longer, she'd explode, "Jesus, Mary, and Joseph, leave off! You're tougher than everyone in Boston. You'd run the world different. Alright! Leave off." It was the only point in the week that I saw a use for the poor creature, except as a draft animal, and protecting her baby kept her going.

Only after the Mrs. balked would Sean restore order and then only if Billy and I were well done. Just livin' among 'em was difficult, and they made sure it was well rubbed into the pair of us that we were too gentle for their taste. And it made no difference in whose flat we were eating. Well, maybe it was a little worse if it was Mike's.

Every other week, we'd take our drive to Burlington, and just as I was gettin' comfortable with the routine, we had our first incident. The convoy, about ten cars—with me at the tail—had been rolling home from Shelburne for about an hour, and my nerves had settled down to as close to zero as they got. Passing through a little village on a picturesque section of Route 14 on one of the few straight-aways, we were sailing at a good clip when I heard a siren. In the mirror, I saw a cop car and an arm out the window waving me over. My heart in my mouth, I pulled up.

The officer parked and walked up. Saying not a word, he gave the Packard I was driving serious scrutiny. Dropping to a knee, he examined the undercarriage. He couldn't miss the false bottom, and I was on the verge of a stroke. Rising without a word, he continued around to the passenger side and, reaching into the open car, knocked on the seat with his knuckle. It didn't sound like pure moleskin to me or, based on the sly grin, to him either.

"I had ya at fohty, mista. Twenty-five's the limit."

Shocked, I failed to notice that the Guinea had pulled up on the other side of the road, and before I could reply, Paul intervened. "We're together, officer. I didn't realize we were goin' that fast. We didn't mean to speed through your town. This fellow has a perfect record, and I'd appreciate it if you could let him off with a wahnin'. It was my fault."

The officer, a kindly soul, said, "It's an easy mistake. That's a straight stretch, but you fellas hold it down in the futchah. Not all the boys are as lenient as me."

As he walked back to his car, he tucked into his pocket the small object that I saw the Guinea pass to him.

"You okay?"

It took an effort, but I got it out, "Yeah, fine."

"The bastard's just free lancin'. Somebody'll talk to his chief. Everything's ok. Take a deep breath, and let's go."

The rest of the trip passed in a blur, and the twenty I got for that run wasn't such easy money.

The next Sunday, Sean and Billy and I quaffed ale in the back-yard when Mike came strolling down. After very cursory small talk, he started in on us. "They're shippin' one of those murderin' Guinea bastards to Charlestown. Now you boys buck up those sissy guards and grind that anarchist sonofabitch."

I asked, "What are ya talkin' about?"

"Goddamn Vanzetti is bein' sent to ya. Who else? The friggin' assassin's intent on tearin' down everything we've worked for."

I'd come to believe that Billy had a half-decent head on him, but, at that instant, however, he made the most stupid statement I'd ever heard.

"They say there's a chance he and Sacco were framed."

Mike choked, the veins in his scarlet neck were so thick I thought they'd cut off his wind or pop right there. "Twelve men of Norfolk listened to that red shit. They were innocent until proven guilty. The prosecutors couldn't touch 'em. The judge couldn't make 'em find 'em guilty. But, goddammit, guilty they were. But right here in our own house there's a snake ready to betray us."

Sean leaped between 'em. "Mike, he never said they didn't do it. He said there's a `chance'. Right, Billy—a chance?"

Mike wasn't waiting for Billy's defense. Before Sean was half finished, he spat new accusations past his father. "Look at the both of 'em. They can't wait to meet the Guinea bastard. To tell him how much they admire him—how he was railroaded. They ought to fire every one of the goddamn guards and start over with some real men."

Good God, we were dependent on Sean Moynihan for our safety. "Come on, Mike. It ain't like that. Billy and Emmet know he done it. How he's treated till they fry him don't make no difference."

"You're goin' soft, too, Da. They ought to be toasted right now."

"We'll be goin' in in a minute. Settle down now. We can't be fightin' in front of the women."

Billy was shocked into silence, but I was just two seconds from tellin' the bullyin' bastard what I thought about his heavy handed hectorin'.

The meal was taken in silence. None of us could find a way to start the small talk or to react to the efforts by the women.

Later, Millie demanded an explanation, and she was wild that Mike had picked on Billy so terribly.

"But, I swear, Billy should know better. A vicious Guinea killer, and he says somethin' stupid like that."

The first volcanic eruption in the Moynihan house caused by Bart Vanzetti had been recorded; it would be followed by many more.

For a long time, I wondered why Mulligan invested in such big and expensive cars for running the booze. After a few runs, I saw that the other fleets were the same—Packards, Cadillacs, Franklins, Reos, whatever—nothin' but the biggest and the best. It soon became obvious that they were the only ones worth buying. An examination of the sales of expensive cars during prohibition would lead you to think that America was rich as could be, but it was bootleggers and smugglers who bought half of those big cars. Their solid construction and powerful engines were the reason. Just try taking a Model T and welding a false bottom on it that would hold a hundred bottles of the best. God, two runs and you'd be junking the poor little beast. Running booze was for big strong cars—and men—with exceptions, of course.

One morning, I walked into the tailor shop and knew something big had happened. The warden and Captain Healy were flutterin' like a pair of old biddies. There was a new worker on the floor, Bartolomeo Vanzetti, a celebrity. The shop superintendent was demonstrating a sewing machine, and the con was nodding and agreeing like it was the finest thing he'd ever seen. He had his own interpreter, a Guinea who usually worked shoveling coal, but I saw that the new man understood English, too. The warden, Healy, the super, and the interpreter hovered like midwives over a newborn. I faked disinterest, but the show was so spectacular it was impossible. As I made my rounds and came up on him, Vanzetti gave me a big smile, and I half returned it.

His was a friendly face—intelligent, sparkling dark eyes with deep and friendly crows feet constantly breaking toward a smile, high cheek bones, a great domed forehead, and a walrus mustache that drooped to his chin and fit him very well. He was smaller than expected—Christ knows he'd have had to have been less than the monster Mike Moynihan described, but he looked strong and vital with broad shoulders. All in all, he fit my vision of an anarchist, except for the constant smiling, bowing and deferring. The guards thought he was marvelous. Today, it would take a rock star to turn heads that way.

One night shortly after Bart arrived, I took the long way home and dropped by Clancy's for an ale. Entering the new restaurant, I saw several young families eating. That might not seem like much, but it nearly floored me. Women and children had never darkened the door of those sacred premises, and, except for the barmaids, I never recall seeing a female in the place. One youngster was digging into a pizza like it was food fit for Micks. I sighed and moved to the club door and knocked.

Jimmy peered at me like I was a germ under a microscope, revolting me, as there wasn't a chance that the place would be raided without warning. "It's a great act, Jimmy, but I could'a had two down waitin' for ya."

Clancy buttered me up. "Nice to see ya, Emmet. We can't be

too careful, you know. The feds send in fronts lookin' to get served just so's they can close a place and axe the stock."

"Whatever you say." My tone was none too subtle.

At least in the speakeasy proper, it was like old times with only men in sight. Mike Flynn and Batty Ryan were at a table up front, and I gave 'em a meager hello as I passed to a spot not far from where John Moran was holding court. Grampa and Da were in his train and waved me to a chair nearer the center of gravity. Da went through the hand signals that led to an ale being dropped before me, and I nodded thanks. It's amazing what can be communicated by loquacious Gaels without them ever uttering a sound.

John, at the height of his standard anarchist tirade with Mulligan playin' straight man, fired up the crowd. "Boys, I was never much on the war or Wilson—of course, we supported him because we're all democrats. But, at least now, he's doin' the right thing by them anarchists. Right, Mike?"

"I don't know, he ain't deportin' 'em fast enough to suit me," said Mulligan between pulls on a sad lookin' stogie. There were muffled giggles for that riposte.

Without a blink, Moran went on, "Take it from me, the Attorney General—Palmer—he's our kind. He put a couple o' hundred o' those bastards, includin' America's sweetheart, Emma Goldman, on a boat and dropped 'em off on the doorstep o' them Bolshevikees in Russia. We need more spunk like that. Right, Mike?" John looked around to assure that the boys were payin' attention and approvin'. Like him, I read their eyes and knew they were in his pocket.

Big John went round the room again and again with his tirade on how half of the Polacks, Greeks, and Russians were communists, but it wasn't till I'd had my two ales and half a dozen weeds that I realized that all them big bad immigrants no longer included Guineas. God, had I been blind. John had to hit me between the eyes before I broke the code. We were in bed with the Guineas from the North End. Of course Big John was the linchpin of bootleggin' in the Irish neighborhoods. I felt stupid for not seein' it from the beginning. The Magawleys and Moynihans would never have danced Mulligan's tune without John's blessing. And, certainly, Da would have to have been a lot deeper into his cups before he'd have queered Moran unnecessarily. I was makin' my twenties, and that was all I needed to know.

Moran was a talent, ranting and raving about his favorite targets and never once hitting the Guineas he'd been sightin' on for the past two years. Solidarity may have been the foundation of our success, but flexibility wasn't far behind. I smiled away an hour before headin' home to my little buzz saw.

The pressure in the penitentiary office was nonexistent and plenty of time was available for socializing. One morning, a few of us guards and civilian clerks were chewin' the rag when the telephone rang. I picked up and discovered Paul Revere. By this time, I knew that he and the Guinea convoy chief were one and the same, and I readied myself for the usual, but it was two lanterns in the Old North Church. We were going to sea. I passed the word to my confederates and found they were as anxious as me to see how the Italian Navy operated.

Tommy had acquired a Model T and, shortly after dark on the appointed night, picked up Billy and me. In the clear, windless night, we headed for South Station. I'd tell you that the time was selected because of the phase of the moon and after heavy pondering of weather reports, but, long go, I'd concluded that everyone who had to be was paid off and that the Guinea just didn't give a thought to being caught. I was wrong, but that's a tale for another day.

In spite of the seeming solidity of the fix, our nerves forced us into playin' bootleggers, and, as Tommy pointed the Tin Lizzie toward the water, Billy and I nervously scanned every doorway and alley, but spotted nothing more suspicious than a stray mongrel, head and tail drooping, trotting busily along Harrison Avenue. Turning left from Kneeland Street onto Atlantic, we coasted slowly toward the darkened behemoth, South Station, and stopped near one of the great loading docks at which the teams and trucks transferred the goods in and out of the city. Simple as that, Tom cut the lights, and we headed, separately, for our destination.

Rounding the corner of the station, I watched Billy cross the Northern Avenue Bridge. Tom had already disappeared into Sleeper Street, and I dogtrotted after them.

A smallish dragger was tied at the channel wall, and, under the watchful gaze of two tough looking Guineas, I hopped aboard. Pushing my way to the darkened stern, damned if I didn't bump into half a dozen boys from The Bush and Little Dublin and helloed all around. For the love of God, among 'em were Flynn and Batty. My first reaction was disgust, but I softened when I thought how loyal Mike was to his poor buddy and how hard he must have had to lobby to get Batty on board.

By this time, we new sailors were jumping out of our skins and chain smoking, and I suspected that we'd burn up our twenty bucks before the night was through. The others had made the run several times and tried to comfort us, so, to show that we were men, there was no choice but to stifle our fears. I smoked a full pack that night, even while working like a damn donkey.

Fishing was no more profitable in the twenties than it is today, so the poor boys, like us, had to get in league with the devil if they were to put food on the table. The boat, the Genoa, was but a decaying rust bucket, and, as I surveyed the quality of the rotted planking in the bulkheads, fear of drownin' drove out all problems of violating the Volstead Act.

Kevin, if you and the professors ever get to wonderin' whether you've got it good or bad in life, take a stroll around the docks of Gloucester or New Bedford and give a hard look at those boats. There's little doubt about the source of those cenotaphs bearing the names of those poor Portuguese and Guineas in the Seaman's Bethel and the churches of fishing villages everywhere. The poor cruds lived—and died—on the edge. Prices for their catch were always so low that, by the time they paid for milk and bread for their little ones and the liquid courage needed to board, there was rarely enough left for essential maintenance.

In Paul's navy, my trio served on only two boats, but at least half the fleet was active. A guy named Sal, a very nice Guinea, who had been born in the old country, owned the Genoa. The other, the Rosa, was owned by a native of the North End. He was the most surly bastard that I met in the years I ran whiskey, and I thought that he and Mike Moynihan would have made a great team. There could be no doubt, the Moran/Mulligan syndicate was in bed with the Black Hand—the Mafia.

The motor coughed to life as if on two packs of weeds a day, and we eased into the harbor. I thought the engine would settle down after a while, but, if anything, it got worse. By the time we passed Castle Island and Fort Independence, she was wheezin' badly, and I could tell Billy was thinking that the Mrs. was about to lose her second child to a bad end. We struggled past Boston Light and headed for Spain by way of the last islands of the harbor, the Brewsters. Not a minute beyond the far reaches of the harbor, I felt a great increase in the swells, and my stomach sent up reminders of the Mauretania.

Moving forward to an open space on the rail, I soaked up the cool breeze in an effort to settle my nausea. Paul came out of the cabin and asked, "Havin' a hard time, Emmet?"

It was the first time he'd used my name. "Yeah, I'm an army man at heart, Paul. I doubt that I'll be much use in the boats."

He looked at me kindly and said, "You'll do fine."

Immediately bolstered, I rejoined the lads in the stern. Things had loosened up, and, if the Genoa hadn't sunk already, there was hope for our safe return.

We headed due east past the rum line, the three-mile limit, beyond which the Coast Guard couldn't touch us. After half an hour, lights appeared in the distance; a freighter was ablaze. A tiny ship—sure, it was ten times longer than the Genoa, but I wouldn't want to face any kind of weather on it. It was low in the water— low. They'd take a chance on going under before refusin' a bottle. Sal cut the engine, and we stood by while others loaded.

While the lights from the ship were bright, they lit up little of the vast sea, but I sensed many boats flitting about like bees to the hive. The sounds told me that they were of all sizes and types, from speedboats to trawlers larger than the Genoa. Many strategies for beating the feds had been developed.

After an hour adrift, it was our turn. The engine sputtered to life, and we came along side. The language was English and, in minutes, it became obvious that they were out of Halifax, Nova Scotia. The crew swore and strained to guide a hoist from amidships to the side near us. The load looked like a round fronted barge, and they plopped it into the sea to our stern. When she hit, two Guineas, carrying lines, jumped aboard and secured the two vessels. At their signal, the Irish stepped into the low slung tow.

It was small, maybe thirty-five feet long by twelve wide, but I guessed that it was too much for the Genoa, except under ideal conditions. The hands on the ship began lowering pallets bearing cases of liquor. Atop each case of booze was a box, and we stacked them carefully assuring that nothing was jammed too tightly together.

Paul gave the rookies a rundown. "This here's a submarine. The two lines—one's for towin', the other scuttlin'. Loaded, she's just inches above the water. If the feds ever waylay us, we open the valves and she's a rock. The boxes on the crates have fifty-foot lines buried in salt. A couple o' hours after we convince the feds we're just fishin', the salt dissolves and we pull up a boat load of forty pounders. Stack em' carefully."

Before we cast off, every square inch of the barge was taken up by whiskey cases. The engine sounded better than it had all night. Sal hit the gas and the Genoa moved out, but, when the line tightened, I knew that she didn't like the feel. She might have been made for hauling nets, but this barge was right at her limit. Sal jammed the throttle through the pain.

It seemed an eternity, but, finally, I spotted a bow wave on the barge. The city lights rose in the distance, and we made for them at maybe a mile or two an hour. After ten minutes, Sal cut the running lights and turned south. Obviously, we weren't taking the direct route.

Paul passed, and I asked, "What gives with the left turn?"

"It ain't like the cars. The Coast Guard means business. We have to play it safe and head for a small harbor. Tonight, it's Cohasset, but we switch all the time.

"Relax. It's a milk run."

Easy for him!

Two Guineas stood by at the stern. One had an axe for the hawser pulling the barge and the other held the line to the valves; peering into the night, they looked like they hadn't a care in the world. Only when we came dangerously close to Strawberry Point, did Sal hit the lights, and, very slowly, we inched our way into the narrow channel. Two trucks waited on the pier, and we closed on them at a glacial pace.

The Guineas secured both craft, the donkeys—the prison guards—muscled the cases onto the dock, and the rest of the Micks loaded the trucks. It took about an hour.

Wasting no time, the Italians waved and headed back to sea. We piled onto the top of the whiskey cases for the ride to the warehouse. It had been a learning experience.

One morning in the winter of '22, I crawled up the stairs after the night shift and found Millie sick as a dog. She was bearin' her second and was payin' a price.

Millie and Emmet Magawley were settlin' in for the long ride through life, still in love. Like many Irishmen, I was a better husband than suitor. The Gaels are terribly sentimental, but it's difficult when your best promise to the one you love is for a life of drudgery. But she was game, and it was us against the world. I had a decent job, a supplementary source of income, and the finest companion the world could provide. For what more could I ask?...Not havin' to live among the Moynihans might be a place to start. But I had to go easy on that, for they weren't out after me alone. Sean and Mike were classic Irish and spoke well of no one, at least behind their backs.

CHAPTER 10

Vanzetti's arrival in Charlestown, signaled a dramatic change in prison life. The number of visitors on Saturdays and Sundays doubled weekly. A chance glimpse of Bart gave long abandoned inmates cachet among loving family and friends, and, reveling in his fame and the injustice of it all, he smiled on all whose eyes met his.

As Mike Moynihan had set the parameters of Bart's guilt on behalf of the police, Brahmins, the American Legion, upwardly mobile Irish, and even many leading Italians, so it was that in the first days of his incarceration, the guards and inmates settled on his innocence. That many Italians were lined against Sacco and Vanzetti has always dropped jaws, but they, like the Irish, were being assimilated, and many of their leaders were currying favor with the establishment by supporting the convictions.

Over the years, the keepers had listened to pleas of innocence from thousands of guilty convicts and smiled as prisoners swapped yarns on gross injustices. But, for once, members of the prison community believed this Italian immigrant, except, of course, for the tower tigers who cared not about guilt or innocence but patiently waited for the opportunity to shoot someone, anyone. Outside the walls, it was a different world for the warders, and wearing other hats across the river, they became observers in homes and halls dominated by strident voices demanding vengeance.

The trial of Sacco and Vanzetti permeated every nook and cranny of the globe into which tales of injustice might be squeezed, and, in a blink, the binary worlds made their choices. The fish monger and shoe maker were either innocent, railroaded by an overzealous police and court system as a warning to immigrants that they better speed their way to assimilation, or cold blooded killers whose lives should be extinguished as a lesson to those intent on destroying America. There was no middle ground; in speakeasies, jackets were flung and fists raised as evidence of where the participants stood on Nick and Bart.

Most of us are open to persuasion, but in the Sacco and Vanzetti case, the factions were so shrill that rational review became impossible. Lines drawn, members stood with their tribes. Pawns, the guards caught in a no-man's-land had to trip lightly. A few brave souls among the Brahmins, mostly women, stood for the truth, as they saw it, but they were lonely indeed. Many neighbors of Vanzetti from Plymouth, Italians and many Swamp Yankees, never flagged in their support of their townsman, but they were the only ones who knew him. Certainly the Irish were too insecure to throw up such sports in any number. Most Gaels had put radicalism behind by the mid-twenties, and only one Celt, Mary Donovan, a born fighter, was on their defense committee.

Most ordinary Italians believed in Sacco and Vanzetti, but the criminal and political leaders whose ideas were more compatible with the Brahmins and the Irish undercut them. Even the Italian government was for getting beyond the incident—Mussolini was always a stickler for justice.

In Charlestown, there was no such thing as Sacco and Vanzetti. Bart was serving fourteen years for his conviction for an attempted-armed robbery in Bridgewater on Christmas Eve of 1919. Sacco, a suspect in the case, had an iron clad alibi and was never tried. But together, they were found guilty of murdering the paymaster and his guard during the April 15, 1920 shoe company payroll robbery in South Braintree. The convictions were appealed, and Sacco was held in the Dedham jail during the seven-year course of the review, while Bart was sent to Charlestown for the Bridgewater caper. Over the years, I saw Sacco at hearings, but not until knowing him was pain incarnate did I come to see him as a human being.

Around the globe, anarchists, Bolsheviks, and socialists raised money for them, and there was never a shortage of lawyers meeting with Bart on his defense. Vanzetti, a one-man circus, enlivened Charlestown with the balls that were tossed in the air on his behalf and by the activity that trailed him everywhere.

From the first, the prison community determined Bart's anarchy was that of books and not the bomb throwing variety that prosecutors painted. Like all theologians, he bored us to slumber on the canonical differences of Sorel and Kropotkin. Stopping at his cell, I nodded as he preached on the inherent goodness of man, and, on my next round of the block, I'd have to strain to remember what he'd said concerning my fulfillment during the previous circuit.

Notwithstanding the hoopla, Bart was extremely shy by nature. He had a quick smile, but it was difficult for him to initiate interactions. We worked together in the tailor shop for many weeks before we screwed up the courage to speak. As he bumbled his way through sewing the khaki uniforms worn by the inmates and I made my rounds of the floor, we exchanged hesitant smiles.

Finally, he spoke, "Good morning, Meesta." The opening was punctuated with a warm smile.

Returning the greeting, I moved on about the factory. This sparring went on for days before he formally introduced himself. "I'm a Bart a Vanzetti. What's a you name?"

The ice broken, our familiarity developed rapidly. Vanzetti's friendly nature and the atmosphere of innocence in Charlestown permitted the effortless breakdown of social barriers after that.

On the home front, Millie's kind heart shone through, and she made sure that I was not cut off from the Magawleys. Every month, we bundled up the heir and traipsed into The Bush. Like Mrs. Moynihan, Ma was a fine cook, and she worked tirelessly to prepare for the return of the native.

The Irish have been pounded by dilettantes for their terrible cuisine, but it is a bigoted label. The Celts were an oppressed agrarian people with little opportunity to develop gastronomic wonders. Certainly, they never sought to curry the favor of those who stole their land by creating fine sauces and such for manor house tables. Their task was to take the limited foodstuff available to them and create wholesome and satisfying meals for hard working families. In America, they began with the chickens from their backyards, the cheapest cuts of beef, pork and mutton, and, together with native vegetables, they produced nourishing plates for their progeny.

The top of the line in the Magawley household, as in most homes, was pot roast of beef. Mother of God, they had to give a mortgage for it, and having it placed before you was evidence of the deepest love. Always, it was simmering when we arrived; the rich aroma filled the house, and we salivated from the first whiff. My Millie, with none of the guile of her male kin, flew to tackle the least desirable chores in assisting Ma and Eileen. As they worked, they tossed little Bobby between them, while Da, Uncle Bob, and I did the heavy work of bending elbows, smoking, and solving the world's social and political problems.

Da opened with, "Have you seen Vanzetti?" It was the first question from those who knew I worked in the prison.

"It's like incarceratin' the governor; there're lawyers everywhere. The prisoners and guards are already for him."

Bobby snapped, "The bastard murders two men in cold blood, and we make him a celebrity? For the love of God, we can't let scum like that get away with it."

"Are they guilty?" Da tentatively sought my feelings.

"If you want a reason to kill 'em, pick up a Transcript. If you don't like that one, try the Globe. How should I know? But guilty or not, they're bein' hustled straight into the chair."

Bobby was on me, but with none of the Moynihan anger when faced with a batting practice fastball. "The bastards have got to see that if they want in, they've got to change. There's no room for bomb throwin' in Boston.

"Christ, you're not for lettin' 'em off, Em?"

"Hell no, but suppose they're innocent. Could ya pull the switch?"

Bobby returned the fire but in a measured way, "Nobody's for that. But, Jesus, they were convicted. How can ya be for 'em?"

"I'm not for 'em. The Yankees, the cops, and the lace curtains are out to burn them, but they don't know the facts."

Da stabbed me. "Twelve men determined the facts for them—and more than one of 'em was Catholic."

It was nice to be among my own. We could discuss such things and not boil into the rage that lurked just beneath the surface in my new abode.

When I first took up the trade, visitors' day was nothing. The central hall of the prison, not at all unpleasant, was filled with rows of chairs waiting to welcome the guests. Wives, children, mothers, and fathers would queue up outside waiting for the hour, and, on pleasant days, they were serenaded by a brass band of Christian volunteers. 'Home Sweet Home', a particular favorite, was pumped into the milling crowd—a none too subtle reminder for felon and family that they'd better fly right if they didn't want to hear it again after their homecoming reunion.

When visitors were seated, the prisoners were loosed into the great room, and little groups huddled together around the hall. The guards, decent fellows, tried not to interfere in the few moments of pleasure afforded the unfortunate devils and were as discreet as possible as prisoners held loved ones close. No one ever criticized me for it, so, ever more emboldened, I leaned on a wall and read books during the hours of socializing. The primitive library inside the walls was a great benefit for the few prisoners and guards who found solace in the written word.

After Vanzetti came aboard, the atmosphere became charged. The lines of visitors backed up far into Rutherford Street, and even the band seemed inspired. Rules were bent to accommodate him. He had more visitors than permitted to others, and they stayed longer, as well. The weekends became holidays, and guards and inmates alike were enlivened.

For men rediscovered by their families, it meant time away from the darkened eight by four-foot holes. The dank cellblocks gave way to the airy central hall, and everyone was indebted to the anarchist for putting a little life into Charlie Bulfinch's wondrous pile of rocks.

Millie and I, ever inspired by history and by our illustrious families, called the dear little girl with the soft features, Helen. The lady from Troy followed in the path laid out by Robert Emmet Magawley. She was a pretty thing with lots of bone and a smile that could launch ships. In the scheme of things, we came to believe that she would fit right into Little Dublin and would mother her own brood in twenty years. Bobby, true to his clan, looked more like me every day—and his Grampa and his Great Grampa. That sonofabitch, Mike, let few meetings pass without an allusion to spearing fish or splash landin's or whatever other images he could conjure.

Millie was devoted to her Ma and Da and would never break from them because of Mike, but, on edge whenever he was lurking, she had to stand at the ready when his funnies were loosed. Poor Billy was intimidated by his bullying, and only Sean was able to stand up to him. The Mrs. hadn't a chance and cringed while waiting for the attack on her baby that impelled her into unwanted action. But with the arrival of Bobby, Mike discovered a target that would wound Millie and me with a single shot. Direct assaults on me diminished, and I thought that he might be growing a little afraid of me.

With the passing seasons, the affinity between Bart and me ripened. Early on, spotting me scrunched up on the wall with a book, he pointed with pride to the tome he held. "What you read, Meesta Magawley?"

"What's in front o' me...I guess history'd be my choice."

"Heestoree good. I read about great men, too, Dante—Saint Francis, no?"

It took months of chattin' in the tailor shop and at his cell for him to get up the nerve to call me Emmet, but, at last, he took the plunge. A more conventional person than ever I dreamed, it took me many weeks to return the intimacy.

Vanzetti fancied himself an intellectual and loved discussing the finer things. Father Murphy, the prison chaplain, began visiting in his cell, and they'd gab by the hour. Bart, a confirmed atheist, was full of himself for considering the Father's points. Opportunities for Murphy to exercise his noggin' in Charlestown were few, so, at the drop of a hat, he'd run up to the block. They sat side by side on the bunk and went at the saints or anarchy or whatever.

The talks with Murphy did wonders for Bart's English. The father, a typical Gael, spun yarns with as many usages as he could shoehorn into a sentence, and Bart had to step lively to keep up. Between the lawyers, the Brahmin ladies who visited with him, his reading, and Murphy, Bart's flair for language came to the fore. During that first year, he went from very modest facility in English to a first rate talker and writer.

When on the block—often, since I sought the shift, I'd stroll by as Bart and the Father palavered over esoteric points of medieval philosophy or other such relevant topics. Occasionally, I'd stop, and we'd all go at it, but, quickly, I'd tire of the malarkey and be off on my rounds. They loved it. And, when Bart wasn't working in the shop or didn't have sufficient light for reading—his first priority—he welcomed the priest to his cell.

One winter evening, as I made my rounds, a terrible commotion broke out behind me. Bart shouted wildly, "Meesta Magawley! Meesta Magawley! Come queeck!"

I flew to the cell and found Bart drawn up to his full height facing me at the bars; if his uniform had been other than faded khaki, I'd have thought it was Il Duce, himself. Murphy was staring vacantly at the wall as Bart made a formal statement, "Father Murphy has finished hees visit. Please let heem out."

I hastily freed the priest. With his eyes on his shoes like he'd been caught playin' with himself, the priest skulked away.

"What happened?"

"Father Murphy ees not welcome heere."

After digging for a few minutes, it was obvious that Bart had made his pronouncement on the matter for the day. On the next shift, I pursued it with similar success. Weeks later, after I'd given up on solving the mystery, we were chewing the fat up at his cell when it popped out.

"Never let that priest near me again. We discuss Tolstoy. Hee knows nothing about Russian writers, but hee's smart fella, so I don care. Priest turn to me and ask, `Tell me, Vanzetti, who drove the car in South Braintree?'

"Emmet, I no believe but never blaspheme. I almost curse that Murphy. Hee's a no good."

For weeks the priest avoided me, and we were never again on the same easy terms. I felt sorry for him; if he'd been raised in The Bush, he'd have known enough to leave the roadwork to those charged with handling it.

In the war against the feds, the Italian general staff grew bolder with each run. One Saturday night, Sal gunned the Genoa, and—every trip was an adventure in sound—I suspected consumption deep in the engine's lungs. The crew that black night was the usual collection of Micks and Gineas, with a unique exception—my Da. I had no idea that he was up to rum running or how he got himself to Sleeper Street. Be that as it may, I had difficulty stifling a laugh as he squirmed through his explanations of the finer points of moral law. My first thought was that he'd make a perfect visitor for Vanzetti.

It was nearly impossible to concentrate on both the sick engine and Da's definitions of laws that might be ignored. In my mind, I replayed the painful day at St. Michael's and, smiling inwardly, determined to give him no quarter. A sea of bobbing boats lay before us, and it would be very late before our turn came. Only when we were secured alongside the freighter, did I agree. "You're right, Da. Puttin' up with prohibition would be stupid—and a mortal sin to boot." He seemed very satisfied with that response.

The sea was calm; maybe Paul Romano—references to the Old North Church and its lanterns had long disappeared with our growing confidence in the enterprise—had paid more attention to the weather than I'd given him credit for in selecting the timing of our runs. Apparently, it never crossed my mind that we simply sprang into action on the day the ship appeared off Boston. The pallets were lowered, and we worked like dogs to stack the crates of liquor. The crew of the Genoa was now expert at loading the booze, and soon we were underway to rendezvous with Mulligan's trucks waiting for us in Scituate Harbor.

Sal steered, as usual, for Boston Light. The Genoa balked but could not resist all night, and we began. Nothing seemed out of the ordinary. Sal cut the running lights long before we recrossed the three-mile limit, and we pushed on and, after another few minutes, made our sweeping left turn to the south. We were operating at full throttle at about a mile and a half an hour, and, still, the bow wave on the barge was only inches from swamping it. Suddenly, out of the blackness there came a light; we were in the blinding beam of a powerful searchlight.

"Coast Guard. Give me the wheel, Sal," Paul shouted as he sprinted into the cabin. He added with a nod to the other Guineas, "Move."

Sal and two others shoved the Micks aside and prepared for action. The gunboat was bearing down at flank speed, and, in this tubercular slug, only the Celts dreamed of outrunning the law. We were caught, and I thought I would die right there. Over the years, I found that flaunting the law for fellow plotters was as easy as pouring cold beer down my gullet. Explaining to feds what you're doing in the open ocean in the middle of the night with a crew of Irishmen who didn't know the difference between a pollack from the sea and a polyp on your seat was another matter altogether. That we wouldn't go to jail was known to all, but the shame and embarrassment were already gnawing at my entrails. As Tommy and Billy shared the rail, I sensed that we were all in the same pickle.

But when I turned to Da, I couldn't contain myself. He was doing the St. Vitus Dance right on the Genoa. The poor man was pinballing off bulkheads, the crew, and every piece of equipment on deck. He hid behind the wall and darted out to observe the closure the gunboat was making. With each look the distance was halved, and he held his stomach as if to suppress nausea. Although panicked, I had to laugh at the poor man's fix.

"They won't open fire, Da," I said through a grin.

"It ain't funny. All my life, I've done the right thing. I'm ruined."

"Jesus, Da, we're just fishin'."

"They'll buy that?" he asked in a tone so plaintiff, I thought I'd split my gut.

"Easy now. Paul'll take care of it."

"Let us pray."

Romano eased the throttle to the audible relief of the Genoa. As one of his North End pals struggled to free the towline, the other stood at the ready with an axe in case he couldn't make it. Sal held the rope to the valves and waited his turn.

Above the pounding racket of the Genoa, came, "Heave to! Coast Guard. We're comin' aboard. Heave to, now!"

We were making little headway as it was, and Paul ignored the order shouted through a megaphone. The law was only a hundred yards in our wake. After what seemed hours, the line to the sub came free and was tossed into the sea; my chest almost burst when the cord was silhouetted in the beam. Sal gave a powerful yank on his lanyard, while the Micks did their share by internalizing a collective rosary. Ascertaining no desire on the part of the barge to slip to her watery grave, I turned helplessly to Da. He had the answer; his prayers had become audible as he shook in time with the engine.

The feds were within fifty yards, and the megaphone blared on about heaving to—but for all of our speed it had to look like we were cooperating. Shading my eyes, I tried to make out what was going on aboard the enemy craft, but, blinded, I lowered my gaze to the sub in one last hope of finding her missing.

As my pupils recovered, I saw the bow wave breach the gunnel. "She's gone, Da...'Twas your prayers."

Da stepped to the stern and watched as she nosed down. "Blessed be God," he said angelically.

Phosphorescent bubbles rose from the great burp as the ocean digested our treasure. Paul killed the engine and came out to us. Sternly, he said, "We've done nothin'. Leave this to me."

The cutter reversed her engines and, like an enormous hockey skate, skidded, spray flying, to a stop not thirty yards off of our starboard side. A cockboat dropped into the water, and a cox, four oarsmen, and a boarding party of three took their places. "Everybody on deck! We're boardin'," shouted an armed chief petty officer. He, an ordinary seaman, and a young lieutenant scrambled onto the Genoa.

Paul's sure grip on his nerves eased my angst, and I felt the tension subside in the others. But when I turned to look for Da, I almost fell down. The poor man was choking his crotch with both hands to suppress his wild shaking.

"We're fine," I said only loud enough for his ears.

Under his breath, I made out, "...heartily sorry for havin' offended Thee. . ."

The chief and the seaman charged below, and the officer confronted Paul. No direct accusations were made, but there could be no doubt of the reason for the apprehension. After many minutes, the sailors came on deck and quietly reported. A cross look and a snarl sent them for a second and longer look, with the same result.

After going over the Genoa with a fine-tooth comb, they prepared to return to the cutter. The lieutenant was all sarcastic smiles and jibes and promised to see us again, and the chief stomped before us like we were in his boot camp company. But he said nothing until he spotted Da.

"This ain't for you, old timer. Pull any harder on that and the taproot'll give."

Stifling a laugh at that juncture remains among the greatest acts of love of my lifetime, but, sadly, no one else on board could be so proud of himself. Not that I was ever first to broach the topic, but the tale of Da's defiance of the feds that night served as an ice breaker at family gatherings for decades.

The engines on the gunboat roared to life, and she was off with a great wake into the night.

Nerves shot, we smoked until first light, requiring all the soothing the weeds could provide. Da, the only one not puffing, walked off his adrenaline overload on the tiny deck, dodging the great winches and nets.

In the hours following, Paul stayed at the helm, and Sal flashed a signal at well-lit boats that had already dropped their cargo and were heading home. Several came to our aid. One was a beautiful mahogany speedboat that should have been cruising a quiet lake in the Adirondacks instead of being eaten away by the harbor brine, but that was the fate of lovely machines in those days of speed and profit. As the dawn rose, the boats zigzagged over the area trying to spot our boxes while everyone on board the Genoa willed the whiskey into rising, but, after about an hour, our friends abandoned us.

With Sal back at the wheel, we continued the long traverses across the suspected area. Beside me, Paul said to no one in particular, "The fuckin' thing must'a dove in a hole. This is supposed to be forty feet. What a friggin' waste. The floats are a joke...All those runs, we should'a loaded more booze."

But as the sun broke free from the sea, Tommy shouted, "There!" pointing off the port side.

As Sal eased toward the object, we saw that it was our treasure. Paul reached with a hook and dragged the box aboard. The line was loose and about ten feet came aboard before it grew taught. Up it rose from the depths—a case of beautiful Scotch whiskey— and a cheer went up from all on board.

With renewed faith, we stood watch at the rail for still another hour before hope flagged again. Such calamities were the price of doing business, and every gang was self-insured.

"One fuckin' hole in the harbor. We find it." Paul was disgusted. "One friggin' case of Scotch. Shit!"

After still another eternity, Romano gave the signal. We wouldn't waste any more time. He sulked in the cockpit for a few minutes and then came alive; full of smiles and good cheer, he pulled two bottles and passed them around, and, in the hours it took us to get back to Sleeper Street, we became buzzed out of our minds by killing the entire case. Da did more than his share of drinking, and, by then, he and the crew were rewriting the most embarrassing parts of the performance.

As I stepped to the pier, Paul whispered, "You're from good stock, Emmet, but, if your dad can't make the next run, we'll settle for the shell shocked guy."

Again, I controlled my laugh, but, as it turned out, it was Da's only trip on the Genoa.

In my other life, driving Bart from the prison to the Norfolk County Court House in Dedham was a wondrous adventure. In front hunkered into the wind, three state troopers on motorcycles were trailed by a car of police officers; one of our Chevy Royal Mails with three guards and a captain; the car carrying Vanzetti, two guards in front and a guard in back cuffed to him; and, bringing up the rear, another state police car and three more bikes. The only things missing were the secret service agents trotting beside Bart and the Marine Band playing 'Hail to the Chief'.

The Royal Mails, similar to the ones we had with us in France, were called torpedoes, a term that has disappeared from the lexicon. They had integrated lines that, while primitive by today's standard, extended from the radiator to the rear bumper with no sharp stops along the way. The look was most appealin' and seemed very streamlined to me; most manufacturers had examples in all their price ranges.

The open car provided Bart a clear view of the route and the people. In turn, he could be seen easily by the public. As you can imagine, he reveled in his celebrity—never thinking it notoriety or infamy—and enjoyed the give and take with people along the way—anything to forward the causes of his dear anarchy and 'joostice'. The route carried us through both working class neighborhoods and some of the most scenic parts of the city. It was my impression that most of the curious along the way felt little hatred toward Bart. The occasional shouts of 'murderin' bastard' deflated that view, but he ignored those and smiled and waved to all.

When driving Bart's car, I couldn't keep up with his patter on the beauty of the route—the museums, the fens, the houses of the wealthy, and a myriad of other observations—but, when cuffed to him in the back, it was like a ride in the country. People no longer drive for sheer pleasure of motion as we did then. Those with cars would pack up the family and motor over the back roads enjoying the rustic sights of woodland, the still innocent workings of village life, and the glorious smell of new mown hay. That's how we felt as we skimmed over the road to Norfolk County—especially the Irish lads who'd abandoned the agricultural life for the cities of America.

The towns, today, are integrated completely into the Boston metropolitan area, and, were it not for the boundary markers, it would be virtually impossible to tell when the city is left behind and the towns, like Dedham, begin. Two generations ago, however, the drive from the Charles, through the Back Bay, and out Huntington Avenue to the court traced a road evidencing a spectrum of change from city center to the totally rustic.

We'd pull up in the rear of the huge classical courthouse, so that Bart could enter through a protected portal. Only the captain and the guard cuffed to him went inside, as Norfolk County deputies were charged with security in the court. State troopers guarded the perimeter of the building, and those of us from Charlestown without a role remained with the cars.

At every proceeding, a crowd waved placards detailing the miscarriage of justice, and, over the years, the demonstrations increased in size and intensity. Half of the state troopers worked to keep agitators a reasonable distance from the courthouse, while the rest did what they could to quiet the half dozen real Americans armed with baseball bats who wanted to teach citizenship to the anarchist bastard.

During one of my earliest trips to the court, as I smoked and leaned against the wall of the granite monster, a party approached. A beautiful woman, short but well curved, wearing a stylish black dress and a hat with a brim so wide that it seemed to extend beyond her square shoulders, was at the group's center. A little boy held her hand, and one of the two men flanking her carried an infant. They walked directly toward me at the pace set by the boy.

As they neared, the woman looked up and, meeting my eyes, her face broke into the most radiant smile that I had ever seen. I returned the favor and gave her a half salute. She was close enough to touch, and I saw rich auburn hair beneath the brim and friendly freckles dotting a rich creamy complexion. As she turned to enter the court, the shadow of the monolith fell across her, and the lovely smile crashed into a look of terror and panic. I wanted to reach out, but she was gone.

"That's Rosa Sacco," said Alfred Shaw, who'd come up in the car with me, "It's sad."

Stunned by the incongruous juxtaposition of cheer and fear in her dark eyes, for the first time foreboding for Bart entered my thinking. It was never far away after that.

Back on Mulberry Street, young Bobby and Helen put an end to our naming the babies for modern heroes and classical figures. I had begun to think Bobby was destined for a life in Charlestown in which he'd wear khaki and not gray. Helen, also a handful, seemed intent on a lifetime in diapers, and she had the richest voice that I'd ever heard in one so tiny. Whenever chastised, she practiced shattering glass with a lovely soprano blast, so, when we were joined by still another boy, we settled on Patrick in hopes that he would be saintly. That didn't go over at all with Sean and Mike, and they put on their longest pusses when it was announced. Only when they recognized the marsh bird in the little fellow, did they find value in the choice.

There was little need for demonstrating facility in genetics for Millie and me, but Mike was never one to wait for demand before attempting a sale. It was bad enough that he pointed out with

Bobby and Paddy that the apple doesn't fall far from the tree, but Millie's complexion ripened when he insisted on detailing a comparison with fledglings in the heron nest. I think that was about as close as I ever came - up to that point anyway - to lettin' him know how I felt about him but, for Millie's sake, held off.

A real observer of human nature, it took three years of living with the Moynihans for me to see that Billy was a mama's boy. He was a great friend, like my own brother, but, chicken as she was with Mike, the Mrs. dominated her baby. That was the price of defending him from the bully, and, since Sean was always on the go with politics, she needed a man at home for protection. Billy, too shy to chase women—and maybe he didn't have need to—fell naturally into the role required, while Mike, the lovely soul, constantly rubbed the poor lad's nose in his need to hide behind the old lady's skirts. Millie said as much as she could on his behalf, but the family environment consigned him to home. What a lovely way to pass a half a century.

On the cellblock one evening, I played checkers with a very nice Italian who never had visitors. He wasn't as proficient as me— how could he be, I'd learned from masters all over the block—and I stumbled occasionally for his enjoyment. When the light failed, I began my rounds and came on Harry Faxon, an embezzler, sitting in the darkest shadows of his already dim cell. This was out of character as he was always at the bars waiting to greet me. "Under the weather, Harry?"

"Just pissed...paper games on an insurance company and I wind up in this hole, but, every night, the guards run rum, and nobody gives a shit. I don't get it."

"What d'ya mean?" I asked in my most innocent voice.

"Walk on...You're like the rest of 'em. Christ, they're laughin' about it."

I was angry. "What am I supposed to do, turn ya loose. You stole money. Can't ya see the difference, for Christ's sake?"

"No. Wrong's wrong. The friggin' cops are on the take, and their relatives deliver it. You should be in here instead o' me."

"Get the off the high horse. Runnin' booze ain't a crime. You stole. Agh!...In two years you'll be at it, too."

"Yeah. Fuck you."

It took months of buttering up before I again gave him the time of day.

A star among the visitors, Betrando Brini, a lively lad, regularly came to see Bart, and, over six years, I watched his transformation from a child to a rambunctious teenager. Every few months, his folks brought him up from Plymouth; I got to know them all. The subject of most of their conversations with Vanzetti was the old neighborhood, but, occasionally, a great sad anger clouded their meeting.

Betrando had provided Bart's alibi for the Bridgewater robbery, and, when they touched that exposed nerve, the visit degenerated to tears and then outrage. As much as anything, observing the Brinis when they thought themselves alone led me to believe in Bart; it was they who equipped me with more than the simple knee jerk reaction of most of Vanzetti's other supporters.

The crux of Vanzetti's defense for the Bridgewater job was an old holiday custom among the Italians in Plymouth of serving eels on Christmas Eve, and he, the local fish monger, had purchased the fish in Boston. They were delivered early on the morning of December 24, 1919, but, because there were so many orders, he needed help. Betrando was only too happy to help Bart, a boarder in the Brini house and the boy's caring friend and mentor, with his rounds. The unusual delicacy gave the lad, his mother, and other neighbors an absolute fix on the time and date that coincided exactly with that of the robbery.

But it was the lad's love that undid the alibi, and Bart's kindness toward the boy worked against him. The prosecutors twisted the deep affection and caring of the Brinis and their neighbors into a tale of perjuring immigrants protecting a murdering anarchist from justice. Whenever the tale slipped into the visits, Bart was crushed, and the Brinis left the prison in disarray. The youngster's frustration was absolutely convincing.

It was an awful task for the Brinis, balancing their belief in Bart with the terrible impact their visits had on Betrando. Occasionally, they made the trek without him, and it broke Bart's heart that the meetings were so difficult for the lad. For years, these simple people were the only links between Bart's life as an unknown fishmonger and his new role of murdering anarchist.

CHAPTER 11

From the somber darkness of his cave, Vanzetti, in a near whisper, spoke past me, "They must keel us." Despite the outward calm, I perceived a caged tiger, brimming with power and moral outrage ready to spring.

The black lines of the bars fell across his face leaving only his right eye and cheek highlighted in the fading sunset. Shaken and apprehending that his gaze penetrated the future, I tried, unsuccessfully, to rally him. "You'll get a new trial."

"You nice man, Emmet, but part of bad business. They weel keel us. No way out for them."

"There're checks. They have to make sure you had a fair trial."

"I theenk cowards—they never show mercy. But remember St. Augustine, he say, 'The blood of martyrs is the seed of leeberty.'"

This meeting occurred only days after my disturbing encounter with Rosa Sacco, but, quickly, I willed myself to reject Vanzetti's horrible conclusion as impossible, and my concern began to ease. But, try as I might, within weeks, I, too, detected an inexorability of events that, python like, constantly tightened to crush him.

And soon, I began suffering terrifying nightmares. Varying only slightly, uniformed men burst into the block and ordered that Bart be turned over for immediate execution. I trembled through explanations that his appeals had not been exhausted, but the brown shirts laughed in my face and demanded the keys, so that they could drag him to the electric chair. I was alone, always alone, and every time shrieked for help, but no sound was emitted.

Invariably, I awakened to my own wild screams and Millie's touch as she eased me back to life.

"Emmet, it's alright. You're just dreamin'."

"They're here! Help!" The shriek was at the top of my lungs.

"Nobody's here. It's just a terrible nightmare."

Sweating, it took long moments for me to comprehend that I was in my own bed. For hours, sleep would be impossible, and, often, I walked the floors till dawn.

At first, the terrors occurred only sporadically, but, as the years passed and the noose tightened, they came with greater frequency and intensity. After the second or third episode, I explained the scene to Mil. "They come to take him to the chair, and I can never stop them."

"If he's innocent, everything'll work out. It's not yer worry, love. You're just a guard. It's none of yer doin'. You know that—don't ya?" she asked while stroking my hair ever so gently.

"They're goin' to kill 'im."

"Love, you didn't find him guilty and you're not goin' to take any part in killin' him. It's not for you—none of it."

"We're all part of it."

"What if he killed those men?"

"He couldn't have. He couldn't."

"Bein' with him is killin' you—effectin' yer judgment. Don't ask for that tour again. Get out of the tailor shop, too. You've no responsibility."

Millie's love beat back the beast for weeks at a time, but once while pacing after a particularly difficult bout, a bang came to the floor—my loving brother-in-law complainin' that I was interruptin' his beauty rest. I moved the wandering onto the living room rug until I was able to return to bed to at least lie next to Millie.

That morning, as I went downstairs, the second floor door opened and the archangel bearded me. "You alright, Em? The commotion—I thought you might be sick."

"I'm fine. Just a nightmare...Fine, really."

"A nightmare? Jesus, sendin' that bastard up in smoke would be no nightmare. It'd be a dream come true."

My rage rose. "You prick. Can't you let one fuckin' thing go?"

"Easy, brother. Millie'd be mighty pissed if I snapped your scrawny neck."

"Crawl back in yer hole, you friggin' snake."

"Much more and I'll forget that you're family." He laughed and slowly closed the door.

I charged upstairs. "Did you tell Mike about the nightmares?" I asked in as quiet a voice as could be mustered through tightly clenched teeth.

"I told Ma. She must'a let it out."

"Thanks, Ma. Thanks, Millie. That shithead'll never let me live this down."

Needless to say, Millie was extremely saddened, and, like any good Irish wife called down for something that was her own doin', blamed the victim. The fight lasted an hour, and, of course, I was sent to the couch to examine my conscience. Suffice it to say, my affection for Mike grew with each such incident.

Among Vanzetti's regular visitors were Brahmin ladies uncowed by the rhetoric of their husbands, fathers, and brothers. In twos and threes, they were delivered to Rutherford Street by family chauffeurs and, while the band played, stood stoically among the rabble while waiting for the gate to open.

Always, when the ladies entered, the warden greeted them, bowing and scraping as if it was Victoria and her ladies, personally escorting them to the great hall. At last with Bart, they hovered like sodality matrons fluttering about the priests—flirtatious but chaste. He loved them too; vessels to be filled with his great learning and passion. Bees swarming the flower of grand pronouncements, they'd tell him what a great man he was and praise his soul, as he dropped bon mots about Dante and Hegel.

It was a wonderful show, and the prison community lapped it up, except me. I thought it a joke, but I'd have talked anarchy or anything else with at least a couple of them young vessels. One in particular, Maude Hayes, with the face of an angel, a waist you could circle with your two hands, and the two most perfectly formed apples I'd ever lusted to bob for—was heaven sent to discuss philosophy.

Vanzetti was none too easy on me or others who cared for him. He'd push and pull on the finer points of Dante's hell, art—you name it, but just a hint of disapproval, and you were out of his life for weeks at a time—forever if he didn't respect you. He could go longer than Millie in not speaking, but, by nature he was a forgiving fellow and, knowing that I truly cared, slowly opened up to me again. No matter what you hear, he wasn't the Francis of Assisi the socialists made him out to be, and he kept you guessing which loop of the roller coaster you were on.

"Emmet, you Catholeec?"

"Yeah—but a little thin." For the thousandth time, I learned there was little use in being easy on him, for despite his quick smile and gentle ways, his sense of humor was not at all of the earthy variety that Celts thrived on. You certainly couldn't tell a dirty joke in his presence, or it would be off to Coventry for a long vacation.

"When I was leettle boy, I beeleeve, but when my mother die, my heart break, too. Now—like Nietzsche—I theenk God, hee's dead."

"Your problem ain't with God; it's the truth that's gettin' its ass kicked. You oughta pay more attention to your lawyers than to them ladies who're bowin' and scrapin' like you're the second comin'. It's the law that's after ya, and those dead guys and them women ain't handlin' your appeal."

It goes without saying, I wasn't welcome at the Vanzetti residence for a good while after that one. He drove me crazy. Important hearings would be bearing down, and he'd want to talk about a circle in Dante or how Jesus would have acted. It was easy to see why he didn't have a wife; Millie wouldn't have put up with his nonsense for a minute. He cared more for 'joostice' than he did for his backside—which was what they were intent on frying. I've read that it's the single man for the revolution, and, knowing Bart and Mil, I concur.

After zinging him, when I could stand it no longer, my guilt would lead me to his work station or his cell and into a deep discussion of philosophy or religion. I'd have to spout my opinions—most of them manufactured on the spot—on free will or if there was a heaven, whatever. Many's the day I cursed Father Murphy for his stupid mouth.

Da was my rock. I'd stop by the house, and we'd pull on a quart. Other times, I'd catch up with him in the back room at Clancy's. More times than warranted, I'd drop my load on him, and he'd give me his best advice. Bart's view that he was headed for the electric chair, regardless of the facts, gave Da no trouble, and he laid out the possibilities without emotion. He even found ways out for all of the players. Amazingly, a few of his scenarios didn't include my demise.

Tom Mullins, Billy Moynihan, and Millie saw only absolutes if any of us were to openly challenge the conventional wisdom on Bart. The Moynihans would disown us. We'd be pariahs in the neighborhood. The priests would label us atheists. We'd disgrace our families. Big John would never forgive us. We'd have to quit our jobs—the most foolish thing an Irishman could do for principle. The list of adverse impacts was endless.

But Da saw little openings for John Moran and thought that Grampa might find a stand for conscience a brave thing. Maybe John could find something in another state office for me. But most of all he loved me and, without ever saying it, would stand with me.

"In the end, it'll be your choice, and the world won't give a crap which way you go. But the goddam Micks will," he said while slowly pouring another glass.

"You're right; maybe John can find me somethin' else." It was an awful thing that had already been done to me; I was drinking not for pleasure but to ease pain. Jesus, the creature was gaining.

"Whatever, Em. You're caught, and, either way, there'll be recriminations and guilt." Da's pain for me was as great as mine for Bart and Millie.

Once, Da and Grampa met me at the bar, and the old man,

nursing his single ale, became for the moment only seventy. His eyes sparkled as we turned over the old days. After we'd talked about the long departed neighbors, Da started on the heroes of the uprisin' like Dev and Michael Collins. Gramps became more animated by the minute and, with broad sweeps of his arms, laid out the role of man in times of moral crises.

It was then that Da put it right between the old man's eyes. "Emmet believes that Vanzetti's got no chance, regardless of the facts. What's he to do."

The old man looked pained, and his eyes became glacial ice. "Are ya sure?"

"Yes...No...No."

"Dammit. Are ya, or ain't ya?"

"I'm sure he didn't do it, but that's not what's killin' me. It's that he never had a chance. They'll electrocute him because he's a Guinea anarchist."

Grampa recited the facts. "Twelve men of Norfolk found him guilty. But Emmet Magawley says he didn't do it. What makes you smarter than everybody else?"

His voice rose. "That the guards think he was railroaded ain't news to us. We're with the cops in thinkin' you're too soft over there. John checked with the big Dagos from the North End; they'd be happy to watch him go up in smoke and put the whole thing behind 'em."

Looking the old man in the eyes, I spoke as sincerely as possible, "That the big Wops don't care has nothin' to do with whether he killed 'em or had a fair trial. It ain't the ordinary Dagos who want him dead, it's the pols and the Black Hand."

Grampa's voice grew even more shrill. "Whether he murdered 'em has little to do with why the state's puttin' him down. The bastards have to see they can't rob and kill to further their rotten aims.

"He's goin' down. Everyone's got to fall in line." He slammed his bony fist on the table, takin' care—like any good Magawley—not to break already brittle bones. "But no, Emmet Magawley, graduate of the girls' typin' academy, is defendin' an anarchist murderer—one of them killed was a Guinea, no less—because the state failed to dot an `i' or cross a `t'. The Clarence Darrow of the typists knows more than all that protected and nursed him.

"Hear this. Get on the side you're on—now."

Pat would have fought me right there, but I backed down. There was the party line. Deviation would lead to retribution—not the kind you see in movies—the Irish Catholic kind. I'd be a pariah, sitting alone at St. Ann's, Clancy's, and Hibernian Hall. My kids would be shunned. Poor Millie would be welcome nowhere. If the line's not toed, we are revealed as the race of insidious bastards we are. It was tribalism that saved us in the darkest hours in Ireland and in America, too, so if a few had to suffer unfairly for the preservation of the group, so be it.

Later, when they thought the subject had been left behind and that we'd settled down to road work, I foolishly tried out the old canard that it's better ten guilty escape than one innocent man suffer, and a blast of gale force anger again roared into my kisser. The leaders of the Irish and Italian communities were falling in behind the Brahmins. Vanzetti must die, the sooner the better.

The fire was banked before Grampa spoke again, and it took me back to the day long before when he granted me initiation into the tribe. "It's my fault. The Magawleys are flawed, and none more than you, Billy. I never had the gift of faith, but I tried to make it available to ya. No matter how well you went through the motions, it wasn't in ya. And you," he said pointing a shaking finger at me as a look of disgust crossed his face, "you never even tried to hide your contempt. It was obvious what you were made of with the `Our Father' thing. Sad. What could you expect from the likes of that." The old man's fire blazed again. "Dammit, for once in your lives understand somethin'. He's guilty."

Neither Da nor I said a word. The old man drained his mug, and Billy led him out. I sat for few minutes facing the bottom of my glass.

As I went over what I might have said differently, Jimmy Clancy placed a fresh one before me. "There's many around who think he didn't do it, but the big fellas are unrelenting."

Nodding thanks, I drained the pint and went home.

I rarely shared these conversations with Millie. Wiser and more practical than her man, she wouldn't have required that the process of humiliation be spelled out. Regularly, she counseled me to put distance between Bart and me and that there was no hope of getting support from the Moynihans. Mike took his direction from the police hierarchy and Sean from King John. That the pair of 'em were bastards didn't have to be underlined.

Oftentimes over the years, I rode in motorcades to Dedham with Bart, but only three or four times was I cuffed to him in the back of one of the old Chevys. On those occasions, I was obliged to go into the courtroom with him. He was full of bull during the drives, and, by the time we pulled up in the rear of the courthouse, we'd both be in fine fettle. On my initial trip—it must have been sometime in 1922—I first laid eyes on Nick Sacco.

When there was a hearing of any import, crowds of Sacco and Vanzetti supporters gathered in Dedham, and interest was rekindled in the papers. The demonstrations grew in number and intensity with the rise in stakes and immediacy of the danger. To shield us from the crowds, the sheriffs and bailiffs swarmed like bees, and we were hustled into the court like a prince and his entourage.

Inside the courtroom, Bart was uncuffed and I stepped back from the action to observe. A door on the right side of the courtroom opened and in walked the man I knew instantly was Sacco. Shorter and stockier than Bart, he carried himself like a prizefighter. I learned later that he'd developed an exercise program to keep from going crazy, and he looked to be a marvel of conditioning. However, the regimen of being caged for twenty-two hours a day in the near total darkness of the basement jail drove him over the edge, and, during the middle of the seven years of waiting, they carted him off to the mental ward in the prison at Bridgewater for a long period of rehabilitation.

Rosa stood in the right hand corner of the cavern as Nick was led in, and I didn't spot her until the action began. Her dress was similar to the one worn the first time I saw her, except that it was dark gray, and her hat was of the wide brimmed variety that she obviously favored. She was beautiful. As the sheriffs accompanying her husband neared the dock, an unstated signal was given and Rosa ran to him. He called her name, "Rosina." It was said lovingly and sensually. They kissed passionately, as if in a motion picture. My eyes could not remain trained on such desperate emotion.

Sacco, clearly a swarthy type before this, had a pallor that gave him a tubercular look that contrasted sharply with the power and presence he exuded. His tight single-breasted suit looked ready to burst in its poor attempt to contain him. While the fitness program maintained his muscles, his eyes were those of a frightened deer. Unlike Bart, Nick was not suited for a life in prison.

Bart was cerebral while Nick was all animal power. Vanzetti loved manipulating the arguments to be made on his behalf and relished the role of martyr, but, I suspected that Sacco was better suited for an attempt at a wild escape.

As the pair prepared for court, Bart smiled for his lawyers, the sheriffs, Nick and Rosina, reporters, and the audience. But Nick had eyes only for Rosa and the two children, and he looked nothing like a man who could hardly wait for the crisis that loomed before him. As I look back on that day and a thousand other instances in Charlestown, Bart played for the galleries, and I suspected that the saddest scene for him would be the end of the play rather than the retribution of the state.

The hour approached; Nick and Rosa were separated, and he was guided to the dock. As the comrades embraced, I tried to identify the principals. The defense lawyers were well known to me—no surprises there. On the other side, I expected the prosecutors to be wearing horns or other satanic marks, but, as they lined up behind their table, I saw nothing but ordinary men in expensive suits.

From the opposite side of the room, a door opened and in

strode the judge—finally, a participant who looked the part of a sonofabitch moved to center stage. Webster Thayer appeared tall, but that might have been because he was as thin as a cadaver. His was that slim style the Yankees had been seeking for as long as they had money—but on him it was all wrong. Where the Brahmin smile was to be benign and solicitous, in lieu of a mouth, a cruel sneer was on his face. At first glance, he bore the aspect of the race horses they'd been seeking in their selective breeding programs—long head with flaring nostrils that supposedly demonstrated intelligence and sensitivity, but on him it was distorted to that of a broken hack with fearful eyes and ticking cheeks.

Other guards who'd gone to court with Bart reported on the sparring between Thayer and Vanzetti and how Bart bested the old bastard at every turn; I waited for the pyrotechnics, expecting Bart to rattle off one of those eloquent speeches he constantly practiced in the guise of casual talk. But it wasn't to be; the great show fell apart with nothing but bowing and scraping before Thayer. Motions were denied or taken under advisement. It was over in five minutes.

We piled back into the cars. Bart, experienced at courtroom behavior and expectations, enjoyed the jaunt back to Charlestown almost as much as the drive to Dedham—a break from the prison routine, accepted as just that, while I sat, crushed and silent, as we retraced our route.

Tom and Billy, feeling the heat at Clancy's, looked to bolster the case against Bart. They worked hard at revising their positions. They 'Twelve men of Norfolk'd' me to death and, dog like, submitted to the wills of Moran, Sean Moynihan, and Mulligan, even if the three of them were five miles away and out of earshot.

Tom's most successful trial balloon began, "Sacco and Bart dodged the draft. They ran off to Mexico to avoid the war."

Sardonically, I blasted back, "Yeah. Stupid bastards. Immigrants were exempt from the friggin' draft."

"But they were tryin' to undermine us." Tommy had his eldorado for squirmin' from under Charlestown's verdict of innocence.

"What's that got to do with the murders?"

"...and they had guns when they were pinched."

"Three weeks after the shootin's? You know goddamn well that a Guinea without a pistol is a naked man. Did they shoot the poor bastards is the question?"

"Stop twistin' my words. They ran to Mexico while we were fightin' in France."

"Right. The fightin'...awful. Remember when the Kaiser, himself, gassed us in Madame LaBonte's cafe? God, the sufferin'."

"Don't be a bigger asshole than ya are."

That Tom and Billy were seeking a way out galled me, but I should have been kinder. Billy, in particular, had no cause to stand with Bart. Vanzetti treated him with disdain, as the lad had no interest or capacity for arguing the finer points of socialism or canon law. And at home, there was the constant crossing paths with the grand inquisitor on the second floor.

But times were changing. No longer did the tables at Clancy's absorb the months and years. Vanzetti, the flywheel, sped the lives of those believing in him—gilding all with guilt in the process. His lawyers did their damnedest to make the legal system respond, but Bart reveled as civilization failed. That the system was crushing him served as an absolute tonic. "The workers, Emmet, they deevoured. All weethout power bee crushed. They weel see." He smiled, an innocent child revealing the raiments of an empire.

Naturally, I wasn't in the meetings with his counsel, but I watched as the vessels redoubled their efforts. Some of the guards, me among them, were vulnerable to his preaching and didn't know which way to turn.

Unlike most, I was angry with Bart half of the time. He'd been convicted of murder and was headed for the chair. I didn't ascribe the injustice to capitalism but to corrupt and frightened men, panicked by the philosophies that had already toppled governments in Europe. If they had grabbed two Saccos, they'd have been in great shape, but they got the second comin' of Jesus Christ. He was much more than they had bargained for, and they could find no way out. He had 'em right where he wanted them.

One Sunday in '24—or was it '25?—no matter—the
Moynihan families were gathered in Sean's flat for dinner, and the
men were in the parlor drinking. Billy, as usual, was reacting to
Sean and Mike, fearing, correctly, that anything he said would be
used against him. Sean was doing most of the talking, and I served
as his straight man. Surprisingly, Mike was quietly sipping an ale
and casually observing the prey, a seemingly sated carnivore.

After what seemed half an hour, he came alive. "You think I'm
the meanest bastard in Boston—that I want vengeance on Vanzetti?
Fact is, I couldn't care any less for him than for a fly. I just don't
want other families gettin' crushed like ours when Johnny was
gunned down.

"I know what the guards think—and why." He stopped for a
pull.

I'd never seen him in anything but a hectoring position and
was shocked by this show of thoughtful insight. In turn, he calmly
looked Billy and me in the eye and went on, "But there are dozens
of anarchists runnin' around. The Bolsheviks in Russia and others
are sendin' money and firin' 'em up. To you, they may be nothin'
but a bunch of ignorant malcontents, but they're intent on revolution. Oh, that's ridiculous to you, Emmet, but it doesn't stop
them from robbin' payrolls and killin' cops.

"This is beyond the pair o' ya, but they're just vermin—rats
carryin' the plague to be eradicated without feelin'. No hate—
they just have to be exterminated."

Poor Billy didn't know what to say. I could tell that he thought
it a trap and was afraid to step into it. Sean, too, was catatonic, and
it was up to me to respond.

"Well not the meanest; there's a Guinea we run the rum line
with who's a bigger prick than you," I said, trying to move it along.

Mike let out a bellow of laughter, shook his head, and said,
"You say I can't let anything go. Christ, Emmet, you're the biggest
asshole in Boston.

"Really, Em, I don't hate him. It could be like those assholes
say, he's the gentlest man to walk the earth since Francis of Assisi,

but, if he's a hero to those rats, we have to put him down. For the love of God, can't you see that?"

I tried to answer in kind. "I'd have no trouble executin' the bastard who shot John—or Vanzetti for that matter—if we gave him the protection we've been fightin' the Yankees for."

Suddenly, the real Mike Moynihan was among us. "For as long as I've known you, you're just on the other side. You've a slick style that fools these innocents into thinkin' you're doin' the right thing, but you're not foolin' me. You can't stand authority. We've spent generations tryin' to stop bein' Irish, but you. . ."

"That's bullshit. You pervert everything. You're makin' a man walk the plank without a fair hearin', and you're blamin' the messenger."

His color rose, and his eyes bulged. "You four eyed jerk, you've always been the last one in line. You've sung that live and let live shit till I'm sick up to here with it," he said, raising his quivering hand, palm down, to his throat.

Ordinarily, Sean would have waited until Mike had gone too far before joining the fray, but he leaped in with, "He's right. We've come too far to let malcontents like you spoil everything."

I was boiling. "It's out! It ain't Vanzetti. It's me. You'd put him down to teach me a lesson. . ."

Mike was on me. "You twist everything. The Magawleys are geniuses..."

"Twist, my ass. I've got it. Fry the Wop and we pass as Yankees. Cook the Dago and my Bobby will marry a Cabot and..."

He was totally deranged. "You love the bastard because he's against everything we've worked for. You're still in the bogs. You ain't like the rest tryin' to get along. You just want to fight. Good thing you're a friggin' midget, or you'd be dangerous."

"Screw you."

"That's your answer to everything. Screw the law. Screw the cops. Easy Emmet Magawley—my ass. Beneath that crap is an angry man. Christ, no wonder you love the bastard, you're just like him. . ."

Millie and the Mrs. charged in. Mil screamed, "Stop! Can't you even sit in a room without fightin'. What kind of children are ya? And the language, I've never heard such talk. For the love of God, what'll the neighbors think? We're supposed to be settin' an example."

Too much had been said, and we were seeking a way to stop. Thank God the outburst occurred with the women around or I'd have sported a pair of shiners. Well at least the pair of 'em had been exposed as the bullies they were.

We suffered through a silent dinner, and, when we arrived upstairs, Millie turned into a hellcat. "Mike's right. You're an angry man. They're bullies—they are—but anything that comes from above is too much for ya. . ."

"That's bull. Sure. Take their side. You're all alike for Christ's sake."

"Emmet, you never hear anything. Everything that enters the space between your ears is processed so that you're always dissentin'. You've decent instincts, but you're a maverick. I'm not sayin' this to hurt you, but you're wrong—wrong. You've no special knowledge on Vanzetti, but you're happy to put me and the little ones on the line for principle—yours and yours alone."

I was too tired to fight. I was already destined for the couch as it was, but it pained me that even Millie couldn't understand where I was coming from. There's something perverse bred into the Moynihans, and, while loving her dearly, I knew that she'd inherited their blindness and certainty in all matters.

The pressure on Bart grew steadily from his first days at Charlestown, and he thrived on his role in the causes of anarchy and justice. But in the fall of '24, he began to lose control of the situation. The repeated denials of motions and rejection of his appeals by Thayer took a toll. The lawyers and many guards noticed a change in his personality—he wasn't himself. No matter how strong, facing execution is no easy task—especially for an innocent man.

Bart's health, not nearly as robust as his frame and musculature indicated, began to deteriorate, and he entered into a hunger strike to protest Thayer's discrimination. As conditions worsened, the prison doctor agreed that he was in danger of a breakdown and arrangements were made to transfer him to the facility for the criminally insane at the prison in Bridgewater.

Just before Christmas, we mounted up and drove south to the hospital—the nut house. I drew the job of riding with him. It was bitterly cold, and we huddled against the freezing blasts hardly slowed by the canvas curtains enclosing us. Bart spoke only sparingly, with little of the normally non-stop observations of the passing scene. The only comment that stuck in my mind was made as we passed the city hall in Brockton. "That ees where eet began," alluding to the tiny square brick police station and jail in the shadow of the Victorian government center.

After signing him over to the guards in Bridgewater, we headed home. It was dark before we got to Randolph, and, alone in the back seat, I thought I'd freeze to death. When we turned into the prison, I sensed an altogether different institution. Without Bart, the backwater hellhole that it had been created to be was resurrected. During his three-month absence, the prison returned to the easy period of my arrival.

Wrapping our long coats about us even in the office, the granite and the ocean conspired to torment us, and the building became a place of silence. Perhaps the harsh climate that I had observed as unique to the military obtained to prisons as well. Those working in the yard were in constant agony, but, silver lining, much of the heavy work was performed more efficiently as inmates struggled to stay warm.

In the spring, Bart came back; it was the welcoming of the prodigal. His spot in the tailor shop gone, he won the honor of shoveling coal into the great boilers of the heating plant. Busy with my beloved khaki uniforms and typing, we met only rarely during the work day after that. But on the few occasions when I passed him in the yard, it was easy to see that he was better suited to the new assignment. The labor absorbed his energy, and soon the man of action who had originally shown up at the gate was among us again. Above all, the look of prison retreated from his eyes.

Once again typing came to my aid. Not that I was nosey, mind you, but I reviewed Bart's file. The psychiatrists at Bridgewater confirmed my amateur appraisal that he suffered delusions of grandeur and had a messianic complex. The docket was replete with the historic characters that he'd regaled us with over the years. He compared himself, favorably, with Jesus, John Brown, Galileo, Socrates, and a dozen more. It was easy to see the problems that the government had created for itself in railroading this canny lunatic.

Kevin, don't get yourself caught up with the professors on whether I should have been tappin' the files. Sure, it was out of line, but I was a master at such tricks. Besides, the chances of gettin' caught were less than zero.

That Vanzetti could talk was never in dispute. The press hung on his every word. His original lawyers were hacks, but, later, as the case became a cause celebre, he had top of the line counsel. While they were writing and arguing briefs that have stood the test of time, Bart was dropping polemic bombs that are right up there with the big boy martyrs of history.

Communicating with the press and his supporters was no problem for Vanzetti. While prison rules limited the number of letters he could mail, there was nothing that said others couldn't drop them for him. The man was prolific—turning out quality tomes almost on a daily basis, and his lawyers or the lady visitors posted them. He was in constant contact with his family in the Old Country, and one of his sisters wrote weekly.

All the while, Da pushed for me, and, after much anguish, old Pat arranged a meeting with John Moran. When I pulled up the chair in the back room of Clancy's, both of 'em knew I was going to ask for a job with another agency. Late as usual, John charged in, Grampa in tow; Jimmy barely had time to open up before them. Moran waved to the small afternoon crowd and ordered a round, drawing huzzahs from every corner.

With little of his usual preliminary bantering, John spoke quickly and directly. "Your Grampa says that you're unhappy at the prison?"

"Maybe not so much unhappy as needin' a change," I stammered, trying to put the best face on sedition.

"Change is a luxury. Most with steady work are happy to have it," he said with a hint of cold steel. "It's Vanzetti. Ain't it?" he asked without a trace of his natural bonhomie.

"I can't stand the thought of killin' him." There it was out.

"What the hell are ya talkin' about? Nobody who's uncomfortable with it has to lay a finger on him."

"I know, but I'm part of the system."

"For the love of God, have you lost your senses? We're all part of the system. You're with us, or you're with him. As far as I'm, concerned, you've a damn nice job—that you've extolled to me many times—and now I'm supposed to use up valuable coin to get you out of somethin' you're not even in."

There was no point in going on. Moran had made up his mind, and he wasn't prepared to change it.

John was getting into it, with force and volume. "Count your blessings. You've easy, clean, and honest work, and I understand that it's supplemented quite well. Isn't it about time you started thinkin' about those who've supported you since you were a pup?"

He repeated the ancient canard about gettin' on the side I was on and looked for a response. It was simple from Moran's perspective. I was the grandson of a knight, and I'd been taken care of. What was the question anyway? I made no reply.

We finished our beers, and John took off for more important appointments. I trudged home tryin' to make sense of the situation. As I approached the house, I saw Millie standin' in the window. Haltingly, she waved, obviously, hoping against hope that John had offered a way out that would leave our situation intact. When I described the meeting, she flew into an angry frenzy—not with Moran—with me.

"God give me strength, haven't you heard it enough ways to

penetrate that thick Mick skull? Jesus, Mary, and Joseph, are all the good people wrong and you and a Guinea murderer right? In fact, from what you've said, you're alone. Vanzetti will win when they pull the switch, and you'll be left with the anarchists to bury him—and us with him."

I wasn't angry. From a certain warped perspective, what she said was true. I wasn't even made to sleep on the couch that night, and, as usual, the affair was left to fester.

As the years passed, the rum line was extended, and the feds decided to wage a personal vendetta against Emmet Magawley. I was just runnin' booze—that everybody agreed with—and the law was doin' its damnedest to stop me. The worst and most personal was extending the territorial waters from three miles to twelve. That may seem like nothing, but the difference in the size of the swells from the old limit to the middle of the Atlantic was enough to make me sick, literally.

In the summer of '26, I made up my mind that I could no longer be of use to Mulligan and Romano in the North End Navy. I would restrict my felonies to driving the cars to Vermont. On my next to last trip—I'll skip the sickening details of the last voyage— Paul and I had a lengthy conversation as the Genoa pushed ever so slowly to meet the Canadians, anchored just off the Azores.

"You're a friend of Vanzetti's?"

"I guess...Maybe...Yes, but he really can't be friends with any-one. But I don't think he did it...And I know he didn't have a fair trial."

Looking directly into my eyes, he said, "I know your people have been after you on this, but I, too, must talk with you about him.

"Hear this. I've been ordered to speak with you. This man must die. Your people—Moran—Mulligan—all of them—hold little prejudice against us beyond ignorant and hateful words, but they created the stupid Irish who see us as nothing but animals with strong backs and wild ideas." He spoke as softly as possible in the face of the fresh breeze from the east as we moved through the clear night toward George's Bank.

"We are Americans. This man is destroying us. Important people in the North End know that you bear no hatred for us. But you do not help us by aiding this man."

"I'm not on Vanzetti's side because some stupid Irish think that..." I hesitated, "...that...Italians...are the scum of the Mediterranean. They're fuckin' him, Paul. I wouldn't care if his name was Callahan. He's bein' railroaded."

Paul smiled. "You ought to practice more, Em. You can't even say Italian without `fuckin' as a modifier—or was it Wop or Dago you were diggin' for?"

Deadly serious again, he spoke, "You ain't hearin' me. Important people, Irish and Italians, think he had a fair trial. Just because the fuckin' communists say he's been screwed, don't mean he should be let off. Life ain't fair—O-fuckin'-K—life ain't fair. This guy's rapin' all the poor Dagos by bein' a goddamn anarchist."

Paul spoke even more softly, "An important person—a very genteel man—you've heard of Raymond Galento?—a close friend of important people in The Bush and Little Dublin—asked me to tell you he believes Vanzetti is guilty. You ain't signin' the warrant or pullin' the switch. If there's been a mistake, the judge or the governor will pull his chestnuts out. If you want to help us, relax."

It was a direct order from the Black Hand. Galento was the big boss in the North End. No physical threat was intended. The important people in The Bush and Little Dublin to whom Paul referred obviously bore the surnames of Magawley, Moynihan, Moran and Mulligan, and they were displeased to the point that I had to be sent a message from another major constituency.

Paul simply could not comprehend how a flexible private soldier in the Irish gang could be so thick headed.

In late winter '26, I had my first encounter with the death house. A virulent strain of influenza struck, and half the prison was down. Paddy Sullivan, a notorious bad boy from Charlestown, was to be executed for a string of brutal killings in the old town. The mandatory penalty for first degree murder in the Commonwealth was execution by means of the electric chair, and there was nothing unusual about Paddy's case, except for his local antecedents. I won't go into neighborhood lore beyond saying that Charlestown has been famous for toughs since its first boat load from Ireland and it continues to be to this day.

On the night in question, fully half the boys scheduled for the death house detail—and the rest of the prison for that matter—failed to report for their shifts. Executing a man was difficult work, and those with no stomach for it were not required to participate. None of the Charlestown guards had to kill anyone, as a contract executioner from New York committed the deed in their place. He came by train from the city on the night of the killing and was spirited into the prison and, when the job was done, left the same way. There was no mask—as in the Middle Ages, but it would have been mighty difficult for anyone in Charlestown beyond the warden and his closest associates to identify him.

The manpower needed to put down a man was extensive, with many posts in the death house and elsewhere to be manned. The tasks were endless: a guard had to keep a constant eye on the condemned to assure he didn't cheat the Commonwealth by doing himself in; several managed and secured the witness area; two dressed the murderer in the death uniform—black cotton with slits for the electrodes—and shaved his arms and legs where the current would enter his body; others escorted the chaplain or outside clergyman for a last chance for absolution; dozens manned the perimeter walls to defend against outside assault; and security in the cellblocks had to be very heavy as executions created great anxiety among the residents. These were just the tip of the iceberg; an execution was a major production.

For Paddy's party, prison resources were overwhelmed by the bug, and there was no alternative to seeking help from among the squeamish. That morning at the posting of the guards, Healy went as far as he could in cajoling volunteers for the various jobs, and the perimeter posts went quickly. He and the warden worked to pare the numbers to a bare bones level, and, by mid-afternoon, every assignment except for a second guard in the witness section was filled. Returning to the office in a dither, they lamented their luck. Casually scanning a report that I'd just typed, I paid little attention to their ruminations as they paced near my desk. Suddenly the room went quiet, and the stillness forced my eyes from the paper.

Healy spoke, "Emmet, we need a favor. Will you help us out in the witness room tonight?"

With the alacrity of my move to company clerk at Camp Dix, the calculations were rapid and simple. If a newspaperman could do it, so could I, and, if I didn't, this pair had the power to put me in the cold coal yard for the winter. Besides, I harbored more than a little fascination with the process. "Sure—once."

I called Clancy's, and, not surprisingly, found a Magawley present, in this case Uncle Jocko. He promised to get word to Millie that I'd be home in the wee hours. Few had phones in those days, and neighborhood bars and grocery stores were the communications centers. Since the police strike, I'd been more considerate about gettin' word to her when I expected to be late.

At four o'clock, my tour began. I entered the death house and passed three holding cells on the left. I had planned to avert my eyes from Sullivan as I passed, but curiosity got the better of me. Paddy was in the pen nearest the execution chamber. His cell and the two empties were lit very brightly, and Alfred Shaw sat on a simple straight chair looking directly in on him.

Shaw and I nodded silent salutations, and, as I passed in front of the cell toward the bile green door to the execution chamber, I stared in at Paddy. But there was little to see, as he was lying on the slab as if already dead.

I was granted entrance to the witness area that had already been cleaned and set up with chairs. To my surprise, Billy was already on duty. Obviously, Healy and the warden were at the bottom of the barrel when they got to this assignment. We compared notes on our shock and revulsion but found that we both were more than a little intrigued by the prospect of our first execution.

Tommy Mullins had skipped out by coming down with the flu, and that caused him some to suffer more than a little cursing. Actually, I'd screwed him over so many times in Chaumont by getting out of unpleasant chores that fell to him, my oaths, tempered by guilt, were mild indeed. We sat in the witness chairs and waited for the process to unfold.

We had an unobstructed view of the chamber and the electric chair. The room was painted a very bright and shiny white illuminated by a single powerful bulb hanging directly over the condemned's head. The chair was nearly pure black from bein' singed so many times. Capital punishment was not a big deal in those days, and the chair was put through its paces on a regular basis. While we'd gotten far more civilized since the days of Charlie Bulfinch and no longer flogged or maimed our nasty friends, there was little of the call to eliminate capital punishment that became so common with the passing years.

About an hour before the execution, activity picked up. A shadowy figure worked behind a screen on the far side of the chamber beyond the chair—the executioner had arrived and was testing the equipment. The warden came through, nodding to each of the guards, checking all of the posts on his route. Healy followed about ten minutes later, repeating the process. With approximately half an hour to go, witnesses arrived, including male family members of the condemned, and were seated in the chairs between Billy and me. The rest of the family, including his poor Ma who couldn't bear sitting through the execution, had said their good-byes earlier. There would be no further contact between them and Paddy.

With only minutes to go, the pace quickened, Paddy was dragged in. In a stupor and well past resisting, two guards gently maneuvered the package into the chair. Earlier, he had refused communion and was not accompanied by Father Murphy in these last moments, and, in any event, he appeared well beyond making a rational change of heart at this stage of the proceedings. The guards, Freddy Glavin and Kevin Gilbride, moved expertly to strap him into the chair and attach the electrodes to shaved portions of his arms and legs through the slits in the death uniform. Like a grotesque beanie, another wired mechanism was placed on his head. When finished, they stepped away.

At about nine past midnight, the warden looked at the clock and turned to Captain Healy stationed at a telephone on a small table near the wall inside the chamber. Healy shook his head. There would be no clemency. The warden asked if Paddy had any last words, but there was no response from the slack figure before him. The warden waited for what seemed an eternity before his next motion. At that, Glavin walked to Sullivan and dropped the leather mask attached to the electrode on his head. Once more the warden turned to Healy—this time with an imploring look. Obtaining no reaction, his shoulders slumped, and he wheeled toward the screen and nodded.

A shadow slipped from the edge of the screen and pandemonium broke loose. At that instant, the extraordinarily bright lights that we had been bathed in dimmed to near total darkness and Paddy leaped into action. All of his muscles convulsed at once, and the straps containing him grew taught. A primal scream blasted forth from behind the mask, and he was launched into a state of suspended levitation, a kite in a hurricane. Sparks flew, smoke rose, and an odor that I'd not smelled since returning from France, burning flesh, filled my nostrils. After an intolerable period—probably not more than ten seconds, but an eternity to those watching—the process reversed itself. Paddy dropped back into his chair and the fierce light returned to its previous brilliant level. I breathed normally for the first time since the switch was pulled.

But the circus wasn't over. After another long interval, the executioner acted again. Another burst of current coursed through what I perceived to be an already dead body, and, once again, we held our collective breath. I swear that I saw Paddy's eyes bulge through the mask. The corpse dutifully danced, but, this time, there was no scream; no air had returned to his lungs after the initial aria. When the lights came up, Paddy returned quietly to his seat, a thoroughly chastened schoolboy. From the direction of the holding cells, the doctor entered. He placed his cold stethoscope on Paddy's chest, and, after a quick touch, nodded to the warden. The guards in the death chamber pulled a curtain in front of the window of the witness box, and for the first time I looked at the faces of those in attendance.

The two pool reporters bolted into the night to file their stories. Three cousins of the dead man bore the look of Mike Flynn and Batty Ryan on that awful day in France when they'd seen death close up. The whites of their eyes shown and their jaws were slack from the strain of clenching their teeth. They spoke not a word but touched each other repeatedly as if to be sure that there was a reality to this nightmare.

When they were gone, Billy and I slumped into chairs and relaxed our overly taught bodies. Billy spoke, "Jesus, Em, have you ever?"

"God, when he jumped, I thought he was headed to Revere for a swim."

"Christ, he'd still be goin', if they hadn't tied him down."

I said for both of us, "I don't see how those guys can do this. Once—whew! Twice—no way...But old Paddy won't be scarin' the good folks of Charlestown anymore."

Suddenly, we found ourselves laughing hysterically, unable to control ourselves for what seemed half an hour. I resolved again to raise hell with Tommy for leaving Billy and me in such a fix. He must have been faking the flu.

For days, as we traveled between home and work, Paddy's latent athleticism was the principal subject of our entertainment. But through the laughter, the specter of Bart sitting in that ancient charred chair filled me with trepidation.

CHAPTER 12

One afternoon in the dying days of 1925, I was engrossed in my typing when two men, William Thompson, Vanzetti's lead counsel, and a young associate returned to the office after visiting with Bart. As they prepared to check out of the prison, contrary to their usual crisp professional demeanor, they were full of smiles and chatter.

Looking up, I said, "You're mighty chipper, Mr. Thompson."

Startled by the unusual intrusion by a clerk, Thompson was taken aback until he recognized me in my unfamiliar role. "Magawley, I didn't realize you worked in the office, too. I suppose we are more lively than usual. There's been a break. A man in the Dedham jail has confessed to the Braintree murders. It's very early, but we're convinced he's telling the truth.

"To top that, the New York World is running a series in support of Bart and Sacco." He paused. "Finally, it's possible to think that the stars may be aligning our way."

"It's over?" I asked while scrambling to the railing.

"Not by a long shot. But, until now, we've never had reason to hope for support from outside the judicial process.

He went on. "The man's conviction for another murder is under appeal, and there's much to be investigated in the meantime."

His tone darkened. "Bart doesn't seem to comprehend all this. Try to buck him up, will you."

As soon as they departed, I raced to Vanzetti's cell and found him reading by the fading rays of the late winter sun. Ordinarily, this would have been not at all unusual, but his languor in the face of the wondrous news was shocking.

"I saw Thompson. You'll be free soon."

He broke into a broad but joyless smile—a father patronizing an innocent child. "He say we saved. The man confessed…That we weel be veendicated."

My heart stopped. I grabbed his hand and almost tore it from his arm. "Mother o' God, that's the best news I've ever heard." My mind leaped straight to the nightmares, and I was filled with relief at the prospect of their cessation. For half an hour, we talked about the long ordeal, but Bart failed to muster any enthusiasm.

"New York paper say we eennocent. Lawyers say we weel be free. Me—I don believe.

"But would be nice for Rosa. Thees has been terrible theeng. Nick could be father and husband again. That would make me happy."

"Bart, it'll work out."

"You happy, Emmet. Nick happy. Thompson, he ees happy. That's a nice, but, beleeve me, thees weel make no difference. They must keel us. Cowards must destroy objects of their fear."

After trying repeatedly but failing to raise his spirits, I staggered back to the office.

Driving back to Little Dublin that evening, I shared the dark reaction with Tom and Billy. "The poor bastard can't pick himself off the canvas no matter how good it looks."

Billy saw the good news as support for his tenuous position at home. "The World story will make life easier for us."

Tom was bolder. "The Post has jumped on it—about friggin' time." Maybe he could support Bart after all.

Without cause, other than I'd been too nice for too long, I turned on Billy and made it horridly personal. "This ought to quiet your asshole brother." It was said not as a fellow conspirator but as if Billy were responsible for Mike's malice. Despite that unkindness, which I attempted to paper over as we rolled, it was the easiest ride home in years.

The car had barely stopped before I leaped out and raced to the door and flew up the two flights to engulf Millie. "A man's confessed. Vanzetti didn't do it."

After a short pause, Millie kissed me. "I'm happy for ya, Em. I am. All along, I thought he did it. I'm sorry, but I did."

"It's not over. Nothin' can be done for months. The fella's a murderer, and his appeal's pending. When that's decided, Bart's lawyers will go to the prosecutors, and they'll move on it."

The following Sunday was to have been one of the great days in the history of the Moynihan household—at least for old Mary, Billy and me. The worms would turn, and Sean and Mike knew it was coming. God, I never looked forward to a feast so much in my life.

The Mrs. bought a corned beef, and, when we arrived downstairs, she was humming Irish ditties and dancing through her chores. The rich aroma of the meat and the boiling carrots and cabbage filled the air like never before. She loved her first born, but, bully that he was, she couldn't help but enjoy laying in wait for him. Naturally, the prospect of a free shot at the old man gave her more than a little pleasure, as well.

I pushed into the parlor where Sean and Billy had drained the first quart and where glasses sat on the sideboard for me and the prince of darkness. I had a feeling that he'd be fashionably late for this gathering, so I cracked a fresh bottle and joined in the talk of the neighborhood. I wanted to lash out, and Billy's desire to jump his Da was obvious, but we suppressed our needs until Beelzebub presented himself. Applying a match to a camel, I tried—and failed again—to blow the smoke rings that I could never create as a boy.

Sean was handled with more respect than warranted, permitting him to dictate the topics, as we stored the best for later. A sly one, he touched on nothing that would give us a chance to punish him. As the hands of the clock neared perpendicular, the line between early and late dinners in Irish households, I listened to Mike and Dolly stomping above us, readying to face the music. When it could no longer be postponed, the door to the kitchen squeaked open, and honey dripped from his lips as he lathered up his Mum on the tempting scent of the meal. He went on and on—it seemed like hours—giving thanks to the beast that had given up the ghost that we might feast. Never was a beer so mellow as that I swirled about my palate in anticipation of his entrance.

But the bastard would not step into the pit, and, when I could bear it no longer, I lunged into the kitchen to drag him into the killing field. "There won't be time for another quart if you don't stop kissin' up to these women." The ladies, including innocent Dolores, laughed uproariously at the repartee and parted like the Red Sea so that Mike could enter the promised land. Dolly expected that we'd soon emerge for dinner, never realizing our plan was to leave her man dead on the floor.

Billy poured the victim ten ounces of rich golden lager with a perfect half-inch head and presented it as if it were the lubricant of his last meal—which was our intent. Billy's grin betrayed him, but Mike said not a word.

The victim thanked Billy and turned to face the gunners. "Well, what say the warders about the World story and the confession? The papers love it. They'll jump on anything to sell copies."

I struck. "Sell papers—bullshit! They didn't do it. You'll all look like jackasses for not givin' them at least a nod."

Mike was ready. "You would fall for that malarkey. A Portchagee from New Bedford—holdin' a ticket to the beyond—figures a way to postpone what's comin' to 'im. Could ya think up a better way?"

Instantly, I realized that facts would never mean anything to the bastard. He and his buddies would fry Vanzetti, no matter what. "Mother o' God, surely you'll consider the confession before you kill 'em? If he gives up facts only the robbers could know, you'd follow up wouldn't ya?"

The drama wasn't proceeding as scripted. Mike and Sean savored their brew as Billy and I hung draped over the ropes.

The unctuous tones made me want to puke. "You're not stupid. You're not. Just too close to him. We've got the killers, and the judge has 'em headed in the right direction. Vanzetti's a slick talkin' S.O.B., so there's no shame in havin' been takin' in by 'im."

Billy was done, hunched over the half-drained glass. But I was damned if I'd be decked by bullying jabs with nothing behind them. "Dammit, what if the poor bastard was your own brother?"

"Don't give me that. He ain't, and he done it. Case closed." The talk died for lack of passion, a first round knockout, and Billy and I were on the canvas. Sadly, the dinner—the tastiest damn corned beef I'd ever put in my mouth—went down like the Saturday night cold cuts at Camp Dix. I had enough left only to feel sorry for the Mrs. For once, her Billy was to have gotten the best of the despot, but damned if the whole shebang hadn't blown up in her face. At any moment, I thought she'd break, but she struggled through. When we got back upstairs, Millie said little, instinctively knowing what had happened. That night, I slept fitfully, realizing that Bart had reason for his gloomy outlook.

But by the time we returned to Charlestown, the sky had brightened. Thompson and his troops were filled with energy, and it was infectious. The warden, Captain Healy, and the guards haltingly began to envision a future in which they would not have to kill an innocent man. All at the rock pile, prisoners and keepers, breathed more easily, as we gleaned hope from the droppings that Bart might not die in the charred old electric chair.

A false normalcy spread through the prison as the appeal of Celestino Madeiros, the man who confessed to the crimes in Braintree, wended its way through the courts. During the interregnum, Thompson brought in a bright young lawyer from Harvard, Herbert Ehrmann, to lead the defense's investigation. Ehrmann's enthusiasm buoyed Bart's believers even more.

The youthful attorney's confidence raised a glimmer of hope even in Vanzetti. Often, at day's end, Bart related what he had learned about Madeiros. Languishing in the Dedham jail with Sacco and observing the sad tale of Rosa and Nick unfold before him, his long forgotten conscience reappeared, and, when it could be borne no longer, Celestino sent a note to Nick confessing to the killings.

Initially rejected as a cruel hoaxer, Madeiros persisted and con-

vinced Nick and the deputies that he was telling the truth. Condemned to die, he had no trouble confessing to save Nick, but his
loyalty to his confederates never slaked, and he refused to give
them up.

Madeiros, despite being one of life's losers, had a little luck
and, because of a technicality, won a retrial, but in the spring of
1926, he was convicted again. Life wants to live, however, and his
lawyers pressed new appeals.

Ehrmann ran all over Southeastern Massachusetts and Rhode
Island searching for evidence. Each time he returned with new
revelations, Vanzetti's spirits rose—and ours with them. Bart
dropped tidbits, as he had loosed the theological bon mots, on his
friends—including the lovely vessels—and we spent hours gluing
them together. The facts pointed to a gang of robbers from Providence and New Bedford, including Madeiros. I arrived home evenings pumped high with renewed optimism—not so much that I
braved thumbing my nose at my brother-in-law, not yet anyway.

Good news piled on good. A famous Harvard law professor,
Felix Frankfurter—at the time, I'd never heard of him—wrote a
magazine article that tore the prosecution case apart. All involved,
from the chief of police in Bridgewater, who'd started the ball rolling, to Judge Thayer and everyone in between was systematically
rended. I devoured Bart's copy. For the first time, I grasped the
essence of the defense's position, and it fired my outrage. The most
egregious injustices included Bart and Sacco being arrested without probable cause, their being forced to reenact the Bridgewater
payroll robbery in front of eyewitnesses, and the foreman of the
Braintree murders trial jury openly tampering with evidence during deliberations.

The weeks passed quickly, and soon it was time for the final
appeal on behalf of Madeiros. He'd been more fortunate than most
murderers by having his first conviction overturned, fending off
Old Sparky in the process. But, as expected, this time the Su-
preme Judicial Court of the Commonwealth took little time in
rubber stamping the second conviction. The State's mandatory

punishment of death in the electric chair for first degree murder would be carried out, as usual.

With his remedies exhausted, Madeiros, sentenced to death, came to spend his last days in Charlestown. He was sent directly to our Cherry Hill unit. Can you imagine calling death row by such an awful name? The only time I'd ever been near the place was the night I skirted its periphery to watch poor Paddy Sullivan's effort at the tethered long jump, but, from all I heard, it was a medieval dungeon. Not only did the most enlightened state in the union snuff out its killers, it provided the beasts with the best possible environment for contemplating the consequences of their vile acts.

But Madeiros was not through. Agreeing that he had potential value as a material witness in the Sacco and Vanzetti case, the State determined that he would not be executed until the fates of our anarchists had been decided. It wasn't much, but it was better than being sent on his way. Six years, and still Nick and Bart were among us, but who knew how much longer it could last?

The Sacco and Vanzetti team moved aggressively; Thompson petitioned the prosecutor to drop the charges or, at a minimum, agree to a new trial for Nick and Bart. Horrible as it seemed, the government, after one short meeting, cavalierly refused and threw the case back onto the courts. Broken men, the lawyers returned to Charlestown to inform Bart.

Thank God, Vanzetti had steeled himself for this, and, when I dragged myself to his cell a few hours later, except for his jaw muscles, which danced wildly, his rage was under control.

"I'm sorry."

"I know. Sorry for Rosa and Nick and all you who beleeve in joostice. Thompson say I must get new counsel. He no have to withdraw, but hee say he must eef ever we are to be free."

That was how I learned that Mr. Thompson, a noble man, had resigned—another blow for the pair.

"New trial...The injoostice, the errors, the prejudice be laid out—in full view. Cannot be. Prosecutors and Thayer know that we must die. They must deestroy us."

I wept silently, helpless as the day my heart broke on the bank of the River Marne. For the first time in my adult life, I shed tears before another man, but Bart was detached and very calm, at least outwardly.

"By our deaths we weel stop theese theengs. Our lives weel have meaning eef thees cannot happen again."

In the surreality of the moment, I wondered if I might be in the middle of one of my nightmares. As usual, the scream was in my throat, and I fantasized ripping the bars away and pulverizing the granite walls to spirit Bart to freedom. But all I could do was blubber uncontrollably.

"Go home. Not on you head. Go to wife and babies."

I refused to acknowledge finality. "They can't win. The courts...The governor..."

"You right. Go home. Everytheeng be fine."

That night, Millie rocked me in her arms as I drifted away, racked with sobbing, toward another rendezvous with terror. Several times, I awakened in the pitch to find her still stroking my aching body and kissing my sweaty brow. "Easy, Em. You're a lovely lad. But you've done your all."

"Jesus, Mary and Joseph, yesterday, they were practically fittin' him with street clothes, and, tomorra, he draws a black death uniform." I was too weak for further remonstrations and fell back into a fitful slumber.

Appeal followed appeal and hearings merged with one another, and, after all the years, I can't keep them straight any longer. Tommy, Billy and I no longer talked of Sacco and Vanzetti during our commute, and the subject was avoided in the Moynihan redoubt as well. Even Mike seemed less cruel. The press, however, could not print enough about the case—whether in fits of moral outrage or simply to sell papers I couldn't tell, nor did I any longer give a damn.

Around the world, public demonstrations increased in size and despair with each court date. In Europe, communists, anarchists, and tens of millions of ordinary working men and women from Spain to the Soviet Union who cared for nothing but justice awakened to the reality that the glacial pace of events in the case would no longer hold. Giant rallies were staged in New York, Chicago, San Francisco, Boston, and in dozens of other American cities. For seven years there had been little visible change for Sacco and Vanzetti, but, in just weeks, the case progressed from the rejection of the confession of a credible man and the reversal of media opinion to the delivery of Nick and Bart to the edge of the abyss.

In March, 1927, we learned that Sacco and Vanzetti would be sentenced to die on April 9. I was ill. I avoided Bart and busied myself in the office. On the second of April, when I could bear it no longer, I approached him. While outwardly calm, I determined from his grip on the bars and his clenched jaw that he was seething, but he continued to shelter me from further pain and did not mention sentencing or execution.

As we were about to part, he asked most gently, "My friend, you ride with me to Dedham?"

Through great resolve, I held myself upright, but the urgency in the understated request could not be missed. Almost without pause, I replied, "I'll ask the warden."

I made my plea, and it was arranged. I would ride cuffed to Bart to the sentencing. The week before and the trip itself passed in a fog, and I wallowed in self-pity. I have almost no recollection of events from that last meeting with Bart until the motorcade drew into Dedham. As we neared the courthouse, masses of people fought at police barricades to reach out and touch Vanzetti. Their plaintiff screams for justice and placards decrying Thayer danced everywhere, invading my torpor. American flags waved wildly while hundreds of women and many men wept openly.

In the rear of the granite monolith, dozens of state troopers fought to clear space for our vehicles, and a corps of sheriff's deputies struggled to shelter us from the overarching mob and wedged us into the mouth of the giant carnivore. As we spilled into the courtroom, the crushing ceased, and we were loosed in the bowels of the cavern. The cuffs were removed, and Bart, of whom I had been only vaguely aware during the ordeal, was escorted by bailiffs into the dock. I remained at the rear in the standing room only section.

Only slowly did I become aware of my surroundings and gain self control. The obvious difference from previous visits was the mass of humanity swarming among and between ever changing gaggles across the hall. In addition to the small army of police, sheriffs and bailiffs, dozens of reporters scurried like rats to seek audiences with lawyers, court officers, and those I determined to be supporters of Nick and Bart.

Again, Vanzetti was first into the box, and, as in prior hearings, he played to the crowd while waiting for Nick. I searched for bravado but found nothing false in him. Each time he made eye contact with a supporter, he smiled and waved confidently. It was obvious that this man was not going to make it easy for his tormentors, but the recipients of these salutes proved to be another species altogether. There was none of the cheer seen earlier, and the hollow smiles and weak waves betrayed them as tears and pain were suppressed only poorly.

Rosa was in her usual place at the right front, but I caught only glimpses of her through the crowd—for that I gave thanks. The side door opened, and Sacco and his bailiffs entered. Conversation died as the spectators surveyed him. While only of average height, Nick strode in at full measure. His eyes sought and found but one in the multitude, and, after a fleeting encounter with Rosa—again, thank God, mostly hidden from me—he joined his comrade.

"All rise." The circus began.

Absolute silence descended as we waited for the judge to speak. He acknowledged the prosecution and identified the defendants and their counsel. Again, near total quiet. I had trouble catching my breath.

The clerk rose and faced Sacco standing before him in the

dock. "Nicola Sacco, have you anything to say why the sentence of death should not be passed upon you?"

A gasp rose from the mass. With his anger carefully curbed, Nick spoke directly to the Judge, "Yes, sir. Eet ees not very familiar with me the English language, and my comrade, Vanzetti, weel speak more long.

"I never know, never heard, even read in heestory anything so cruel as thees Court." The power and confidence of the man rallied his friends and family, and they, too, turned to face Thayer, squaring their shoulders.

"I know the sentence will be between two class, the oppressed class and the reech class, and there weel always be a collision between one and the other. We try the education of people always. You persecute the people, tyrannize over them and keel them. That is why I am here today, for having been the oppressed class. Well you are the oppressor."

By now the anger in his voice was clear to all, and, while I could not see his eyes, he faced Thayer without flinching. The judge blinked and lowered his glance to the papers before him. "You know, Judge Thayer, after seven years that you been persecuting me and my poor wife, and you steell today sentence us to death. I would like to tell you my life, but what is the use? You know all about what I said before, and my friend—that is my comrade—will be talking." For the first time, Sacco's fears overcame his courage, and I watched his shoulders sag, ever so slightly.

"I thank you all, you peoples, my comrades who have been with me for seven years."

He turned to Vanzetti but hurriedly faced back and continued, "I forget one theeng to say...Judge Thayer know all my life that I am never been guilty, never—not yesterday, not today, not forever."

The audience and the judge were stunned. No one spoke.

After much fumbling the clerk rose again. "Bartolomeo Vanzetti, have you anything to say why the sentence of death should not be passed upon you?

In a clear and resonant voice, Bart began, "Yes...I am an eennocent man, not only of the Braintree crime, but also of the Bridgewater crime. Een all my life I have never stole and I have never killed and I have never speelled blood. I have struggled all my life to eliminate crime from the earth." A woman's voice cried out—Mrs. Brini, from Plymouth. Her husband embraced and supported her.

Vanzetti showed no sign of noticing the commotion and continued to bore in on Thayer. "Not only have I struggled all my life to eliminate crimes—official law crimes and moral crimes—the exploitation and the oppression of man by man. Eef there ees a reason why I am here as a guilty man, eef there ees a reason why you can doom me, eet ees thees reason and none else.

"They all steeck with us—the best writers, the greatest theenkers and statesmen een Europe have pleaded een our favor.

"What we have suffered during theese seven years no human tongue can say, and you see before you, not trembling, you see me looking een your eyes straight, not ashamed or een fear.

"Not even a dog that keel the chickens would have been found guilty with the evidence that the Commonwealth have produced against us. Not even a leprous dog would have hees appeal refused two times—not a leprous dog."

Sobbing rose from many points, and my own added to the swell.

"They have given Madeiros a new trial because the judge forgot to tell the jury that they should consider the man eennocent until found guilty. The man has confessed to murder and to murders een Braintree. There could not have been another judge on the face of the earth more prejudiced and cruel than you have been against us. You know een your heart that you have been against us from the very beginning. Before you see us you already know we are radicals, that we were the enemies of the institution that you believe een.

"I have suffered because I am a radical and because I was Italian. I have suffered more for my family than for myself, but I am so conveeenced to be right that eef you could execute me two other times, and eef I could be reborn two other times, I would live again to do what I have done already.

"I must say about Sacco. Hees name will live een the hearts of the people when your bones will be dispersed by time, when your name, your laws, your institutions, and your false god are but a deem memory.

I have finished. Thank you."

Thayer paused and swallowed. In a shaky, cracking voice he began, "Nicola Sacco, it is ordered by the Court that you suffer the punishment of death by the passage of a current of electricity through your body."

Gasps went up. Rosa collapsed.

"Bartolomeo Vanzetti, it is ordered by the Court that you suffer the punishment of death by the passage of a current of electricity through your body."

Sacco was out of control. His lawyers could not restrain him. Lunging for Thayer, he screamed, "You know I am eennocent. You condemn two eennocent men."

"All rise."

Thayer turned and walked out. Pandemonium broke loose. Bailiffs and police fought for order and moved to hustle the condemned to a side room. I wiggled through the teeming throng to the room where Bart was being held. Already, Sacco had been spirited back to his cell. Although I should have known it and was almost certainly told, I was shocked to learn that Vanzetti would not return with us to Charlestown. He was hustled off by the bailiffs to be kept with Sacco until their delivery to us weeks or months hence for execution.

I stumbled out of the court to the car and found the return trip to Charlestown being organized. The crowd had diminished, but a hard core stood by and jeered us, but as we drove away from Dedham, the cries and shouts receded. As we passed through the Fenway, Bart's defiance and the cruelty of the sentence alternated in my thoughts and occupied me as I sat fumbling with the empty handcuffs in the back seat.

As usual, with Vanzetti gone, a false normalcy returned to Charlestown. I swear, I might have been able to work there all of my life had I not become close to Bart. It seemed not nearly so cruel a place for a person to work, if you didn't think about what you were doing—checkers on the block, cards, it was a snap.

When I arrived at work on June 30, 1927, I found, again to my total surprise, that, in the middle of the night, Sacco and Vanzetti had been secreted from the Dedham jail to Charlestown and hustled into the dank dungeons of Cherry Hill. Naively, I had expected Bart to be returned to the cell that had been his home for so long. How all this could have shocked me confounds me to this day. Vanzetti was a condemned murderer and would remain with Nick in the inaptly named death house until the sentence was carried out. They were placed in adjoining cells next to Madeiros.

Since the death house was off limits for me, it was all but a certainty that we would never see each other again and that we would never have the opportunity for good-byes.

CHAPTER 13

During the summer of 1927, the world watched and waited as the Commonwealth of Massachusetts made ready to kill Nicola Sacco and Bartolomeo Vanzetti. Absent intervention by the Governor or the courts, in turn, each would be strapped into the electric chair and suffer a current of electricity through the body until dead.

After returning to the prison from sentencing, they languished in the dank dungeons of Cherry Hill, and I had no contact with either of them. I retreated to the false ease of my regular assignments in the office, the tailor shop, and the cellblocks, functioning much as I had for the previous seven years. By that time, however, it was clear to me that I could not continue as a guard and determined to leave Charlestown at the first opportunity. A good Celt and family man, I decided to stay until something better came along, but my objective was irrevocable.

While there could be little doubt of the guilt of the vast majority of the inmates—many of whom had openly confessed, my association with Bart and the time inside the walls convinced me that he was not alone in his innocence, and I could not bear another such series of nightmares. That I was part of a system that not only incarcerated those carelessly convicted but which regularly killed a number of them was too much even for me, and I was far from pleased with the countenance in my mirror. Of course, this thinking never went beyond the prison walls, and I would have contemplated gladly a job with the Department of Public Works or any other State agency.

Calculatingly, I resolved to reestablish myself in the good graces of the Moynihans, Magawleys, and—especially—John Moran and do everything possible to assure that I would quietly fade into the woodwork of the State House and permit all thoughts of Sacco and Vanzetti to recede from my consciousness.

In late July, the Governor came to Charlestown to interview both men, and I was unceremoniously booted from the office and sent to oversee work details in the yard while the meetings took place. The grapevine whispered that Sacco refused to cooperate in his discussions with Fuller, believing, perhaps with more prescience and intelligence than we'd credited him with, that he was doomed and that the process was a mere charade. Nick was also in the early stages of a hunger strike in protest of the abominable use of the legal system against him.

Vanzetti, on the other hand, cooperated fully with the governor's program and took instantly to the charming politician. The guards who stood by as the principals talked were impressed with the sincere interest and solicitous behavior of Fuller. As I mulled over the contradictory information, once again hope leaped into in my heart.

But indeed it had been a sham, on August 3, 1927, the governor announced that there would be no clemency for them, and the prison administration began the count down to their executions which were now set for shortly after midnight on August 8.

Kevin, I've tried not to talk about things that I didn't know first hand or learn from people who were directly connected with the case. There are more than enough books to give the professors all the background on the case they'll ever need to make their own judgments of guilt or innocence and about the horrific tales of official misconduct, but let me tell you a few things about Fuller that I knew only from rumors and newspaper stories.

In the late Twenties, because of its large population and its lofty intellectual status, Massachusetts was a more important state than it is today, and success in public life in the Commonwealth could very well lead to even greater glory. Cal Coolidge, by adroit manipulation of his role in the Boston Police Strike, had wound up in residence at 1600 Pennsylvania Avenue, and poor Fuller, a far less able politician, saw Sacco and Vanzetti as both his test of tests and his opportunity to follow the silent one to Washington.

According to contemporary accounts and books I later read, the governor, an automobile salesman lacking both legal training and intellectual depth, came to believe that by emulating Coolidge and demonstrating his mettle in the case, he might become president—heady stuff for the price of the lives of two murdering anarchists. He was unable to fathom the subtle differences between doing what had to be done in a true public crisis and bowing to the demands of panicked grandees and their lackeys that the more cunning Cal would have perceived instinctively. Fuller's shallow nature was one of the principal road blocks facing Nick and Bart, so the announcement came as no surprise to anyone familiar with the governor's limitations. The executions would be carried out shortly after midnight on the eighth of August, and the warden and his associates, including me, put the plan into action. In view of the extraordinary global attention focused on Sacco and Vanzetti, the logistics would be far more complex than those for doing away with garden-variety local killers like Paddy Sullivan. State troopers, city police, and the State Guard would augment the prison force to extinguish the lives of Nick and Bart.

The execution chamber at Charlestown was a bubble on the outside wall of the prison, and a paranoid mind could easily believe that a successful assault might be made upon it. With thousands of anarchists, communists, and Bolsheviks expected at the scene, together with the all of the wild tales that had circulated over the years, it's no wonder that the security forces of the Commonwealth spared no expense in readying for war. The warden and Healy, decent and sensitive men, worked out a schedule that protected the guards closest to Bart. Obviously, poor Sacco had no friends among us, and, knowing his destiny, none was seeking him out. The plan for the fateful night called for me to be posted as a reserve in the office; I would do little more than run errands and relay messages to and from the warden to points throughout the plant.

The buildup began immediately after the governor's announcement. It would be a show of force to discourage anarchists and their communist cousins who were surely plotting to intervene on behalf of their doomed comrades. The State Guard arrived first and set up tents on the grounds and mounted the walls and towers to position machine guns and searchlights and lay out concertina wire to thwart any direct assault.

If the anarchists wanted war, they would have it. They would have to scale heavily protected parapets and defeat almost impregnable strong points merely to enter the prison yard and approach the vulnerable death house on the outer wall. Like ants, the soldiers busied themselves in stringing the cruel barbs around the already impenetrable citadel.

As liaison between the warden and the officers of the guard, I found the young men on the heights vacillating between the thrill of participating in a great event and the worry that they might actually come under siege. I remember well many of the comments made by the lads as they went about the business of preparing their redoubt but can't bear to recite them. Had we been preparing to kill the likes of old Paddy, many of the better lines would have caused me to keel over in raucous laughter. But it was not poor Sullivan who would be a kite in the night winds, but my own dear friend. Smiling and waving off the young soldiers, they surely thought me some kind of freak for not joining the frolic.

On the afternoon of the fifth, the leaders of what would become a immense contingent of state and city police ultimately totaling more than eight hundred arrived to survey what the military had accomplished and to plan the melding of the forces. Walking the walls with the guard commanders and the warden, I marveled at the institutional paranoia.

The State House and the prison were expected to be besieged by hundreds of thousands of demonstrators. Already, they were arriving from around the world. Trains and buses from up and down the East Coast were depositing Sacco and Vanzetti sympathizers onto the hostile streets of Boston. But, good God, the preparations under way were sufficient to battle the Kaiser's army at its peak. The only weapons I'd seen in the streets were signs proclaiming the crucifixion of justice. No doubt there would be armed and dangerous anarchists among the throng, but the State was preparing to wipe out a force greater than the Boches had ever loosed against the allies.

State Guard officers calculated every angle for their machine gun emplacements, assuring themselves and us that no one could reach the walls without being raked by murderous volleys of thirty caliber bullets. A hundred mounted policemen wielding weighted batons prepared to run down mercilessly anyone who crossed their final lines in front of the main gate, and their horseless comrades promised that every perceived weak point on the prison perimeter would be guarded by patrolmen and State Guard soldiers wearing bullet proof vests and sporting riot guns with bayonets. In turn, they would be supported by vicious dogs encouraged by half trained handlers.

In a vacant lot across from the yard, one of several contingents of firemen, deputized as lawmen, readied to leap into action to either blast with high pressure hoses any demonstrators breaking through the lines or fight any conflagrations caused by anarchists' bombs. It mattered not that ninety-nine percent of the demonstrators would be unarmed and intent on non-violent protest and that maybe a third of them would be women. We'd show these godless bastards just what the hell they were up against.

Sacco and Vanzetti represented the worst fears of the establishment. Fuller, the police, the American Legion, the Brahmins, one hundred percenters, the Irish pols, and the Italian community leaders worked tirelessly to get these cancers off the planet before their godless doctrines metastasized into the waves of immigrants threatening to overwhelm all decent people, and so that loyal Americans could sleep peacefully. Only as I surveyed the preparations, did I come to understand what Bart had known all along—the leaders of the Commonwealth of Massachusetts would never consider themselves safe so long as these two vicious men were alive.

Walking back to the office after a survey on the sixth, the warden said quietly, "No doubt, all of the women in the demonstration will have pistols in their bloomers."

When I replied, "I'll frisk the most dangerous among 'em," the old man performed a perfect double take and chuckled. It was one of very few light moments that day.

Passing the State House on our way home that evening, we saw that the preparations were almost as extensive as those in Charlestown. As the Common came into view, an encampment of tents being erected in great haste met our eyes. Canvas structures were everywhere and the young soldiers looked as untrained and anxious as those who had broken up the police strike years before.

"They'll be lucky to get through this with only Bart and Sacco sayin' goodbye," was Tommy's observation.

When I arrived home, everything was ready. Millie had prepared a corned beef supper that looked and smelled as nice as any Sunday dinner. By working so hard at making life easy and normal, it was worse than if she'd invited Mike up to share it. We did our best, but the kids, unable to fathom the undercurrents, sat quietly as we ate with hardly a word passing between us. Ma and Da might not be fighting, but there was something seriously amiss.

After we polished off the slab of beef, Millie scurried to get the kids into bed and to wash the dishes, assuring that there was no interference with my thoughts, as I scanned the Post which was full of Sacco and Vanzetti. Every permutation was laid out, and there was an analysis of all of the options available to the governor. I tried to get into the details, but, having heard them all at the prison, I found it difficult to concentrate. A quart of ale and half a pack of weeds disappeared before I turned in.

At first light on the seventh, I was alert to the fact that this was the day I'd dreaded for all these seven years. Marshal law had been declared by the Governor, and, as Tommy, Billy and I drove to Charlestown late in the morning, we surveyed a city overly armed and under siege.

As we passed one particularly youthful nest of nervous privates, Tommy worried aloud, "Jesus, one friggin' boo, and those jittery bastards'll fill half of the socialists with lead." Along our path, young men and women shouted insults at our uniforms. We shut our ears to cries of murderers and pushed on...But we heard them.

Crossing the bridge into Charlestown was like assaulting an enemy shore. Only after we identified ourselves to the satisfaction of a half dozen of the State's finest were the barricades protecting Rutherford Street shoved aside. Saw horses draped in razor sharp concertina wire were carefully swiveled only sufficiently to permit the flivver to squeeze through. Huge Alsatians snarled and lunged at us, and I compressed myself into the smallest package possible in the center of the back seat, gladly offering up Tommy and Billy as meals for the hungry dogs. Checkpoints followed on one another, and we flashed our credentials at any uniform that even turned in our direction. Only when we reached the main gate did any semblance of ease cross the brows of police and soldiers. We parked and made our way past even more armed policemen in the corridor to the prison headquarters. In the office, Tommy and Billy made their final comments and headed for their posts on the cellblocks. While these positions were assigned to guards not actually participating in the execution, they were far from easy compared to the task of sharing a tower with a Home Guard youth and smoking freely in the night air. Pain was taken to keep word of an execution from the prisoners, but never successfully. Prisons, even more than most government institutions, leak like sieves, and it was difficult to say that nothing was up when the remains of the AEF was setting up its encampment.

When the death sentence was carried out, the prison population came under great stress, particularly if the condemned was well liked or perceived to be innocent. Bart was both, so upheaval was expected. The guards were ordered to use all of their authority and any reasonable coercive measures to keep the moaning and groaning down. Any prisoner charged with creating a ruckus would be sent to solitary confinement with no guarantee that the sentence would ever end. The warden had no desire to face a prison riot on top of his other troubles. Besides, with all these armed rookies, lives were at risk—warders and penitents alike.

Sacco and Vanzetti, along with Madeiros, had been removed from Cherry Hill and locked into the cells adjacent to the execution chamber. Undoubtedly, they had been outfitted with the black death suits and shaved on the arms and legs for the electrodes. With little to do, I imagined the horror.

Just after dusk, Healy dispatched me with a message for the State Police lieutenant commanding the southeast wall. Making my way along the walkway on top of the revetment past the police and young soldiers, the rising tension was obvious—far greater than that which had reigned when the sun blazed. The night had magnified the fears of the young soldiers and amplified the paranoia that had been goading them. Those manning the search lights aimed the powerful beams into every nook and cranny of the interior yard and swung them up and down every yard and alley along Rutherford Street. Machine gunners shadowed the torches as they probed the tiniest of corners and sought out every noise and movement, real or imagined. God pity any mangy hound that upset a swill bucket near Rutherford Street as twelve o'clock neared, and I hoped, for the sake of the police and soldiers in the streets, that the safeties were locked on the weapons.

By this time my own demons were making themselves known, and on the way back to the office, I stopped in the guard room and took a long pull on a pint of Four Roses that I'd stashed for the occasion. There was no immediate relief, but I hoped that by midnight the creature would aid me in getting through the darkest moments ahead. To be sure, I poured down several additional ounces. The burning was intense, and I coughed and choked. Had anyone seen my contorted face, they'd have wondered how sitting alone in the office waiting for a switch to be pulled could be any more painful than this self-torture.

Composing myself, I walked to the office and sat at my desk. By the time I was alone in the large room it was close to eleven, and I hoped against hope that the rotgut would hurry its dulling mission. I propped myself upright and hung on the end of a Camel, so that Healy and the warden wouldn't notice I was beyond their reach. Only the waiting remained.

Toward quarter of twelve, as the flush rose in my cheeks on its way to my forehead, the door burst open. The warden, looking for all the world as if he'd won the Irish Sweepstakes, could barely contain himself. "It's off, Emmet. Call all the posts. There's been a stay. I'll get the soldiers and the troopers. Get with it. Hey, let's go!" His joy was unmistakable as he raced for the parapets with the good news.

By this time, my speech was badly slurred by the finest pint available for under a dollar from the drugstore, but I fought my way through the happy tasks required for the stand down. It took several hours to undo all of the security measures for the postponed execution. The warden made it absolutely clear that the governor's order was merely a ten-day stay and not a commutation. While the brilliant searchlights were extinguished and the machine guns unloaded, the emplacements were untouched and a small cadre of the Home Guard and police settled in for the duration.

As we escaped fortress Charlestown and crossed the bridge to the city in Tommy's car, we were forced to a crawl by the huge throngs dancing joyfully on word that Sacco and Vanzetti were saved. Only hours earlier, this same mob that had so reviled us as we made our way to the slaughter offered joyous smiles and good cheer even for those in uniform. There appeared to be little room in the hearts of the revelers for considering the difference between commuting the death sentences for Sacco and Vanzetti and a ten-day stay of execution. No doubt, ten days from now they'd do it again, if need be.

As we rolled, Tommy stopped near a young hawker of Globe extras, and we set up beneath an arc light to get the latest. Naturally, it was all headline and no story, but we learned from the two sparse paragraphs that a commission would be set up by the governor to determine once and for all the guilt or innocence of Sacco and Vanzetti and the fairness of the process that had landed them in the death house.

As I climbed the steps to the house as quietly as possible and prepared to settle in for a few hours of sleep, my joy was unbounded. Perhaps there was a chance yet for Bart to escape death. As I slipped in beside her, Millie murmured a sleepy acknowledgement of having heard about the reprieve. I patted her shoulder and closed my eyes, drifting toward nirvana by filling my mind with the pleasant thoughts of a high paying job as a clerk in the State House, relaxed for the first time in a week.

At virtually the instant I was about to let go of the happy day, I bolted upright. Jesus Christ, I had gone through with the executions. I had fully completed my part in the killings of Sacco and Vanzetti. Had it been up to me, at this minute, they'd be rolling toward the crematorium. I'd done as much to help them on their way as any who'd have attached an electrode or pulled a switch. Only the action of the governor, their acknowledged enemy, had checked the executioner's hand. I might as well have pulled the lever. I'd have killed them as look at them. But for a stroke of fortune, I would have participated in killing my friend and another man whom I believed, with all my heart, to be innocent of the crime for which they had been condemned.

Millie, as usual, rose from her slumber to help, but this time it was no dream and I pushed her away. "Sweet Jesus, I'd 've killed them. I would."

She started with the exculpatory nonsense that had worked so many times in the past. But, for the first time, the cataracts clouding my vision cleared, and I was naked in my guilt. No amount of soothing would ever again hypnotize me. At that instant, I vowed to never move against them.

New thoughts and problems seeped into the recesses of my excited brain. Where could I turn? Poor innocent Millie and the little children were totally dependent on me. At this minute, my family in The Bush slept secure in the knowledge that I would never betray them. Even Mike Moynihan, as he snored beneath my feet, knew that, for all my faults, I was true to the law, my duty, and my tribe. Mother of God, what to do?

The days flew. Hope was on every lip—at least inside the prison and among those marching in the streets of Boston. There was no time for either hope or despair; I had to develop a plan for when Bart again faced death. My brain raced to find an out.

The governor appointed President Lowell of Harvard and two other distinguished citizens to weigh the fates of Nick and Bart, and the papers were full of stories of how there could not be assembled anywhere in the land a fairer or finer panel. When these three finished, whichever way it went, there could never again be doubt about the quality of justice for Sacco and Vanzetti. But I'd been around the case long enough to acquire a sense of foreboding whenever good news was in the air. According to the newspapers, virtually all of the original witnesses still alive had met with the commission and were grilled by Lowell and the others. On the street, we read that the trio was leaving nothing to chance and was intent on establishing a record demonstrating even handedness and great care for the rights of the condemned. While Nick, Bart and Madeiros, having been returned to the dungeons of Cherry Hill for the duration of the inquiry, were brought out to meet with the great panjandrums, it was reported that Sacco continued his refusal to cooperate and defied them to condemn him, understanding, at least in his mind, that he was done for any way. Friends working in Cherry Hill later confirmed all of this for me.

Although the condemned moved back and forth from death row to the office for questioning, I never set eyes on any of them during these days, and, for that, I wasn't sorry in the least.

Newspapers competed for sales with stories of the great care being taken to keep the commission's proceedings secret and to assure justice. Every hour it seemed, a new extra hit the streets with virtually verbatim transcripts of the most damning testimony against Sacco and Vanzetti that had escaped from behind the closed doors. From the wisecracks loosed through Charlestown, it was clear that I was not the only one thinking the great venture in

Massachusetts justice was little more than a kangaroo court. Rumors, good and bad, filtered through the thick walls of Charlestown, and our spirits rose and fell hourly. All the while, I weighed my options and found only unsatisfactory alternatives. If I resigned immediately, Nick and Bart would gain nothing, and, if by some miracle, the tribunal recommended a new trial or commutation of the sentences, I'd have more than a little explaining to do in Little Dublin and The Bush. Mother of God, if I came walking into the kitchen with the word that I was unemployed and Sacco and Vanzetti were walking away with their skins, it would take walls thicker than Charlie Bulfinch's to protect me from little Millie Magawley and her big bad brother—and old Grampa, too, for that matter.

As the days, at one and the same time, dragged and flew, it was clear that the newspapers in Boston and the rest of the country and public opinion everywhere had shifted in favor of Sacco and Vanzetti, but, from just walking the walls and listening to the State troopers and the older noncoms of the State Guard, I knew that the police and the American Legion would never relent. My guess was that Big John and the Black Hand were at least as intent that the power of the Commonwealth, and those that had made it great, be demonstrated for anarchists in whatever holes and dens they might be plotting. Hope waned as those about me sated themselves with pipe dreams of waving goodbye to the boys as they walked away from Charlestown to freedom.

Public support for Sacco and Vanzetti confirmed the worst fears of the establishment. If the lower classes believed in them, the clear threat to American society was substantiated. The perversity of this circular logic drove me to my Camels and to oneness with the creature.

Sacco remained on his hunger strike and refused to cooperate in his defense. Sometime during the process, however, the powers that be determined that they would end the nonsense and his shenanigans. He was told that he would eat or that he would be force-fed through a tube in his nose. Rosa and his new lawyer talked him into dropping the futile show.

On the other hand, Bart was doing everything possible to work the system as it was designed. I was hatefully angry with him for it and knew that his connivance represented utter contempt for American justice and the capitalist system. He would give his all, and he would fail—an innocent man assuring his redemption beyond the grave. I recalled the anger that filled Millie when I complied with the conscription laws. God, Bart Vanzetti was a hard man to love.

One morning in the midst of the respite as we drove across the bridge to work, totally out of character, Billy turned and asked in a tone of disgust, "What's eatin' you? You ain't said three words in days. What d'ya want, for Christ's sake? They were supposed to fry, and they ain't."

Tommy nodded as he prepared to skirt the narrow checkpoint at the end of the structure.

All that had been bottled up gushed out. "You jerkoffs don't get it. That commission's in business to make Bart jump, no matter what. You're fuckin' Chinks on opium, if you can't see it. That's what's gettin' me."

Mullins jammed on the brakes and flew into my face. "You sonofabitch! You got a monopoly on friggin' justice. Half the guard's are with Bart, but you're better'n all of 'em. You always had a big fuckin' mouth, and I'm gonna give ya a lip to match."

Tommy leaped over the seat, and Billy grabbed an arm as he passed. "Tom! Come on! Tom! He's all mouth. He didn't mean nothin'. Did ya, Em?"

As I'd pierced the hearts of the priests with my minor league cruelty years before, I'd stabbed my two best friends who, considering their limitations, were very real supporters of Vanzetti. The rising tension had hit the fan. The swearing and offers to settle it there and then continued as Tommy and I squared off. I tried to back down—at least a little, but they were deeply hurt. Mr. Sensitivity had worked his evil magic once again. Ah, what the hell, it would all be over soon.

And it was. Silent on our way home, we picked up a Post extra that reported that the commission had found no basis for overturning the results of the trial. President Lowell and the others determined that while there might have been ways for police, prosecutors, and Judge Thayer to have done their jobs better, the panel could find no basis for further detaining the murdering anarchists on this earth. The headlines were as bold as possible—Sacco and Vanzetti would die. On August 19, they were sent back to death row, and in the early moments of August 23, they would be executed.

At that very instant, the plan came to my mind. Like so many stratagems in my life, it was nearly fully formed in its conception, and, over the next days—right to the end, I modified it hardly at all. Adrenaline rushed into my system, and I was both euphoric about finding my way and petrified at the probable consequences.

My first act the next morning was to ask the warden to post me in the death house in the seat opposite Bart's cell for the final shift before the executions. The poor man was incredulous at my explanation of wanting to be near Vanzetti for the final moments and approved the assignment only reluctantly. Nevertheless, he agreed, and the first element of the plan had been executed.

Martial Law was reinstituted. State Guard soldiers returned to their posts high above the yard, and the state police troopers appeared only hours later to cover the perimeter. Setting up the second time was far easier as the searchlights, machine guns and barriers had been left in place. The police and guardsmen seemed pleased to be back and eager to complete their mission.

By early afternoon of the twenty-first, preparations within the prison and in the nearby streets were complete, and I was having difficulty with my nerves. To do what I deeply believed to be right was a powerful tonic, but knowing that I would be repudiating everything that had made me weighed at least as heavily on the other side of the scales. I was far from sure that I could go on, and the idea of begging out with the warden lurked in the recesses of my brain. He would have complied with my change of heart without question.

With all of the turmoil, just carrying out simple assignments proved difficult, if not impossible. Time and again, I found myself at the wrong post on the walls attempting to pass messages from the warden to the wrong officer. Thank God, these people didn't know me and looked on the dolt before them as a mere incompetent, but a simpleton was only half of what I was. At every embarrassing error, I feared my undoing, but, knowing that I had not conspired, it was certain that I could not be found out or undone, except by my own cowardice—a comforting thought for a well established recreant.

The crowds in the city built once again. The newspapers described the onslaught, and our eyes confirmed that the demonstrations to save Bart and Sacco would be even more massive than the last effort. It was clear to all, friend and foe - inside and out, that the chance of another reprieve was nearly zero. Our trips to and from home were frightening; derisive screams and hateful oaths filled our ears. Tommy and Billy hunkered down under the onslaught, but, somehow, since I had hatched my scheme, I felt immune to the barbs.

Life at home was intolerable. Millie was treating me with great care and gentleness, and I kept my final assignment from her and lived the lie. As our paths crossed on the stairs, Mike and I limited ourselves to passing the time of day, and there were none of the usual digs. That even that puffed up bastard might bear a human heart crossed my mind, and my treachery weighed even heavier as the hours passed. Dwelling on my sedition from tribe and family, any innocent comment filled me with adrenaline, and I was ready for fight or flight—well flight, anyway.

In the office, I was unable to concentrate on my typing, and my hands trembled whenever the warden or Captain Healy spoke. I smoked more, but the usually comforting fags did little but burn my throat. I made a great effort not to tap the pint of Four Roses, but, God knows, that was a difficult decision to maintain.

On the night of the twenty-second, I slept not a minute - not a single moment. Poor Mil awakened periodically and assured me that none of what was happening was my fault and that I could do no more for Vanzetti. But I knew it was more than the horrible injustice about to be perpetrated that was keeping me awake; it was that I'd found a plan—a scheme that would do Bart no good and that might ruin the life of the lovely being, innocent and trusting, laying by my side.

After rolling out of bed, two cups of coffee jump started me out of my zombie state, and as I walked down the back stairs, each footfall on the hard wooden steps jarred the base of my already aching skull. In a show of good faith and in apology for my recent actions, I forced as pleasant a 'Good morning' as I could for Billy and smiled and nodded to Tom as he pulled up. Not a word passed between us as we drove into the city, and we drank in the mounting excitement as the car rolled slowly toward the Common.

The taunts of the massive mob bothered me not at all, and I watched for signs that the lads in front were sagging. But unlike the last time, they too seemed beyond the reach of the unruly crowd. Young men and women with fierce contortions on their fanatical faces screamed the vilest of epithets right into our stony visages, but the awful words had no impact, at least on our exteriors, as we continued ever more slowly through the thickening mass of humanity toward the top of the hill and the State House. Tens of thousands of placards proclaiming, 'Justice Crucified' were thrust into our nostrils, but nothing deterred us.

After passing the State House where the moral might of the world was focusing on the seat of government and its head, we dropped down toward Scollay Square and felt the crowd thin dramatically. There were, however, more than enough frantic anarchists organizing themselves at the entrance to the bridge to stiffen the backs of the frightened police manning the barriers. The blue coats blocked our way even more aggressively than on the day of the first scheduled execution, but Tommy was far more in control than on the earlier run and managed the gauntlet without difficulty.

With a stiff legged, shortened stride that gave me the aspect of old Pat, I hobbled to my desk. More cigarettes and another coffee only enervated me further, if that were possible. I sat before the typewriter and the longest day of my life began. With disgust all over his face, Captain Healy tossed back my first report after finding errors on virtually every line. How the hands of the clock could both spin out of control and, at the same time, not advance, further addled my already confounded mind.

But six o'clock came, and the last posting of the guards began. Those of us assigned to the death house assembled outside the office and began the long trek. We passed the three stations securing the route from the prison proper through the wall and into the holding area. Mine was the first spot, and I took the chair occupied by Alfred Warren, who was only too happy to move on to a point on the wall. My assignment was to assure that any suicide attempt was thwarted—happy day. It was getting late to back down, but the competition for my will continued unabated.

Becoming aware of the surroundings, I realized that the warden had done everything to assure that if only one of the three condemned prisoners were to survive an eleventh hour reprieve, it would be Bart. Madeiros had been placed in the cell nearest the forbidding green door to the antiseptically white execution chamber and would be the first to die. Sacco was in the middle, and Vanzetti was opposite my chair in the third. No matter how late any change of heart on the part of Governor Fuller, Bart had the best chance of cheating the executioner. For even that minute advantage, I gave thanks.

The condemned lay on the cold plain slabs in their tiny cells, oblivious to or ignoring the frenetic preparations underway hard by them beyond the bile green door. That gave me time to clear my mind before having to face Bart. But as I waited, it became obvious that while Madeiros was asleep—unconscious would be a better description—Bart and Sacco were quietly reflecting on what had been and was about to happen. I could hear occasional soft exchanges in Italian but kept silent, not wishing to intrude.

"Emmet, my friend", broke the quiet. Bart was at the bars wearing a sad smile.

I rose and reached for his hand. "I wanted to be here."
"Good friend."

We stood for a few seconds looking into each other's hearts but passed only grunts and wan smiles before slowly retreating to our seats and our thoughts. My control of mind and body was surprising, and I began to believe that I might be able to carry out the grand design.

Bart spoke to Sacco, and I interpreted the melodious soft vowel sounds as assurance of my fidelity. My already overburdened, crooked shoulders hunched to accept still another weighty load.

A half dozen cigarettes later, the holding area came alive. The thick steel door from the prison proper slid open. Captain Healy walked purposefully past me toward Sacco and informed him that Rosa was in the office and soon would arrive here. That it was to be their last meeting went unstated. Almost in the captain's wake, the heavy door gaped again, and the warden escorted Rosa, a well-dressed man and an entourage of guards and state troopers into the small area.

A painted line on the floor six feet from the cells, across which no visitor was permitted, served as the final barrier between them. While the safety and security value of this measure was obvious, the cruelty of not permitting final touches between the condemned and his love broke my heart, as well as theirs. They spoke in a mixture of English and Italian, and each professed undying love. I offered thanks to God—I did, truly—that I was not alone in observing this agony and that I could hide like a sheep in the center of the small flock.

The warden could bear it no longer and hesitatingly escorted Rosa across the imaginary abyss. Her hands met Nick's, and they intertwined. Tears obscured my view, but I can hear her words still, "Hands that worked in ditches, in factories, in gardens, and at the shoemaker's bench, but never had done a dishonest act."

"My love, take care of yourself. Eat vegetables and good food. You are the only one left to care for the cheeldren. I don't know what I would do eef anytheeng happened to you.

"Rosina, the children, they must know that I never killed."

"Unteel my last breath, the truth weel be weeth them, my dearest."

Nick implored, "Rosina, our leetle garden, the lovely flowers, the birds, they sing so sweetly—you remember?"

"Rosina, I love you and always will."

The juxtaposition of the prosaic and the profound terrible reality battered us. I began to hyperventilate and had to hold onto my chair for support.

"Nick, I am dying with you."

The warden intervened and gently pried them apart. She swayed, and he and a trooper supported her as she cried for God to intercede. The sight of the beautiful and vibrant young woman breaking as she reached helplessly for the hand of her mate about to be wrenched from her life caused me to become light headed, but I held on. The image that lingers after all these decades is of their fingers, like those of God and Adam in the Sistine Chapel, not quite touching.

The sobbing woman was eased from the chamber, and the man who had come with her remained behind. It was the newest and last lawyer for the two men, Michael Musmanno.

I fell back into my seat unable and unwilling to listen in on the final words between the three men—more thanks were due. For perhaps five minutes at each cell, Musmanno talked very quietly before rushing to his more important duty of attempting to forestall what now appeared inevitable.

Another tasteless, burning butt scorched my throat before Healy entered once again. This time it was for Bart. His sister had arrived at the last possible moment after a frantic and harrowing journey from Italy.

Bart was at the bars. "No! I cannot face her. I weel not be able to face death eef she sees me like thees. Please, Captain," he begged.

"Bart, For the love of God, she's come half way round the world."

The door opened, and a tiny bird of a woman entered on the

arm of the warden. She sought my eyes, but I averted them in shame. They halted opposite the first cell. She turned to face Bart and stiffened. Speaking in halting English, she said, "Oh, God, he ees een a cage of iron bars!"

"My dear Luigia, why deed you come? You should not have seen me like thees." His hands grasped the thick bars, and the cables of his forearms knotted to part them in order to catch the slumping woman. But it would take more powerful arms than those to undo the Commonwealth.

The warden supported Luigia, and, with a demanding, purposeful nod, abrogated the inviolable rule that the death cells would open only for the last walk. Healy raced to unlock Bart's cell, and Vanzetti emerged. The months in the pitch-black Dedham jail and the dank dungeons of Cherry Hill were exposed. The blazing lights of death row highlighted his sallow complexion, wrinkled brow and the deep crow's feet round his eyes. He reached out for Luigia, and the warden delivered her into his enveloping arms.

"My lovely Luigia. Theenk of better days. You look the same to me as in the happy times in Villafallatto. I remember always your beautiful laugh, eet was music."

"I weel never laugh again. They cannot do thees."

"Eet ees not the worst. We die, but we weel live in the hearts of the people. Believe, Luigia, thees injoostice will give meaning to my life. The blood of martyrs is the seed of liberty." Suddenly finding himself in the present, Vanzetti appeared startled by the poppycock that had no meaning for the helpless woman in his arms who had eyes only for Bart, her beloved brother.

"How do you say goodbye, my lovely girl? Oh, Luigia, why deed you come? You have geeven yourself such pain."

"For love. I could do nothing else."

The warden intervened. "It's time."

The life departed from Bart's arms, and, like the wings of a bird shot from the sky, they settled never to rise again. Behind Luigia, I was transfixed by the agony in Vanzetti's eyes, as she, like everything else, was excised from his life.

Like ancient Mongol chieftains whose joy sprang from shedding the blood of their enemies and wringing tears from their womenfolk, I pictured the cream of Massachusetts's society waiting, not in horsehide tents but behind elegant brownstone facades, for word that their barbaric fantasies had been fulfilled. I watched in horror as guilt-riven guards and officers moved to carry out their sworn duties.

At that moment, I felt great need for my pint, but it was too late to remedy that deficiency. I could only smoke, but there was far too little opiate in the overheated weeds to ease my pain. The holding area settled into an eerie silence in which the only sound that reached my ears was the burning crackle of tobacco and paper that I primed with every other breath.

Crushed by their encounters, Nick and Bart fell back exhausted onto the cold naked benches. All was quiet.

No one came to bid farewell to the lump of flesh nearest the green door. Madeiros would die as he lived, unloved and missed not at all. I walked to his cell, but, beyond the shallow rising and falling of his slight chest, there were no signs of life. The killer would be put to death for his crimes, but, like a dumb animal, he had not the power to seek absolution. He would simply be sent on his way, a steer in a slaughterhouse.

But my thoughts drifted from the anguish of my friend to the requirements for final implementation of the plan. It was nearly nine, and there would be three hours of internal struggle until action was required. Serving as a voyeur of the final intimacies of Sacco and Vanzetti bolstered my strength, and my intentions were sound, even if the flesh was weak.

But again and again my thoughts wandered to Mulberry Street and I viewed my deception from Millie's perspective. Undoubtedly, I would be seen as as big a fool as Bart must seem from wherever Luigia now sobbed and prayed.

At this moment, Mil was readying the children for their beds, secure that, while this night would be the most difficult my life, it would end like all before it, safely in the bosom of family and community. So it was, too, with Police Captain Michael Moynihan, Councilman Sean Moynihan, Grampa Pat, King John, and all the rest. The awful task of ridding the Commonwealth of two murdering anarchists would soon be done, and the testing duty required of their three sons on duty in Charlestown Prison would be driven from mind by the age-old bonhomie of Clancy's.

But one of those loyal lads was plotting to stab in the back those who had succored and protected him. An Italian anarchist who had never done anything for him meant more than those who had borne him and his children. And this treachery, would it gain Vanzetti his freedom? Good God, it wouldn't extend his life by even a single instant!

The sedition might not be so great if it would save the man, but there was no prospect of altering anything but the lives of those I loved. Was it merely an empty symbol for the private edification of a malcontent? The archangel would know. So, as the hands of the clock spun out of control, nausea rose and the self-loathing flagellation continued unabated.

Soon it was five minutes before the appointed hour and time to implement the grand design. Marching resolutely to the door back into the prison, I silently implored, "God, give me strength." Raising my fist to bang for John Donnelly, sitting on the other side, I. . .the hand and arm froze in midair. Turning from the door to Vanzetti's cell and back again and again, I did all in my power to overcome my cowardice, but it was not to be. The great plan to resign with the grand flourish of a heroic speech was shelved for lack of character.

Understanding fully that I would participate in the execution of two men, both of whom I believed innocent—one a dear friend, I dropped helplessly on my chair. Healy and the warden, checking the posts, walked past into the execution chamber; I nodded as they spoke, understanding not a word of their directives.

Soon, they returned, hesitantly, into the holding area with Freddy Glavin, Kevin Gilbride and several others in tow. Unlocking the first cell, they spoke softly as they gently eased Madeiros from his slab into the death chamber. My eyes glued on my shoes, I heard little and saw less.

In a stupor equal to Celestino's, I waited, an uncomprehending dumb animal. Suddenly, the lights dimmed, and a barely audible scream leaked under the heavy steel door. I pictured him leaping into the night, a figurehead in a gale.

From the passageway back to the prison proper, through the rank of bars near the top of the heavy door, a faraway groan, the sigh of a primordial beast in its death agony, filled my ears. The prisoners vented sorrow and anger, and, above this, the guards shouted for silence from the now shrieking inmates. But the darkness retreated, and I breathed again.

But, again, the night consumed us. This time, the screams from the blocks were louder and the demands for order softer, with less authority. Celestino Madeiros was dead and gone.

The forbidding green door gaped and the crew returned for Sacco. Alert and ready, he rose to meet them. Turning to Vanzetti, the good-byes were spoken in Italian. Catatonic, out of the corner of my eye, I watched him disappear. By this time, I was praying to God—truly I was—as trembling fingers reached for still another cigarette. The telephone line from the governor ran directly to the death chamber and no instrument was near, but I fantasized grabbing the receiver and racing to halt the carnage. Again, it was too late. It was even darker than it had been for Madeiros; the voltage ripping into the electric chair was determined by the weight of the condemned. Nick Sacco, the most robust of the trio, would take a lot of killing, and the executioner was seeing to it that he got it. The moaning from the blocks was deeper and sadder; there were no more demands from the guards.

By the time the lights came up, I had abandoned hope and sat through the next set of murky shadows without flinching. Nick was gone, Rosa with him.

When they came for Bart, I stood and watched. My last chance to scream for help against the brown shirts was at hand. He came out into the light without incident. Stopping and looking directly into my eyes, he spoke softly, "Goodbye, good friend. Of all the guards, you most loyal."

There were other words, but, comprehending not one more, I could only nod and support myself on the back of the chair.

Collapsing brute like into the seat, I moved not a muscle as Bartolomeo Vanzetti was put to death. No cigarettes were required, and, as the last act played out, I tried to focus on the grim satisfaction of the frightened men who had saved the nation as millions wept. The most dangerous man in America was no longer a threat.

In my mind, I watched as Vanzetti, surely sustained by St. Augustine, leaped with the lightening into the midnight sky, and his words echoed in my mind, "...eef I could be reborn two other times, I would live again to do what I have done already."

The circus over, I made my way slowly to the office. Minutes later, the death crew staggered into the room. Shattered, to no one in particular, the warden said, "He forgave me...He forgave me."

Singling me out, he said, "Emmet, Bart forgave us all. He shook hands with each of us. He forgave us. He did."

The team fell onto the available chairs, and, those without places, supported themselves on the railing. Again and again, he repeated, "He forgave me. He forgave us all."

With none of the carefully fantasized outrage of the speech to have been delivered as they were about to drag Vanzetti to the electric chair, I said in a monotone, "I'll be quittin' now. I can't come back."

Silence reigned for an eternity. Finally, the warden, looking at Healy, said in a flat tone, "Have him clean out his stuff."

Turning to me, coldly, he said, "Don't come back, ever."

I wanted to ease the moment but found no words. Healy and I traipsed silently to the locker room. I put on my old street clothes and stuffed the pint into a brown bag. The captain, never looking at me, escorted me to the main gate. Side by side, we stopped and watched the soldiers tearing down their emplacements. The street clock confirmed that it was just after two. Taking a long pull from the pint and, saying not a word to Healy nor ever looking back, I walked across the Prison Point Bridge for the last time.

Not a single soldier or policeman glanced as I passed through what, just hours earlier, had been impregnable checkpoints. The deed was done. The world was safe. As I passed, all snippets from the soldiers and police were of the final round, the cortege to the crematorium in the morning.

Climbing the hill to the State House, I mingled with the hushed crowd. There was none of the fire of hours earlier, but I sensed the determination to shame the Commonwealth by conducting a mournful procession to the crematorium for the remains of Sacco and Vanzetti. Shouts for revenge were quelled by hard glances and firm grasps. Deeply moved, I determined that I would walk with the bodies.

Fuller, Lowell and Thayer had prevailed. But I sensed there would be a perpetual price for the pyrrhic triumph. For all their days, the happy recognizing eyes needed by public men to feed their fragile egos would seek the pavement and avoid their hungry, colluding smiles.

The granite steps to the Common below the State House cooled my bottom, and I watched as both sides readied themselves for the last act. Pulling several times on the pint, the warmth passed my temples, and I became completely relaxed. The adrenaline coursing my system as the battle for my conscience was waged was fully spent, and the combination of whiskey and exhaustion made it nearly impossible to hold my eyes open. As if under the influence, I staggered for the Public Garden.

Not a hundred paces toward my goal, I stopped, drained the pint, and, turning to the corner office, fired the bottle at the governor's window. "Bastard! Are ya happy now? Bastard!" The missile hadn't a prayer and fell harmlessly short of its target, as I knew it would. It had not been a mighty heave, for I hadn't really wanted to harm my new brother in expediency.

Continuing aimlessly, I crossed Charles Street into the Public Garden. There was no choice but to find a protected spot to rest my worn out being until it was time to march.

An opening under a huge elm tree, protected from the path by several large bushes was less than perfect but would have to do. I slumped onto the cool turf and gave up my consciousness.

Near dawn, a beam of light was fired into my eyes and a familiar voice barked, "That's the asshole."

Two patrolmen lifted me gently and hustled me to the back of a Paddy Wagon. A larger man, yanked open the door, and they tossed me onto a pile of smelly human flotsam. Flying past, I recognized Mike Moynihan. In just hours, news of my transgression had reached Little Dublin, and, undoubtedly, The Bush. Crawling over bodies to an empty spot, I tried to avoid interfering with good Micks carrying out their bodily functions. This was a run for drunken Irishmen, and there would be no talk of anarchy amid the retching. My decision to participate in the funeral procession had been abrogated.

Before I could gain purchase, the truck lurched into motion and careened wildly around corners. The Paddy Wagon rocketed at speeds I wouldn't have believed possible in the narrow city streets, and, with each dodge and turn, another poor Mick hurled his load of cheap whiskey. It was the Mauretania again, and I retreated to a point nearest the bow to avoid what I could.

The ride seemed eternal; one lad, still conscious, begged to be shot, but there was no respite until, as quickly as it began, we shuddered to a stop. The two cops come round to the back and struggled with the door. One called, "Magawley, come out, lad."

Stepping on any number of trunks, arms, and legs and ignoring the sounds of squishing fluids I dared not identify, I escaped the rolling asylum, doing my best not to maim my comrades. The screams were particularly piercing when I squashed fingers with the heavy prison brogans that hadn't been turned in. But out I was, not sure of my footing. Mike stood at the side and directed them to drag me upstairs. Strange, I slowly became aware that this was not a police station. It was the Moynihan residence in Little Dublin, I was home.

The lads gave me a lift. My appearance was surely worse even than the situation warranted, and my only thought was that Sean would be horrified if any neighbors were awake. My feet barely touched the stairs as the lads struggled up the back porch and the two flights. It was a good thing they were young and in good condition, as I was an awesome load for a wee fellow. Millie was at the door waiting and didn't even look at me. Like John Moran at a wake, she expertly directed the traffic into the bedroom.

They sat me down. Millie was thanking them, and they were dropping 'no trouble at alls.' I cannot describe how tired I was, but before I could collapse, Mil insisted on cleaning me up.

Placing a cool cloth on my clammy brow, she carefully washed my bloody fingers—I have no idea whose it was. The words are gone, but the gist of her remarks was that no blame for death of Vanzetti was on my hands. . .If only she knew.

I felt compelled to blurt out the truth of my cowardice, but, like the grand move to bang on the death house door, the impulse was suppressed and never uttered until this day. All the while, a host of words I didn't know the poor woman commanded concerning stupidity and ignorance were unleashed. But the tone, unlike the phrases, was sweet and gentle.

As she drew the sheet over me, she knelt and kissed my brow. Despite the guilt and shame, it was the last thing I remembered that night.

CHAPTER 14

It was mid-afternoon before I stirred, but I pretended to sleep on, aware that my world had changed forever and that awakening would light the fuse to its demolition. Vanzetti was dead, and I was unemployed and no longer a member of my tribe. But the sounds of Millie working in the kitchen intruded, and there was no choice but to determine the extent of the damage and face the inevitable.

After an additional fifteen minutes of introspection, I rolled out and staggered to my destiny. Millie, hearing the steps, rushed to meet me with a tender embrace. There were no words, but it was clear that I was loved and not alone.

Disheveled and wearing only trousers over my underwear, I sat silently as she fried eggs. Forcing them down, I retreated to the parlor and set up to serve a life sentence at the side window through which a gentle breeze carried shouts of boys playing baseball in the street below. Parting the curtains and blowing smoke through the rusted screen, I watched and listened to their cries.

That day and the next, I left my window only rarely, while Mil worked quietly, never intruding. Mute, I watched as Mary O'Reilly, Meg Malone, and Peggy Callahan, women from the neighborhoods with whom I was on only the most casual of terms, separately trudged all the way up bearing casseroles and cakes. Little was said, but it was clear that these were offerings of support. Millie, effusive in her thanks, told them that I was fine—but never brought them in to see me. Obviously, Emmet Magawley was dead and being readied for viewing.

I ruminated on the events leading up to my gazing from the window and of the bravery of these tiny women walking openly before their neighbors to provide succor for a traitor. I concluded that, in many ways, women are more courageous than men. From time immemorial, men have defined valor, and our interpretations are laced with illustrations of bold charges into enemy strongholds and of brave hearts—like Bart—defying death for a cause. But before me, care worn biddies trekked long distances with warm bread and pies for a frightened man perceived to have acted morally. These wives of a shoemaker, a fireman and a longshoreman demonstrated solidarity with me—a less worthy hero than they suspected, and I thought again of the lovely vessels of Charlestown.

Late the first day, Da pulled up, and Millie hurried him in. Drawing me out of the chair, he enveloped me with his arms. "We love you, boy. Are you alright?"

"Fine...Tired's all."

His eyes sped around the map. Mandating a shave and bath was on the tip of his tongue, but he bit it off. "Ma wants yuz Sunday for pot roast. I want ya, too."

"I'm off my feed."

"Come. Everything's ok. You were right, and all of 'em wrong."

Again my confession was almost blurted, but it was stifled in my throat. It was then that my rationalization began. Perhaps what I'd done was indeed a courageous thing. The power of Da's words began to lighten the load. . ."We'll see, Da."

They retreated to the kitchen. I listened to the hushed tones thanking him for coming.

I watched and listened to the boys shout and run a while longer—their summer was ending, interjecting intensity into their play—while a fly on reconnaissance from the kitchen made me his personal target and intruded on my thoughts. At the instant I committed to quit the post, a beautiful Packard pulled up. A liveried chauffeur emerged and made for the back door.

Millie answered, and I heard my name. She—reluctantly I knew—guided him in to the living room. A smooth one, he gave no notice to the wild hair or the three days growth of beard.

"Miss Hayes asked that this be delivered." He handed me a

folded note on monogrammed paper that exuded position in a world of which Mil and I knew nothing.

Standing by, Mil's eyes popped. Maude, the loveliest of Bart's vessels knew. The substance was that a bookstore on West Street needed a clerk, and she had taken the liberty of recommending me.

I thanked him, and, as soon as he left and much to the relief of my loving spouse—and perhaps the neighbors as well, as it was the height of summer—I began a long relaxed toilet. The new Emmet Magawley emerged and kissed his wife.

The next morning, putting on my Sunday best, thin as it was, I headed for West Street and a new life. Entering the dingy Olde Boston Book Shoppe—that was, coincidentally, almost directly under the sign shot down during the police strike—I asked for the proprietor. Albert Hayes introduced himself and indicated that he'd been expecting me. It was a solicitous interview for a lifetime surrounded by books, and I salivated at the description. It slipped out that Albert was a poor relative of the venerable Hayeses, and, instantly, I knew that the position was mine. The real Emmet Magawley swung into action—the leopard had not changed his spots after all.

When it was time to discuss payment for services, Albert sat, defenseless, as the fox surveyed the unguarded nest. "What are your salary requirement?"

Ever the supplicant, I entreated, "I'd be happy to work for what I took home from the prison." His eyes relaxed, and, after a pregnant pause, I continued, "One hundred and seventy-five a month should cover it."

A dark cloud crossed the sky, and I watched his face drop in pain. "Guards make that much?"

There was no sag in my shoulders nor in the Cheshire grin, so Albert, alone, was forced to make a decision. He coughed and asked, "When could you begin?"

"First thing in the morning," I said cheerily and then added solicitously, "You won't regret it, Mr. Hayes." But there was little confidence in his eyes as I turned to leave. The drive home flew by, and I was as full of myself as when the Molly Maguires ran amok in St. Michael's.

While at the prison, my salary may have been only one hundred and ten, but Mulligan was contributing another fifty in peak months. And, of course, just a little slack had to be built in for assuring that additional costs—such as for proper attire—did not adversely impact the net. Examining my conscience, I concluded that the price was actually under what I'd traditionally taken home and eminently fair to Albert.

Before long, however, the reality was that I had made a poor bargain. Albert's wise acceptance was by far the better end. He and his two superannuated clerks did little beyond reading everything in the store. Dusting, stacking, pricing and all other activities relating to running a going concern were deferred indefinitely and accomplished only in extremis. While as anxious as the others to peruse the merchandise, I was at least minimally organized and prepared to work, at some level—and I could type.

Overdue bills were sent with strong messages. I kicked the two elderly, impoverished Brahmin rejects—held over from ownership long forgotten—right where it counted, and the place began to look like we might actually be attempting commerce.

Within months, Albert was taking home more money than ever and began to act is if he'd not been conned. The geezers found that they could return books to the proper shelf without causing heart failure and determined that passing dust cloths actually eased their troubled breathing. Morale rose and business picked up.

The Olde Boston Book Shoppe—New and Used Books—moved into the black. Quickly, we became the best source of all things Sacco and Vanzetti, and those sympathetic to their cause sought us out. There was no mention of any role by Maude, but more than a few Brahmin matrons and lovely vessels began to spend time in the establishment.

And before too many seasons, we determined that our Italian language section was becoming profitable. Gnarled old men traipsed over from the North End and pressed pennies and nickels into our palms for items among our used selections. None mentioned Sacco and Vanzetti, but they were deferential beyond that which came so naturally to them.

All four clerks became valuable resources on Nick and Bart, and nothing on the case entered Olde Boston without being devoured by all; even opponents asked for our help. I read somewhere that booksellers are liberal minded men. That was just one of our curses, but I was the least liberal of the four and kept the bills and the dust flying.

At home it was another story; the reality of my situation was not at all what I'd imagined. Times were changing and, thank God, the cruelest among us no longer held all of the power. The terrible things that I'd been warned about; friends not talking to me, the shunning of my good wife and children, and the rest, thank God, were so diluted as to be nearly meaningless. Looking back, it's easier to understand. Women who warned their daughters about giving themselves up at the price of everything relented and kissed their grandchildren. Boys, admonished that Protestant wives would make them outcasts, survived. Oh, there were the cold hearted who disowned and exiled their children on principle, and there were some—not counting poor Tommy Mullins who had cause and whose loss I still feel— whose eyes never met mine again. They were, however, a tiny minority at whom the ordinary denizens could point in order to constrain the wildest impulses of their offspring.

But for those who actually crossed the line of defiance, life was forever changed. I was not despised—there was even a measure of respect—truly—and forgiveness was granted, however reluctantly. Mike Moynihan was unwilling to give up Millie to spite me, and I came to believe that he was not so great a bully as I had thought.

Grampa could never cut off his Billy and forced himself to embrace me—and, later, even talked about me and Michael Collins in the same breath, as if there were a comparison. Dear Ma never for a single instant thought of anything but her crooked, squinty eyed, little Emmet. But the bravest and most loving shared bed and life without flinching.

Acceptance and forgiveness, however, did not equate to trust. Never again did the phone carry Paul Romano's conspiratorial whispers of wicked deeds requiring my special services—such as they were. Mulligan might be handing out twenties—but not for me. King John and Mary would never again open their hearts and share the agony of what had been torn from them and tossed so carelessly in a field far away. I was saddened but the price was known in advance, and, indeed, it was far less than advertised.

It was time to complete the break with the bogs. The world, not just the tiny ones in the old neighborhoods, had been transformed, and many of us who had seen 'Paree' would no longer bear silly petty tyrannies. Changes were underway in Boston, and young middle class Irish families transformed the trickle to the suburbs into a torrent. These were the salad days of the green belt around Boston, and Millie and I spent our free days driving along the lovely avenues of Milton in our new little Chevy looking for a bower to live out those reachable fantasies.

Albert and Maude called on another cousin who presided over a family owned bank to finance the dream. So in June 1929, Mulligan's lads came to deliver us to a lovely little bungalow in Lower Mills just a stone's throw from Turners Pond and only two more down to the river.

On the great day, Mary Moynihan and Ma fluttered about and cheered the parade, and, after but a few hours of terrible sweating for the lads, we were off. But there were tears among the smiles as the grandmothers waved their good-byes. It might be only five miles to the new world, but it was light years from the flat earth that had created and defined us. A sign of the change was the great Mack moving van with screaming chain drive that carted our treasure to a place where newly minted Irish suburbanites could reinvent themselves.

We were welcomed by neighbors with but weeks more seniority than ourselves and soon realized that the manager of a going book store in Boston—while technically not the manager, I carried out many of the duties of the position—was almost as good as an insurance salesman who'd graduated from Boston College.

Soon the assimilation was complete, and we became the first true Irish-Americans, even as we raised the first generation of citizens requiring no hyphenation.

I vowed, as soon as we were set, to move for restoration of Vanzetti's name. While many of the young couples around us demonstrated republican tendencies, more retained their connections with the old places, and all of them were open and friendly. In time, I thought a campaign to sway them to support the notion of judicial or legislative annulment for Nick and Bart might be possible.

With little choice, I bided my time, and a bizarre schizoid existence resulted. In the world of Olde Boston, the cause of Sacco and Vanzetti was fought from opening till the curtain was drawn, while, in Milton and the old neighborhoods, even mentioning their names became a shameful taboo. It was amazing to me how quickly the perpetrators of a vile deed—and those who supported them—saw it for what it was and attempted to eradicate it from memory.

But seminal events stepped into the road of my good intentions. The Great Depression descended, and families and neighborhoods had to succor their own once again. The transition of middle class Gaels from their working class Democrat roots into the novel worlds of Republicans and limousine liberals was postponed indefinitely. We all had troubles enough without taking on the burden of clearing a man no longer in need of a hot meal.

The bad times didn't end with whimpers but with explosions, and, regardless of the inspiring admonitions of Franklin Roosevelt, there was little respite from fear. Soon, the young men were off to another foreign war, Bobby and Pat with them. Millie and I proudly hung the blue stars in our front window, and each night I listened as she drifted off thanking the Almighty that the stars were not gold.

I proved as adept at growing carrots in our Victory Garden as had my Da before me. Millie volunteered at the USO downtown. Helen served as a welder at the Fore River ShipYard in Quincy, and, beyond belief, with overtime, she cleared more than a hundred dollars a week.

The Commonwealth had no time for the finer points of jurisprudence, and neither did I. By V-J Day, our parents had passed from the scene, and we learned that the Moynihans carried a fatal flaw. When Mike slumped over in his office, my suspicion that he had no heart was blasted. Poor Billy joined him in the family plot only two years later.

After the war, guilt over Vanzetti crawled into the recesses of my brain. The boys graduated from Boston College, and they and Helen moved on to new lives.

When next I considered doing something about Sacco and Vanzetti, Joe McCarthy was bellowing about communists and their fellow travelers, and Olde Boston's clientele was upgraded to include young, crew cut, nattily dressed federal investigator types. Perusing our collections on anarchy and socialism, they took many notes but spent nearly nothing. Fear was palpable among our customers.

Even after McCarthy was destroyed, the Cold War prevented an objective examination of the case, depressing even further the aging supporters of Nick and Bart. The hard core made efforts at clearing them but could never muster the clout necessary to overcome those who had demanded their heads.

One afternoon as I quietly stocked shelves, a clean-cut young fellow in a pressed suit approached. "Mr. Magawley?

"Special Agent Charles Ryan, FBI, can we talk?"

In the office, he began. "You were friends with Sacco and Vanzetti?"

"I barely knew Sacco, but I was very close to Vanzetti."

"We're reviewing the case, and I'm contacting people who knew them."

In but minutes, Ryan saw that I had nothing exculpatory.

"I was with Bart almost every day for seven years and knew him as well as anyone. He could never have killed anybody."

"Everyone I talk with says the same thing. Was he all that they say?"

"As close to a saint as you could ever know. Of course, saints are far from easy to live with. But I'll go to my grave believin' in his innocence.

"It was the Morelli gang from Providence. Madeiros was tellin' the truth." I spoke with conviction, having believed for years that Herbert Ehrmann had uncovered the murderers.

Ryan listened to the entire story without interrupting and said, "I don't believe he did it either, but that won't bring him back or get him cleared."

After he left, I lit a cigarette and brooded on what more might have been said. There was nothing.

Later, the FBI produced a report indicating that Bart was probably innocent, but embarrassment for revered historic figures and lesser players, still living, made it impossible to exonerate him or annul the conviction.

Albert died in '66, and, after assuring that I was set with social security and some small savings, the family closed the store. I retreated to the Milton Public Library for my daily reading. Within months, I returned home to find Millie lying on the kitchen floor. Racing to her side, I knew before I touched her what had happened. I pressed my lips to her forehead and whispered, "I loved you from that first dance, Millie Moynihan."

I brooded for weeks and, only after the kids conspired to drag me back to life, was I able face winter. I moved in with Helen and John Pacella and their three to begin my new existence. Like many previous changes, it wasn't nearly as difficult as we had feared. Blessed with a tiny appetite and a robust constitution, I did my best to make it bearable by spending hours in the library. I also discovered a satisfactory substitute for Clancy's in Mattapan, Barry's, where, initially, I limited myself to two beers a visit.

But, without Millie for ballast, the creature began to gain

ground. Ignoring the disapproval in Helen's eyes, I dove deeply into my cups, and, finally, it devolved upon Bobby to confront me—a happy chore for any oldest child. We met at the bar, and it was during that talk that he came up with the idea to bring me back from the edge.

"Why don't ya try to clear Sacco and Vanzetti? You've been B.S.'n about it for a hundred years."

Indeed, it was time. My sister Eileen's oldest boy, Frank Boyle, a State Representative from Hyde Park, was second in rank on the Judiciary Committee, and Bobby arranged for me to visit with him.

Effusive in his greeting, Franky sought my purpose, but, learning it was to clear Nick and Bart, he nearly threw up.

"Sacco and Vanzetti? Jesus, Emmet, we can't touch 'em. The last guys who tried lost the next time out of the gate."

"It's never a good time, but Vanzetti was fucked, and I can't die without tryin' to make it right." Franky winced at the language.

Aged men can air the most disgusting problems of their digestive and urologic systems but are forbidden to use coarse language. The shock value of four letter words that disappears in youthful excess is restored with spare usage by the old. It worked.

"It won't be on ya, Franky. Get me in with the governor. I have to see him.

"I can't die with this on my head. Vanzetti didn't kill anyone." As he rolled his eyes, I gave no quarter.

"I'll see what I can do." An abscessed tooth extracted without novocaine, Frank's promise was given up in agony.

A week later, the phone rang; it was Franky. "The governor's office is expectin' ya next Tuesday at ten."

"You're a good boy. I'll never forget this."

"Yeah, right."

Sacco and Vanzetti would have still one more day. My life since that night in Charlestown was prologue to this encounter, and I dug out everything from my files.

Arriving early, I walked the Common to ease my nerves. As the sun sparkled on the great golden dome, I whispered my lines, and, at a quarter before the hour, I struggled up the massive granite steps.

In a mob of supplicants, I waited to identify myself to the receptionist. A bench was pointed to, and, although anxious and fired up, I forced myself onto it. An hour passed and the crush of those seeking audience with the great man continued unabated. Doing my best to suppress my anxiety, once more I approached the desk.

"I'm sorry, I haven't been forgotten?"

"It won't be much longer, sir."

Finally, after another half-hour, my name was called. A youth in his twenties wearing the pinstriped, charcoal gray uniform of a budding politician smiled and clasped my hand. "Mr. Browne has been very busy. I'm sorry you had to wait so long."

"Mr. Browne?"

"Fred Browne—a close friend and aid to the governor—he wants very much to meet you."

The young fellow led me through a labyrinth of corridors and cubbies, and, expertly, from one professional to another, I was passed into the office of Mr. Browne.

"Mr. Magawley, nice of you to come forward." Directing me to a soft leather chair, he began, "Your nephew says that you have new information about Sacco and Vanzetti.

"We count on Frank as an ally. When he called, the governor asked me to get right on it.

"Tell me what you have."

"When will I be meeting with the governor?"

"I'm sorry, you didn't hear?" Browne appeared genuinely shocked that I hadn't been told. "The governor was called to Springfield and won't be able to see you, so he wants me to share your evidence with him when he returns."

"They didn't do it."

"From everything I've heard, you're probably right, but, over the years, many have tried and failed to get them cleared. If you have new information, we'll see what can be done."

"But I don't have anything new."

"Oh, that's unfortunate," he said with a hurt expression.

"I know the case backward and forward."

"Frank vouched for that. But there's nothin' new?"

I'd been had. I'd bored in too hard on Franky. To get me out of his face, he set up this farce.

We waltzed through an hour of me offering up the best of the Frankfurter and New York World arguments. He nodded at all the right spots and turned on his sad puss, like me at a funeral orchestrated by King John. It was silly, but I hit all of the major points. This was a favor for Franky, and Browne would have eyeballed every petition and motion and spent a week with me, if necessary.

When it was over, the young man with the bright smile led me back to the front desk. "Thanks for coming in, sir. I'm sure the governor will be very interested in what you said to Mr. Browne."

He pivoted grandly and disappeared in the crowd.

While I'd known for sometime that I was an old man, that morning, for the first time, I comprehended the full meaning of the designation, and I decided to test it. An arrow pointed in the direction to the Judiciary Committee, where two distinguished looking middle age men wearing politicians' costumes were whispering conspiratorially in the hallway. When they parted, I bearded one.

"I was a close friend of Bartolomeo Vanzetti. He and Sacco were executed for murders they never committed. Their convictions have to be annulled."

He looked into my eyes as if I were the only person in the world whose opinion meant anything to him. "You knew Vanzetti?"

"We were very close."

"Amazing. I don't have time right now, but I'd love to hear more about this. Have you taken any steps to clear them?"

"I just met with Mr. Browne in the governor's office."

"That's marvelous. If anyone can help, it's Fred Browne. You'll have to excuse me now. Best of luck."

I needed a drink. Without doubt, I could say anything about everything, and everyone would patronizingly blow me off. My views on Sacco and Vanzetti and everything else were irrelevant.

Attempting to come to grips with the discovery, I'd go into the library and, like the ancient mariner, glom onto an unsuspecting person and begin the tale of State corruption. Within minutes, I had total agreement from the victim and a promise of full support—if only I would excuse them this once. It was clear, I would have no role in clearing Sacco and Vanzetti. The quest ended, one of their last horses had foundered.

One fine spring day during the late sixties, I found myself drivin' John's Chevy through Little Dublin. My first tour of the neighborhood in decades, I was intrigued by the passing scene. Slowing, I sought old faces, but there were none. Surprisingly, I felt not a pang as I passed the Moynihan house. Of course, Dublin was not my native land, and, excitedly, I pushed into The Bush.

Arriving at the center of the universe—St. Michael's—I parked and strolled through the old neighborhood. A surreality settled about me. Pride of home ownership had all but disappeared. Fresh paint adorned few of the old triple-deckers, and, from most, the clapboards begged for protection. Young sprigs had matured, while all of the graceful old elms had been cut off in their prime, many of the stumps still rotting in place. Lovely little gardens that many of the old timers had nurtured were overgrown or paved for the benefit of derelict automobiles.

Suddenly, the high school loomed before me, and, approaching the main front, the old steam plant came into view on the left. I smiled at the memories of youthful transgressions committed in its shadows. But as I closed on the aging structure, it became obvious that great changes had taken place. The second floor windows were boarded up with water streaked sheets of plywood, and chains were on all the doors save the center panel of the main front entrance.

A small sign hanging askew on the side wall of the entranceway identified the building as a warehouse for the public works department. The cement footings, bearing only the rotted remnants of the posts that proudly held the honor roll of its brave sons gone off to fight the Kaiser, were overgrown with weeds. The AEF no longer held even the schoolyard.

Emmet Magawley was a stranger in his motherland. I turned and moved on. The faces on parade bore none of the familiar marks stamped by generations of Irish who had walked these ways. But my natural optimism fought through. Surely, the sight of a wading heron would spark recognition in some old crone, but I reached Mulligan's warehouse without a single hello.

There seemed little point in trying, but I was compelled to knock on the rickety old portal. The door shuddered as it swung open, and an elderly woman looked quizzically into my face.

She stammered, "Emmet, is it you?"

"It is, Peggy. My God, you look lovely." I couldn't help myself; she was beautiful. Nearly half a century had passed, and yet the woman before me was nearly as exquisite as when she was the prettiest girl The Bush had ever produced.

"I'd know you anywhere, Emmet. What a sight for sore eyes. Come in. Come in…Tea?"

"Oh, what could be better, love?"

Stunned that she could have aged so gracefully, I was spell bound. Her silver hair was luminescent and as delicate and full of sparkling highlights as the lovely auburn crown that had made her a princess so long ago.

Her face had not been immune to the marks of time, but her complexion was that of one only slightly past flowering, and her cheeks and lips were still full like those of woman nearly half her age.

"You're still at the business, Peg?"

"Not for long. We haven't made expenses in years, and I stay open only for the sake of the men. But I'm not well, and it won't be much longer."

"I'm sorry, dear."

"Ah, it's nothin' for you to worry about, Em. Let's talk about better times."

The words flowed like fine ale as aged Gaels remembered the glory days. Mike Mulligan, King John, and Grampa spoke and strode again as we filled the air with sentimental revisionism. The tea disappeared all too quickly. As I was about to take leave, she broke the spell by nodding to an aging photograph on the credenza behind her desk. It was Jack Moran, the very portrait that John and Mary and I had cried over so long ago. He was even straighter than I remembered. How could a bullet have gotten past that Sam Brown belt?

"Wasn't he lovely, Em?"

"There was none better."

"I still dream of how it might have been."

Tears flowed. I rushed to support her. "It was not to be, dear. He was the best, and he loved you."

"That's what sustained me. Wasn't he grand?"

"Oh, he was."

The moment shattered, Peggy grasped my hand and pressed her lips to the gnarled fingers. We embraced, and I kissed her cheek as lovingly as if she were my own Mil.

Lovely Peggy, framed by the sagging doorway, raised ever so slightly her right arm and waved a weak goodbye. Her tears and fragile smile intensified the image of her haunting beauty. I gave a bold thumbs up and turned my back for what I knew in my heart was the last time.

Shaken, I moved on and spied the place that I knew could provide relief—Clancy's. Like the warehouse, the true hub of the universe was showing signs of neglect. The outside stairs to the academy had been torn down and, like the school, the second story windows wore plywood blinders. My first thought—where would the young boys learn to swear and smoke? But, a man of great faith, I relaxed knowing they'd surely deal with the loss.

The door swung open, and I found myself in a time machine. My first reaction was that, save for the faces at the bar, nothing had changed. There was no obvious litter, but the place looked like it hadn't been cleaned since my last visit decades before. Hustling into the men's room to prepare for an hour of rehabilitation from the encounter with Peggy, I was reassured of my sanity when I saw that the linoleum squares had worn through in a wider ark.

Emerging, I sought my bearings. The wall defending the speakeasy was still in place—only an atomic bomb could have destroyed it—but the heavy doors were gone. The need for revetments that compared favorably to Charlestown's was surely a mystery for any much younger than me.

The barkeep and the waitress, youthful enough to be carded, lounged lazily in the slow afternoon traffic. I squinted to pierce the smoky haze and determine if just one patron at the bar might be an old comrade, but they were all children. Two cliques bantered easily, separated by three empty stools. The middle one looked safe enough for an old timer, and I moved to claim it.

"Emmet! Hey, Emmet Magawley!"

It was Mike Flynn. While the gravelly voice was that of a stranger, and the blob of flaccid flesh compared not at all to the hard frame stored in my mind's eye, I knew it was him before the second syllable reached my ears. As ever, Flynn was not alone in the dark booth, and there was no need for him to introduce the wizened skeleton gazing at him. Pat Ryan had survived as well.

I grabbed hands and dropped to the bench, custom worn to fit the contours of an Irish bottom. The old defenses created for the nasty old bully fell away, and I strained for his words.

As always, Mike did the pontificating, and Batty echoed the most infallible of the pronouncements. A match made in heaven, their mutual needs and benefits had sustained them while so many others faltered.

The waitress plopped three pints, and, when I sprang, Flynn's eyes popped. He came alive and somehow his heroic tales of socking me in the beak in New Jersey and beatin' the crap out of that no good sonofabitchin' Callahan, echoed punch for punch by the soft little boy voice, seemed less mean. He then recounted his greatest feat, pushin' Paul Romano aside when the Guinea lost his nerve and tellin' the Coast Guard just where it could leap when they found no booze in a search of the Genoa. I had no idea if that story was supposed to have been the one about the night that Da and I had nearly died of fright, for, in my recollection, Mike wasn't even on board that evening. In any case, it was a hell of a yarn. and I roared at the oft-told tales, though much of the load was at my doorstep.

I asked about Tommy Mullins and the others, and Mike related that he and many of the old cops had retired to Wareham or the Cape.

The parting from Peggy was pushed aside by the laughter, and I signaled the waitress to bring three more. Flynn grew somber and recounted the day poor Joe Riley fell headless in France. I tried not to listen, as, even after all the decades, it was still very painful. The glasses from the first round drained, I realized that the barmaid had not delivered. I walked up and placed the order again. She begged forgiveness, and I assured her that none was needed. I revisited the men's room, as she transferred the goods.

When I returned, the pints were still bubbling, and I took my place as one last echo sounded, "...Emmet and Vanzetti spoiled everything."

Horror was in Mike's eyes, as he tried without words to explain. But I tapped the bony old shoulder. "That ain't too far from the truth, Pat. Now drink up. I gotta go."

Flynn was silent, and I did my best to show that no offense had been taken. I bought them each one more, and begged out as they were delivered, pledging to return soon and repeat the happy hour. Strolling to my car, I was thoroughly renewed.

Driving past the old homestead, only the best of times popped into mind as it receded in the vibrating mirror. Any demons that had lingered within me, were exorcised that afternoon.

Good God, Kevin, fourteen sessions. I've used more tape than all the rest of these old coots put together. That's it. There's nothin' else.

From this distance, it's easy to see how innocent fools like Bart could get caught up in the utopian world of anarchy. He didn't have the benefit of knowing the rottenness behind the Berlin Wall and beyond. Most of all, the poor man had no understandin' of human nature and ascribed all of the worst in us to the oppression of the system. Ah, if it were only so.

Bart thought that by his death, the workers would take heart and the exploitive world of capitalism would come crashing down. He had no idea we could reform, and that people would be inspired to stop such wanton executions. How could he know that because of him, Nick, and others like them, we would implement the constitutional guarantees we now take for granted?

Bart Vanzetti, flesh and blood, died bravely that we might understand that police officers are but human beings ever in need of our support; that judges can be misguided in defense of their societies; and that many's the governor who burns with desire to gaze on the Potomac.

It's unfortunate for Sacco and Vanzetti that the last of their champions was simply a poor book seller, a four flusher spotted in his youth as one who always sought the easier way. But damn it, they were the anarchists. I did my best. Who in God's name did they think they might meet and inspire to become their paladin in a hellhole like Charlestown—Perry Mason?

In 1977—fifty years late—Governor Dukakis issued a proclamation that the proceedings against Nick and Bart had been permeated with unfairness and that all stigma and disgrace should be removed from their families and descendants. It was somethin', but didn't clear them, nor could it remove the stain of shame on the Commonwealth. I wish I'd something to do with getting even that much for 'em, but it wasn't the case.

That's it, Kevin. That's the first time I've ever told it all—the real all.

I'm exhausted. I've never been so tired, and I'm ready for my ride to the Cape. The need to get it all out has sustained me, and, finally, I feel released. It's done—and me with it.

I did my best. Oh, I know how I failed 'em. Surely, you believe in redemption for those who do their best—however, ineffectively. Kevin, tell me you do.

If you believe me—it's all true—I beg ya to pick up the banner for Nick and Bart. It's unfair, I know, but, please, Kev, please, say you will. Say it!